Phoenix

IRISH SHORT STORIES 2003

Phoenix IRISH
SHORT STORIES
2003

edited by David Marcus

PHOENIX

First published in Great Britain in 2003 by Phoenix, a division of

The Orion Publishing Group Ltd
Orion House
5 Upper Saint Martin's Lane
London WC2H 9EA

A CIP catalogue record for this book is available
from the British Library

ISBN 0 75381 717 9

Typeset at The Spartan Press Ltd,
Lymington, Hants
Printed in Great Britain by
Clays Ltd, St Ives plc

ACKNOWLEDGEMENTS

None of the following stories has previously appeared in print.

Cashmere, copyright © Jackie Blackman, 2003; *Delivery*, copyright © Lorcan Byrne, 2003; *Tainted*, copyright © Mary J. Byrne, 2003; *Home Run*, copyright © Sean Coffey, 2003; *Glass*, copyright © Gerard Donovan, 2003; *Singing the Blues*, Copyright © Paul Grimes, 2003; *Heavy Weather*, copyright © Niall McArdle, 2003; *October*, copyright © Blánaid McKinney, 2003; *While You Wait*, copyright Mary Morrissy, 2003; *The Moon Shines Clear, The Horseman's Here*, copyright © Éilís Ní Dhuibhne, 2003; *The Hard Way*, copyright © The estate of Frank O'Connor, 2003; *The Corbies' Communion*, copyright © Julia O'Faolain, 2003; *Indian Summer*, copyright © Cóilín Ó hAodha, 2003; *The Fight*, copyright © Dermot Somers, 2003.

Close to the Water's Edge, copyright © Claire Keegan, 1999, appeared only in the US edition of her collection *Antarctica*, published by *Atlantic Monthly Press*.

CONTENTS

INTRODUCTION

Writers are lonely. So they often tell us, because to produce the results of their labour they have to sit in isolation, hour after hour, constantly writing, re-reading and revising. Which class of writers, I wonder, are most affected by their constant spells of imprisonment in their lonely cell of words? Not the poets, surely, even though poets can never leave their labour because their labour never leaves them, always remains with them. Yet I never once heard a poet protest that he or she is lonely. Why not? Because poets are Parnassians whose anointed life sentence is to poetise their loves, their lives, and their thoughts. They inhabit a magic world of self-hypnosis.

Which leaves the prose writers – not the travel writers, the biographers, the critics – but the fiction writers, the world's greatest sitting army of lone page-fillers. The world is all around them, but the irony is that it isn't the world that was created for them. *Their* world is one they must create themselves, and for themselves. Is God lonely, having created His world, our world, which He never stops re-creating? Why, then, is the fiction writer lonely when his world is populated by his characters? Novelists and/or short story writers don't live on Parnassus. They live in the daily grind, but too often they imagine that if they talk about the project they are working on, they risk losing it.

That risk is non-existent. The opposite, in fact. They won't lose it, though they might possibly bin it themselves if they are aspiring fiction writers who find their way, or deliberately make their way, to one of the many groups that exist all over Ireland and Britain to help them with advice, information, and invaluable criticism arising from expert examination of their work. And, what is so important to them, they meet up with other young writers and together can form their own writers' world. For Irish short story writers – novelists too, of course – excellent workshops and story competitions exist all over the island throughout the year. Many writers who have been published in the annual *Phoenix Irish Short Stories* collections have graduated from such literary activities. Be one of them. Be a fiction writer who won't be lonely talking to oneself.

David Marcus

FRANK O'CONNOR

The Hard Way

Introduced by Harriet O'Donovan Sheehy

If someone had handed me this story *The Hard Way* and asked who I thought had written it, I would have been stumped. 'Some Englishman, I guess,' would have been my less than enlightened reply. But actually the story was in a file marked 'Unpublished stories' which I found after my husband, Frank O'Connor, died in 1966. I thought it very atypical and put it aside, even wondering if it had been sent by someone else for comment and then misfiled.

It was a story about the cotton trade in Lancashire, a trade which has long vanished and a people who, even when the story was written, were finding themselves redundant. And how the story ever came to be written is a mystery. Where did Frank O'Connor, a quintessential Corkman, learn the dialect spoken in Lancashire? Could it have been from his friend Bill Naughton, of *Alfie* fame? Did he make a programme for the British Ministry of Information about the weaving trade? He made others (during World War II) about the Nursing Service and about the Lifeboat Service. Did he meet somebody in an English pub who talked about his life as a weaver? We will probably never know.

The only proof we have that *The Hard Way* was written by Frank O'Connor is that he lifted a minor sub-theme from it and expanded it into a story called *Jerome*, which was published in *Travellers' Samples* in 1951. O'Connor spoke about not writing stories that adhere too closely to one place or nationality or religion or profession, but most of his stories are set in Ireland and their characters are mainly Irish. That he extracted from *The Hard Way* one of its sub-themes and published it as a separate story suggests that he might have contemplated returning to the rest of the story at a later date. Whether or which, no revised version exists. Perhaps the story was but an experiment – an experiment with which, clearly, he was never totally satisfied. Fortunately however, what does exist is this intriguing, atypical example of a great writer's approach to his art. As such it has remained too long buried.

1

When Joe Kenyon went into the weaving shed and saw the new girl at the machine, he closed his eyes for a moment. She looked like something out of a dream – or a nightmare; like something you might buy in a toyshop, with gold curls and blue eyes which would open or shut according to the position in which you held her. Joe walked round her once and saw the mirror nailed up behind the machine. Then he turned to old Jim Saunders, the tackler, who seemed to grow gloomier every day.

'Who's t'apparition, Jim?' he shouted.

'Directed labour,' snarled old Jim without even looking to see whom Joe was talking of. 'Given her choice between a mill and a hospital. It'll be hospital all right for her, but not on nursing side. She keeps bumping into everything.'

'How's she shaping?' asked Joe.

'Warehouse overlooker hasn't had much time to see,' Jim snarled at her. 'She's taken it into her head that the warehouse is a first-degree burn. I believe fourteen dropped picks is about her average.'

'Fourteen?' said Joe. 'I knew weavers that drowned themselves in seven, more or less.'

Glaring at Joe, Jim shouted back, his old face suddenly suffused with anger as he threw his arm about the weaving shed. 'I told them they'd have to move her elsewhere. They laughed at me. I'll be the next for moving her myself.'

Worried about the prospect of trouble ahead, Joe went up to the girl. If there hadn't been so much sheer horror in his feeling he might have thought it was love.

'How's it going, lass?' he shouted, putting his arm about her shoulder.

'Better,' she replied promptly. 'I've took two aspirin.'

'No, this,' he said, pointing to the weave.

'Oh, all right,' she said, 'but my assistant is too slow.'

'Whose assistant, lass?' Joe asked, thinking she might be a bit soft in the head.

'Mine,' she replied, pointing to old Jim. 'That old man. He's too old for the job. I need someone younger.'

At that point Joe began to understand something of the old tackler's frame of mind. When a girl who has been six weeks in a weaving shed still thinks she is the tackler's boss, cotton is upside down.

Even when he went home after his work he couldn't get the wretched girl out of his mind.

'How's things in the mill, Joe?' Hilda asked.

'Oh, all right,' he replied. 'Only there's a new girl from Bourne-mouth in the weaving shed who still thinks after six weeks that Jim Saunders is her assistant.'

'More fools they to employ her,' said Hilda.

'But what else can they do,' snapped Joe, 'when girls like our Bella want to serve in shops?'

Hilda flushed, and he knew it was the Irish blood in her.

'We've had all this out before,' she said. 'Bella is entitled to make her own choice. You and I had no choice, but while I live I'll see that Bella has hers.'

He knew what she meant. He remembered the first day he had ever laid eyes on her in the winding room, a gentle, terrified, humiliated child of twelve with a shabby old sailor hat over her mill-girl's shawl, and he knew the hurt of it was still in her, and was angry that all their years of married life had not washed it away.

'But I tell you, woman, it's not the same thing at all,' he said angrily. 'That's always the way with cotton. It's all history. Shops and radio valves and motor-cars have no history; they're all right, but cotton is all history, and I'm sick to death of it. Sometimes I wish we had the old times back. At least they produced people like you and me. Can't you let bygones be bygones?'

'No,' she said quietly. 'Can you?'

Joe knew he couldn't. In his own way, he too was in the grip of history. Hilda would never know how much exactly he had sacrificed to get back as manager of a mill, but she did know how unhappy he was all the time he was earning good money elsewhere. She did know that he could retire in the morning and live in some little place by the sea where they need never see a mill again, and often she had asked him to do it. But it was only a passing depression. She knew he could no more escape from his memories than she could from hers. He had cotton in his blood.

2

That night in bed he thought of it again, and suddenly he felt the throb of delight with which he had first seen his own name in print. It was when he had passed at the Technical School after his first year's examination in spinning. He passed sixth, and there were only six in the class, and he wouldn't have passed at all but that he was the only real mill-hand attending. The other five were the sons of mill-managers. But that in itself was an additional source of gratification to Joe, for the mill-managers' sons had all attended the Grammar School, and had the grounding in math-ematics which he hadn't got.

Even his father seemed pleased, and Joe's father was a hard man to please. He was a butcher with a little shop on the Preston Road. In those days there were no closing times. The shop remained open until midnight, and Mr Kenyon stood at the shop door in his apron and straw hat, calling out to the passers-by to come in and buy a joint cheap. He was never a man to hide his light under a bushel; a hard man, poor and ambitious. In those days they had little custom; the mill-owners' carriages drove up the Preston Road with their fine dapple-grey horses, but they never stopped outside Kenyons. Once or twice, before himself and his father set off for Manchester Market at four in the morning,

Joe had seen the old fellow break open the savings banks of the kids to pay for the meat. A man who never smoked, never took a drink, never paid more than five pounds for a horse or ten for a car. What was no good to anyone else was good enough for him. He learned to shoe his own horses to save the blacksmith's fee, and to take down a car and put it together again to save a mechanic's. Midnight on Saturday was nothing to him. On Sunday mornings he did five-bob flits for poor people who couldn't afford the expense of a furniture remover, and the boys were called in to load and unload. Six o'clock each morning Joe had to be up and out, taking the orders and delivering the meat, and perhaps doing a bit of knocking-up on the side for people who couldn't afford the tuppence a week for the regular knocker-up.

He wasn't an unjust father, though, only hard. Each of the kids had his job. Joe's job was his boots, the old fellow's only extravagance. Fourteen pairs he had in all, and it was Joe's job to see that each was shining when his father went to put them on. If they weren't, Joe got a hiding. There was no sentiment about it; no pretence that it hurt the old fellow more than it hurt Joe. It didn't hurt the old fellow a bit. Bill's job was the car that they drove to the market in, and Bill got a hiding if the car didn't start. Apart from that, Father didn't mind what use they made of it. Once they drove it to Blackpool and back. They had eighteen punctures on the way and arrived home with one tyre stuffed with grass.

They had no entertainments; no pictures, no theatre, but on Sunday nights they went to the 'Appy 'Ome. The 'Appy 'Ome ran a Sunday show for kids with the Temperance Band and lantern slides showing the evils of drink; pictures of girls being thrown out into the snow by their old fellows, and ending up on the streets. Sid Harris, with a candle hidden behind a screen, read out the story of the girl. On Sunday nights when the 'Appy 'Ome wasn't running a show, they went to the Salvation Army. Joe was saved at twelve; the first of his party to be saved, but Joe was never what you'd call modest. He had been brought up to scrap for anything he got.

Joe took the newspaper round to Grandfather just to show him. Grandfather was the only one of the Kenyon family who had made the papers himself. When Joe was a little fellow, a big action was taken against the mill by a German firm who claimed proprietary rights in a certain type of braid. Grandfather had been brought up to London with his old loom which even then was a hundred years old, and the loom had been set up in court while they took pictures of Grandfather weaving the braid on it. Grandfather had won the case for the mill and been presented with a gold sovereign for his trouble. When he was seventy-five the firm had given him a gold watch and fifteen shillings a week for life. Now Joe found the old man on his knees, scrubbing the floor.

'Seen this?' he said. 'They have my name in paper, just like they had yours. Me picture isn't there yet, but that'll come.'

'Ay,' Grandfather said. 'I hope tha gets more out of it than I did.'

'I don't worry,' Joe said stoutly. 'When I'm thy age I'll not be scrubbing floors.'

'When th'art my age, tha'll be lucky if th'ast floor to scrub,' Grandfather replied gloomily.

On Monday morning the news was all over the mill, and Joe was hurt if anyone failed to mention it. Coming on to dinner-time, the overlooker said 'Manager wants to see thee, Joe.' Then Joe got a proper fright. It struck him that perhaps he'd been too cocky. The manager wanting to see somebody had never meant but one thing in the mill, and Joe began to realise that perhaps it had been a little presumptuous for him to compete with mill-managers' sons. When he came in, Harley, the mill-manager, looked up. He was a pale, thin, dark-visaged man.

'I see by the paper th'ast been going to Tech,' he said.

'Ay,' Joe replied in confusion, 'I have.'

'I see th'ast passed,' Harley said in the same expressionless voice.

'Ay,' Joe replied, trying to soften the shock of his offence. 'I was nobbut sixth though.'

'How comes tha wasn't first?' the mill-manager asked severely, and Joe saw then that the man took a proper view of the matter.

'Ah,' he said, 'Jack Rockley and Ted Davies was there as well.'

'What?' Harley asked. 'Mean to say tha could'st not beat Jim Rockley's son?'

'Ah,' Joe said, with growing confidence. 'I could beat him to a frazzle if only I'd been to Grammar School like he has. I wanted to go to Grammar School but Father couldn't afford it. Those chaps learn algebra and trigonometry, logarithms and anti-logarithms, things I was never taught at school. But I have the books. I'll pick them up all right.'

'There's a gowd sovereign for thee,' Harley said curtly.

Joe went out of the office on wings. A gowd sovereign and his name in paper! Everything Grandfather got coming on to seventy, and he a kid of nobbut fourteen. If he was the equal of Grandfather at that age, who could say what he'd be by the time he was seventy? 'Knowledge,' he murmured to himself as he went back to the spinning room. 'Knowledge.'

Joe was hoping that after that Mr Harley would salute him when he passed through the ring-spinners' room, but it seemed that after the gold sovereign he forgot all about Joe, for he didn't speak to him again until the same time the following year, when once more he sent for him.

'I see tha'st passed again,' he said with a smile.

'Ay,' replied Joe. 'I was fourth this time.'

'Tha'rt slow enough,' said Harley with his smile fading. 'There's two gowd sovereigns for thee.'

And again a year passed, and again he failed to recognise Joe when he passed through the ring-spinners' room, and Joe felt secretly indignant. But next time it was three gold sovereigns, and Joe was prepared to forgive quite a lot of forgetfulness for that. But then one day he sent for Joe again, and this time it had nothing to do with the Technical School.

'Winding overlooker's ill, lad,' he said kindly. 'Canst tha take it on?'

'Ah,' Joe said cockily, 'I can cakewalk it.'

'Th'art cocky enough anyhow,' Mr Harley said a bit sourly.

But Joe was expressing only what he knew. He knew the winding room, and he knew what was wrong with it. All the mill overlookers had the same sort of mind as Grandfather. When they had a problem to solve they always worked it out on the machine instead of in their heads. They tried a particular pulley wheel, and if that wasn't right they kept on trying other pulley wheels till they got what they thought they wanted, but they knew no method of deciding beforehand which pulley wheel they wanted, nor did they ever realise how much there was in the machine which they never wanted at all. Joe knew the winding room was capable of producing twenty per cent more than the overlookers got out of it. That evening when the mill was closed, he came back, accompanied by Bill, and they spent a great portion of the night gearing up the machines to produce the extra twenty per cent. Next morning he came in, complacent, but before an hour had passed he realised that something desperate had gone wrong. The machines flew merrily along at the increased pace, but a hundred and seventy women were failing to keep pace with them. They ran from machine to machine, their fingers all thumbs, cursing at him. By noon ends were down all over the place, and by dinner-time forty women were standing idle with no bobbins to wind.

'What else could anyone expect?' they shouted derisively. 'A kid like you in a man's job!'

'All right, all right,' Joe protested in anguish. 'I know now I expected too much of you, but I can put it right. Give me until morning and I'll get it all straight again.'

And again he and Bill worked all night putting things back, but he grudged it. He didn't put everything back all the way, only half the machines; the others he geared about two per cent higher so that the operatives wouldn't notice. They didn't, and next day when he asked 'How's it going?' they replied 'It's a good spin.' That evening he came back and put the remaining half up to two per cent, determined if that worked to put on a little more speed by the following day. He was beginning to learn something about human nature; not much, but a little to be going on with.

3

He had been there a fortnight when a new girl came to work. He noticed her in a flash that first morning; a slight, pretty, terrified child of twelve in a funny dress, a patched frock, a mill-girl's shawl, and a shabby old sailor hat. Then he paid no more attention to her. It was only on the following day during the lunch break that he heard the shouting from the yard, and went to look out. A procession of women and girls was marching across the yard with something on a pole. He looked at it, and then something caught at his heart. It was the shabby little sailor hat which he had noticed on the new girl in the room. Hastily he went back and saw her there alone, wide-eyed in the middle of the room. She wasn't even crying; that was what made it so bad.

'How's it going, lass?' he asked with affected boisterousness.

'It's 'ell,' she replied in a low voice without looking at him.

'Ah, it's not as bad as that,' he said.

'It's 'ell,' she said, 'and I'm 'ere with devils.'

'No, they're not devils,' he said earnestly. 'They're rough and common but they have good 'earts. Tha'll like mill when th'art here a while.'

'I'll never like it,' she said in the same haunted whisper. 'I never wanted to come here. I wanted to be a teacher but we hadn't no food at home. My sister said it was a shame. My mother said I should wear only a shawl like the rest of the girls, but I won't, I won't. I'll die first.'

And suddenly she burst into tears and rushed away from him. It was the first time in his life that anything had touched him so deeply. It was a new experience for him, and he didn't know what to make of it. Partly it was that in the girl he saw himself; he hadn't wanted to come to the mill either, but his father had driven him there for the money. He went out into the yard and strode up to one of the women he knew. It was old Katty Simpson.

'It's a bloody shame how you treated that poor lass,' he said.

'Ah, what is it only sport?' she said with a laugh.

'It's no sport for her,' he said gruffly, 'nor 'twouldn't be for you at her age.'

'Ah,' she said after a moment. 'I think maybe I'd get her a cup of tea.'

After that he noticed a complete change in the attitude of the older women towards Hilda Rooney. The child wasn't strong; she got weaknesses, and Katty or one of the others would take her to sit in the yard, and if that didn't bring her round they took her home. It all meant money lost to them, every minute of it, but they protected her. But Joe soon realised that she was far from being the terrified little creature he had imagined her to be. She put her weaknesses down to the lack of fresh air. She clamoured to Joe for the opening of a window. Joe refused to interfere. He left it to the other women to decide, and they decided all right.

'Foolishness, child,' they said complacently. 'Forty-five years I've been in mill, and I never seen a window open in this room.'

But Hilda Rooney was extraordinarily pertinacious. She continued to cling to her sailor hat and to her demands for the opening of the windows. She even induced two or three of the younger girls to admit that they had heard fresh air was good for the health and seen it admitted without any harmful results. Then one day as he was in the manager's office he heard a terrific commotion from below. He looked through the window and saw several of the women gesticulating from the yard.

'What is it, Joe?' asked Harley.

Joe flung open the window and shouted down a question.

'I'd better go and see,' he said.

'I'll come with you,' said Harley.

When they reached the winding room they saw a knot of women gathered outside. Then they noticed the extraordinary condition of the room itself. It was as though enveloped in a snowstorm. From the roof, from the belts, dark flakes were chipped away and floated in great billowing clouds.

'What is it?' he shouted.

'It's the windows,' replied one of the women vindictively. 'It's Hilda Rooney again.'

And there he saw her again with a set face and fists clenched in the middle of the chaos she had produced; forty – sixty – years' accumulation of cotton waste settling on the machines.

'Ay,' Harley said softly. 'Maybe it's no bad thing.'

From that day on Joe regarded Hilda with a new respect. He set himself to find out all he could about her background from the other women. She was the youngest child of a long family with an Irish father and an illiterate Lancashire mother. Her father was not illiterate. It might have been better for everybody if he was. He had been a bobbin-carrier in the mill, but even that humble job he hadn't been able to keep. Then he became for a while a scene-shifter in the local theatre, where he had got to know a number of the visiting actors and become completely stage-struck. When he was off the drink he spent the evenings reading Dickens and Thackeray to Mrs Rooney. Occasionally he staged performances of Shakespeare in the kitchen. The other girls who had been to school with her called her 'Lady Rooney'. They said she was always telling them fairy stories; wonderful stories in which princesses appeared with beautiful clothes.

When he met her leaving the mill he took to strolling home with her, but she never told him any stories about beautiful princesses.

4

When the winding overlooker came back Harley sent for Joe.

'I see th'ast put up production in winding room,' he said.

'Ay,' Joe said, sticking out his chest. 'I told you I could cakewalk it, didn't I?'

'Ah,' Harley said with a look of disgust, 'th'ast done nothing. Now, see how tha gets on with Bradshaw in carding room.'

That sounded like a warning, and it was. Joe knew Bradshaw, an old-fashioned overlooker with white corduroys, white apron and black cap. He looked innocent and benevolent and wasn't; a man who had broken the spirit of youths more aspiring than Joe.

'Well,' he said with his angelic smile, 'I hear tha's put up production in winding room.'

'Ay,' said Joe sulkily, 'I have.'

'By algebra, I hear,' said Bradshaw.

'Ah,' replied Joe, 'and I could probably do it by algebra here too if tha went sick.'

'Don't worry about me, lad,' said Bradshaw, patting him amiably on the shoulder, 'it's thee as is going to be sick.'

He was right there. Things were going too well for Joe. He no longer had to deliver meat in the mornings; Joe's old fellow was doing well, and now it was another wretched boy who was delivering and knocking up for a few shillings a week. Spiritual pride was the result. The 'Appy 'Ome had only warned him against one sort of temptation. It hadn't told him what follows chaps that go to a disused tip behind the Methodist Chapel after Sunday School for a quiet game of ha'penny pontoon. Joe could have arranged the lantern slides for that lecture afterwards because the scenes were forever stamped on his mind. There was the terrible slide which showed one of the lads – Joe to be precise – looking up from his cards and seeing the figures of four big bobbies coming over the edge of the tip. There was the following slide which showed Joe protesting wildly that they were only playing ha'penny pontoon, not banker, and the bobbies' incredulous faces, for who could credit the word of Sabbath breakers like themselves? Then there was the slide of Joe, a great big lad of sixteen, and his father welting blazes out of him with a walking stick.

It was no use telling Father that they were only playing ha'penny pontoon, not banker. Father had never played either. The three lads had to club their wages and go to a solicitor, a chap called Lacy, a thin mournful chap with spectacles. He knew the difference all right. Joe explained it in passionate tones.

'I believe you,' he said in a depressed tone, as he walked about his office. 'I believe you, but will the magistrates believe you? I don't know. I shall only call you. The police may call your friends, but I won't. I want you to tell your story exactly as you've told it to me, and then we'll see what happens.'

Then came the slide which really caused Joe's heart to sink, the slide which showed him in Harley's office, trying as best he could to make light of his crime, while Harley put on a disgusted expression.

'Serve thee right,' was all he said.

On the day of the trial Joe stayed away from work to go to the court. He got a bit of a shock when he went in. One of the magistrates proved to be an old fellow called Burton, an old carder who was now one of the mill directors. This was worse than anything Joe had expected. He could see only ruin ahead of him. When Lacy called him, Joe told his story with a conviction that almost broke his own heart if not that of the magistrates.

'And you were not playing banker as the constables said?' led Lacy in a tone of horror.

'No, sir,' replied Joe. 'I never played banker in my life, nor never would.'

'Would you know 'ow?' asked old Burton suddenly.

'I wouldn't know well, your worship,' replied Joe, a little shaken.

And then, as he left the box a policeman called Daniels, who was standing to attention by the door, whispered out of the corner of his mouth without even looking at Joe: 'Bluidy liar!'

Joe was overstrung. He knew he had his back to the wall and was fighting for his life. He turned on his heel and went back into the box.

'I want to know am I going to get fair play here or not?' he shouted.

'Fair play?' echoed the Chairman in mild surprise. 'Who suggested to you that you wouldn't get fair play?'

'I've this moment been called a bloody liar,' shouted Joe with a sob in his voice. 'It was by this policeman here.'

'That will do,' said the Chairman kindly.

'I would like to call the policeman,' said Burton suddenly.

'Step into the box, constable,' said the Chairman. 'Now, Mr Burton.'

'Did you call the defendant a bloody liar?' asked Burton in a scandalised tone.

'I told nowt but truth, your worship,' replied the constable, flushing.

Burton sat back and waved his hands despondently. 'I don't

know what we're doing in this court at all,' he said. 'If the police can take the administration of justice out of the hands of magistrates in their own courts, we simply have no business here. So far as I can see, there is only one course open to us. We must ask for a public enquiry into the whole conduct of the police in this case.'

Then the Superintendent rose. He looked red too.

'On behalf of the police,' he said, 'I wish to apologise to the bench for the unfortunate and improper remark made by Constable Daniels. Under the circumstances, I can only ask for permission to withdraw the charge.'

'A very proper course,' said the Chairman.

Joe listened with a beating heart. He heard Burton arguing in favour of an enquiry but it struck him that he was putting the case very badly. It seemed very lax on his part not to demand a thousand pounds compensation for the accused. But when he mentioned this to Lacy, the solicitor seemed astonished.

'Compensation?' he said. 'The man got you off, which, let me tell you, was more than I could have done.'

Next day Burton called at the mill and sent for Joe.

'As th'art such a good card-player, tha'd better come to my place on Sunday afternoon to make up a solo party,' he said. 'I hope it's not against your principles, like banker.'

Joe looked at the mill manager, and saw the shadow of a smile on his face. 'Thanks, Mr Harley,' he said as he was going out. 'I didn't know you'd had owt to do with it.'

'I've better news than that for you,' said Harley without a smile. 'Bradshaw has to go into hospital for an operation. He didn't like to tell you for fear it might break your heart.'

Joe was working out the changes under that man's eyes for the next three days, and he knew it. He was more modest now. He felt he would be quite satisfied with five per cent to begin with. He was only 4.9% too optimistic. On Bradshaw's very first morning in hospital half the machines were stopped, and by noon Joe had stopped the mill. He went along to Harley to report it, but Harley knew it already.

'I hear tha's stopped mill again,' he said wearily.

'Ay,' Joe said, 'I've stopped it all right. It's the human element I overlooked again.'

'It's common sense tha overlooked, lad,' said Harley kindly. 'Tha can change nowt in this world, as long as tha goes round telling people what th'art doing. Canst tha fix it?'

'Ay,' Joe said determinedly. 'I'll put it all right by tomorrow.'

Next morning everything was all right again, and little by little he forced up the pace till the women were all earning seven or eight shillings a week more. Then Bradshaw came back and Joe knew by his beaming face that he had heard all about the changes which had been made.

'I hear tha's been introducing a bit algebra into carding room, Joe,' he said.

'No,' Joe replied shortly. 'It's decimals this time.'

'I never could stand them little dots,' said Bradshaw reflectively. 'I'm sorry, Joe, but it'll have to go back.'

Joe went off in a rage to Harley.

'I don't see there's anything much I can do,' said Harley. 'It's his responsibility, isn't it?'

'Responsibility?' cried Joe. 'How could a man have a sense of responsibility and talk of decimals as them little dots? But you could ask him to work out the calculations for any changes he makes.'

'Ay,' replied Harley with a ghost of a smile. 'I could do that.'

Next day Bradshaw hardly put in an appearance in the carding room. Joe could see him in the cabin with a pencil and paper. Late in the afternoon he came out for Joe.

'There's a few little calculations here tha might do for me, Joe,' he said.

'Ay,' replied Joe stoutly. 'I might but I won't. Do them thyself and I'll tell thee whether tha'rt right or not.'

'Tell the truth, Joe,' said Bradshaw with a mystified expression, 'I don't even know how to begin on them.'

'No,' replied Joe, 'but tha can always begin on those that understand them. Tha'rt like my old grandfather; try a wheel and hope for the best. But I'll give thee thy due; thou knows things I don't know. Teach me how to staple cotton, and I'll do the calculations for thee.'

'Ay,' Bradshaw said with a smile, 'I'll teach thee that, and maybe a bit more. I know a few things that aren't in no book. I worked them out for myself.'

From that out there was no further talk of putting back the carding room. Instead, when Joe went to the cabin he sometimes surprised the old man with Joe's Scott-Taggart or Thornley open before him, a puzzled look on his fat, complacent old face.

5

Then Harley moved Joe to the weaving shed, and he came into regular daily contact with Hilda again. She had asked to be put in the weaving shed, and he frequently walked home with her. The first evening he was surprised when she brought him to a terrace house on the outskirts of the town.

'Ha' ye flit again?' he asked.

'Ay,' she said, growing red, and then she added recklessly, 'we've left me feyther.'

'It was probably the right thing to do,' he said.

'My mother is against it,' she said. 'I know she is, though she doesn't say anything. He broke up the house on us again. I'd ask you in, but we haven't got much furniture inside.'

'Ah,' he said, 'I don't mind about things like that. I wish I could leave my feyther, and he don't drink.'

'Come in so,' she said, and he went into the house with her. Her mother and sisters were in the kitchen at the back. She apologised feverishly for the absence of furniture.

'Tha'lt have to sit on a box,' she said. 'We're only in a month and we're buying the furniture as we go along.'

'I wouldn't mind about the furniture,' said her mother. 'I don't like the house and that's a fact. I was never used to kitchens at back of house. I dare say it's more respectable as Hilda says, but it's not so comfortable. I sit here all day with my hands hanging and look at back wall.'

'You wait until we have this properly furnished, and you'll see how comfortable it is,' said Hilda with an agonised smile.

Joe was drinking his tea when all at once someone knocked at the door, and Mrs Rooney went out.

'I wonder where she's gone to,' Hilda said after a moment.

'I daresay one of the neighbours wanted her,' said her sister.

'But she said she didn't know any of the neighbours,' said Hilda in alarm.

'Only about fifty per cent of them,' said her sister dryly. 'That's solitude to ma.'

Joe could see by Hilda's expression that she was alarmed. About five minutes later their mother came back with her arms folded.

'It's your feyther,' she said briefly. 'He wants to come back. Shall I tell him he can't?'

There was a terrible silence. Then her sister looked at Hilda and Hilda burst into tears and ran up the stairs. Joe got up awkwardly and took his cap. At the corner of the street he saw a tall, mean, crushed-looking man with head bowed, waiting for his sentence.

Joe was alarmed by the change which seemed to be coming over Hilda. There was a new spirit in the mill-girls. Harley would be sitting quietly in his office when all at once he would hear a batter of clogs on the stairs, and when the door opened and a half dozen women streamed in with some fresh complaint, Hilda would always be amongst them. But only Joe knew that she was always the moving spirit. Then one Saturday night he asked her to come for a walk with him next day.

'I can't,' she said doubtfully. 'I have to go to Sunday School.'

'I didn't know tha went to Sunday School,' said Joe. 'I thought tha were R.C. I'll come with thee. Where is it?'

'It's in Labour Hall,' she said, still more confused.

'Labour Hall?' said Joe. 'How long have they got Sunday School at Labour Hall? I'll be there anyway.'

Joe went the following day and got a series of shocks. There were hymns, just as at real Sunday School, but they didn't seem to Joe to be proper hymns. Then the teacher read a lesson that sounded as if it might be from the Bible, but Joe had a vague suspicion that the teacher was making it up, and that it wasn't in the Bible at all.

'Now hearken, I bid you: to the rich men that eat up a realm there cometh a time when they whom they eat up, that is, the poor, seem poorer than of wont, and their complaint goeth up louder to the heavens; yet it is no riddle to say that oft at such times the fellowship of the poor is waxing stronger, else would no man have heard this cry. Also at such times is the rich man become fearful, and so waxeth in cruelty, and of that cruelty do people misdeem that it is power and might waxing. Forsooth ye are stronger than your fathers, because ye are more grieved than they, and ye should have been less grieved than they had ye been horses and swine; and then forsooth, would ye have been stronger to bear; but ye, ye are not strong to bear, but to do.'

After that, he and Hilda had their first real row.

'What that chap read,' said Joe, 'that wasn't from the Bible.'

'No,' she said, flushing, 'it's from the *Dream of John Ball*. Why?'

'I knew it wasn't the proper Bible,' said Joe. 'Nor the hymns weren't proper hymns. They had nowt in them about God.'

'There might be people there who didn't hold with that,' she said feebly.

'Ay,' he said, 'but I didn't think to see thee mixed up with people like that.'

'Tha needn't come unless tha wants to,' she cried, halting and flaring up at him.

'It's no use thy losing thy temper with me,' Joe said. 'I'm sorry to see thee mixed up with people like that, that's all. I always thought thee a good-living religious lass.'

'I were worse,' she said, 'I believed in the fairies too.'

'It's not the same thing,' he said stubbornly.

'It's all the same when you work in mill,' said Hilda with sudden calm. 'I know how you feel about it. I felt the same. I believed in everything till I went to that old mill, and after that I could believe in nowt. I felt as if I was in hell. But then I looked round me and I saw that if I couldn't help myself I could help others. When I thought there was nowt I could believe in, I found safety. I've never been really unhappy since.'

And Joe looked at her under the lamp, and saw that she really meant what she said, that she had found safety, and that her happiness depended on it. It shook his own faith in himself. Several times he found himself going with her on bicycle spins with a lot of the queer believers from the Socialist Sunday School, attending meetings on village greens, and reading the books of H.G. Wells and Shaw. But he couldn't cotton on to it, and he kept on wondering whether his affection for her wasn't all a dreadful mistake.

6

Very soon there was another shift for Joe.

'Tha'd better get them overalls off and put on thy best suit,' said Harley. 'Th'art going to try thy hand at selling. Tha'lt work in Manchester Exchange with me for the future. For the first twelve months tha'lt not open thy mouth. Th'art not to enter a pub while th'art with me, mind.'

'I never took a drink in my life yet,' protested Joe.

'And if I ask thee in, th'art to ask for lemonade. That's all, except that there's a saying on the dome of Exchange I want thee to learn by heart. "A good name is to be honoured more than great riches." '

While Harley was on holidays, Joe took his place in charge of the mill. Each morning Harley phoned Joe from Llandudno, and each evening Joe phoned him back to report on prices. It was the beginning of the slump. While in the beginning he had stood with Harley in Manchester Exchange and sold thirty-six beams at eighty-four pence a pound, he stood there himself some months later and sold the same beams for twenty-four pence a pound. And then left the Exchange to telephone the mill not to open on Monday!

And next day he had seen Hilda come out and grow pale as she saw the notice.

'What is it, lass?' he asked.

'I don't know what we're going to do,' she whispered. 'My feyther is on the drink again, and my mother is depending on my few shillings. I don't know how I'm going to tell her.'

'Ay, lass,' he said. 'That's cotton!'

'Cotton!' she said wildly. 'Cotton! How much did the mill pay in profits last year?'

'I paid £68,000 in Excess Profits Tax alone,' he replied softly. 'This year I doubt if you could get £10,000 for the whole shoot, lock, stock and barrel. But that's cotton!'

'And seven hundred and fifty women like me that doesn't know how they'll eat for the next seven days, that's cotton too,' she cried, bursting out on him. 'Seven hundred and fifty women, hiding from the landlord and the insurance man, that's cotton! And what do the mill-owners care?'

'Never mind, lass,' Joe said. 'We shall pull through. That's what Harley says, and he's seen more of it than we have.'

'We shall pull through!' she hissed, and turned away.

And then next morning in the office Harley showed Joe the yellow veins running between his fingers and said 'I wonder what they are?'

'Th'ad better see a doctor,' said Joe.

'Ay,' he said, 'I'll drop in to him tonight.'

The doctor sent Harley home to bed. Each morning at ten Joe came up briskly with the post, each evening at six he called with the news of the day.

'Prices bad again, Mr Harley.'

'Ah,' said the sick man, 'we shall pull through.'

One evening Mrs Harley beckoned Joe into the front room. 'You know, Joe,' she said in a low voice, 'Mr Harley's not going to live.'

Joe gaped at her. He didn't know what she meant. He merely thought she was being silly in a particularly womanish way.

'But he has to live, Mrs Harley,' he said firmly but kindly. 'The mill can't get on without him.'

'We'll all have to get on without him, Joe,' she said with the tears in her eyes, 't'mill – and me.'

Joe looked at her and then went up the stairs slowly, all the bounce gone out of him. Harley was sitting up in bed and Joe saw that he had been examining curiously the little veins between his fingers. For the first time he didn't ask directly about the mill.

'Tha knows, Joe,' he said, shaking his head doubtfully, 'this isn't what they say.'

'I know that, Mr Harley,' Joe blurted out.

There was a moment's pause while Harley lifted himself in the bed and looked at him.

'Tha knows?' he said incredulously.

Joe nodded. 'I know, Mr Harley,' he said.

Then Harley nodded three or four times and looked at the wall. 'Th'art on thy own from this out, lad,' he said at last.

'What do you mean, Mr Harley?' asked Joe, almost breaking down.

'Don't 'ee bring letters in the morning, Joe,' he said softly.

'No, Mr Harley,' Joe said, and then blundered weeping down the stairs. He stood at the street corner and cried. He was waiting for Hilda, but still he cried, even when he saw her coming.

'What is it, Joe?' she cried.

'It's Mr Harley,' he said. 'He's dying.'

'Ah, don't be daft, lad,' she said in surprise and concern. 'Don't let t'people see thee crying. I didn't know tha was so fond of him.'

'I didn't know it either,' said Joe. 'I was always a scrapper. I had to scrap for everything I got, but I never had to scrap with him. He did the scrapping for me all the time. He had no children. I was his real child and I never knew it. I never knew it, and now it's too late, too late.'

7

After Harley's death Joe felt his youth weighing on him. He bought himself a bowler hat and a choker collar and practised scowling at himself in the glass. The Board met at half past nine every Tuesday morning. On the first Tuesday after Harley's death, Joe put on his bowler and choker, gave himself a final scowl in the glass, and then went off to the mill.

When he strode into the office he got a shock. Sitting there were four men who looked like older editions of himself, all with bowler hats, choker collars and scowls. He felt a curious uneasiness.

'Who are these, Phil?' he asked the clerk.

'Applicants for Mr Harley's job,' replied the clerk. 'Didn't you see the ad in the *Guardian?*'

'No,' Joe said, 'and I don't think I was intended to see it. I'm going to see t'Managing Director.'

As early as it was, Phillips and Burton, who had got him off that day in the court, were both there. Phillips was a bank director as well.

'I hear you advertised Mr Harley's job,' said Joe.

'Ay, Joe,' Phillips said kindly, 'so we did.'

'And you didn't ask me for an application,' Joe cried angrily.

'We considered that, lad,' said Phillips, putting his arm round Joe, 'but we thought you were a bit young.'

'I was old enough to manage the mill while Mr Harley was sick,' cried Joe.

'That's not the same thing, Joe,' said Phillips sternly. 'You must be fair to us. That was Mr Harley's responsibility, not ours.'

'But I want that job,' Joe cried. 'I want a chance to show what I can do. I know what you were giving Mr Harley – fifteen quid a week. I'll take eight.'

'It isn't only the salary, Joe,' said Burton kindly. 'The fact is we want a married man for the job.'

'Mr Burton,' said Joe earnestly, 'you know me. I'm walking out with Hilda Rooney in the weaving shed. You give me that job, and I'll give you my word I'll be married within a month.'

Burton looked at Phillips, and Joe knew he was touched.

'I can't say fairer, can I?' he asked.

'No, Joe,' said Burton, 'you can't. We'll interview the applicants and then consider the matter again.'

The result was that Joe got the job for three months on trial. He went straight down to the weaving shed and called Hilda out. It was no occasion for lip-reading.

'Can you marry me within a fortnight?' he asked.

'I can do nothing of the sort,' she said, beginning to blush. 'I never said I'd marry you.'

'I said I'd marry you,' replied Joe. 'I'm to be manager if I agree to get married. I have a month, but I like to improve on my word. Anyhow, someone is going to marry me in the next few weeks, and I'd sooner it was thee.'

'My mother can't do without me,' said Hilda protestingly.

'I'll talk to your mother,' said Joe, and away he strode through the town. Mrs Rooney was sitting in the kitchen when he went in, and she looked up in alarm.

'I've been talking to Hilda,' he said. 'I was offered the manager's job if I could get married inside a month. Eight quid a week. I'm going to get married, and I'll marry Hilda if she'll have me.'

'Eight quid a week?' cried Mrs Rooney. 'Of course she'll have you. The girl's not daft.'

'She thinks you can't get on without her,' said Joe, 'and you know what Hilda's like when she takes a notion.'

'Eee, I do!' cried her mother. 'That girl's a fair terror. I know what you'll do, Joe. You tell her you'll rent Cox's cottage out the Melton Road. She wanted to bring me out there but I wouldn't go for her. This place is bad enough, Joe, but that place is a terror. Fields in front and behind and nothing else but cocks and hens. You tell her she can have the cottage and she'll jump. Eight quid a week!'

Joe wasn't too happy about the cottage himself, but he could see it made Hilda happy. They married on Monday and on Friday he went to draw the wages at the bank. One thousand eight hundred and forty pounds, twelve and fourpence. He knew well what the figure should be, but he had to wait till he got back to the mill to count it. Then he saw that there was something wrong. There was twenty-five pounds too much – fifty ten-shilling notes. Joe rang up George Sillars, the cashier, and told him what had happened.

'We'll have to wait until three to make a complete check, Joe,' said George. 'I shouldn't think it was our mistake, though.'

At half past three he rang up again. 'Nothing missing at this end, Joe,' he said.

Joe put down the receiver and took up the books. 'I know it's useless,' he said, 'but I'll have to check again.'

It was the end of his honeymoon, such as it was.

'Here,' said Hilda at two in the morning, 'give me those books. You've got yourself into a state where you're inventing mistakes.'

'I should have preferred it if it was actually missing,' Joe said despairingly. 'I could have borrowed the money and put it right.'

'I don't see what's upsetting you so much about it,' said Hilda.

'You might if you were a mill director whose manager had got the books into that state in his first week,' replied Joe bitterly. 'There's nothing for it but to put it on the agenda.'

On the following Tuesday, Burton appeared, just as Joe had suspected, full of suspicion.

'You're sure of this, Joe?' he asked after Joe had explained to the Board what had occurred.

'Mr Burton,' said Joe miserably, 'I haven't slept since it happened. I've checked, and Sellars has checked and my wife's checked, and I'll swear the fault isn't mine.'

'Well, if that's the case, I should suggest that we split it and say no more about it,' said Burton.

'Have the auditors in, Mr Burton!' cried Joe miserably. 'I won't rest easy until it's cleared up.'

'I don't think there's any necessity for that,' said Phillips. 'I've had a talk with the bank manager, and he thinks it may be a mistake at our end.'

Then he smiled as if he had said something clever. Joe looked at him incredulously.

'I don't like that sort of mistake, Mr Phillips,' said old Burton stiffly. 'Sit down, lad,' he said sharply to Joe, who had risen to go. 'And I don't like the suggestion being made to bank officials that the directors of this mill don't trust their own managers. As a sign of our confidence in our present manager I'm going to propose an immediate increase of salary for him. And I don't want any argument about it,' he said, bringing down his open hand on the table.

'Well?' asked Hilda when Joe went home.

'It was a mistake in the bank,' said Joe, smiling. 'And I've got an increase in salary. Two quid a week more.'

'Joe,' she said, 'was that a trap?'

'A trap?' he said with an uneasy laugh. 'What put that into your head?'

'I've been in cotton too,' she replied quietly. 'And if I thought it was a trap I'd go washing with my mother before I let you work another day in that mill.'

And then the mill closed, and for months it hung over the little town like a doom. The women slipped in, week after week, to dust their own machines. Sometimes of an evening they came out to Joe's to ask what was to become of them.

'No news, Joe?' they said when they came in.

'No news, Mrs Wright,' he said.

'She'll know soon enough,' he added to Hilda when Mrs Wright left.

'What is it?' she asked.

'Sold,' he replied quietly.

'Sold?'

'Sold, to a rubber company. For eight thousand pounds. A mill that was worth a quarter of a million. Sixty ring-spindles and three hundred looms.'

'Seven hundred and fifty women,' said Hilda.

'God knows, I have no cause to complain,' he said. 'The new company is taking me over at twice my present screw, and yet I don't know. My heart is with poor old Molly Wright, dusting her loom. That's cotton!'

For three years he was assistant manager of the rubber company's business, but when he got the offer of a managership of a little mill four miles outside the town, he was loath to turn it down. When he came home and told Hilda what he had done, there was almost a scene.

'Oh, you fool!' she said.

'And why do you think I did it?' asked Joe, infuriated by her injustice.

'I don't mind why you did it. We've been poor before, we can be poor again. But you're not happy where you are. You'll never be happy there. It would be better for you to go back as an operative.'

'Ay,' he said miserably, 'I dare say you're right.'

But when next Sunday he walked through the card room and winding room and weaving shed as he used to walk it with Harley, when everything was still, he felt happiness running through him as it hadn't done for years. And that was cotton too.

8

And so when he took Hilda to see the sports at Bentley's mill it wasn't so much for the sake of the sports. He had never liked Bentley's. He had always thought it mollycoddle and window-dressing.

'Show off, that's what it is,' he said to Hilda. 'When we were at Tech, their boys and girls were going to school in the mill, and not to learn spinning either. When grandfather was working his old loom they had automatic looms. I know what Bentley's is – a showplace for visitors.'

Still, he was more impressed than he had expected to be. The mill-children had put on a display of national dances in fancy costumes. They looked well; he had to admit that. He glanced at Hilda.

'Those aren't all mill kids, Joe?' she said, and then it burst out of her. 'They had nothing like this in our time.' He knew the picture which was before her mind, which would always be before her mind; the picture of the little sailor-hat carried by a mob of jeering women.

'Ay,' said Joe, 'but they haven't got mill-hands like us either, lass.'

'I don't know,' she said doubtfully. 'I wouldn't say that.'

It impressed Joe a lot. Next morning he sent for Saunders and enquired about the toyshop lass.

'She wouldn't be so bad if only she'd stop bumping into things,' grunted Saunders, and Joe knew that in spite of himself the old man was becoming reconciled to her. 'She's hoping to make 300,000 picks before half past five.'

'If she does, send her up to me,' said Joe.

At half past five precisely she came to the office. She had two new bruises since Joe had seen her last, and running had become such second nature to her that she bumped into his desk.

'My assistant told me that I was to come to you if I made the 300,000,' she said.

'Listen, lass,' he said wearily. 'He's not the assistant; he's the boss. If tha were in mill in my time he'd have taken a strap to thee. Cotton isn't what it was. There's a quid for thee.'

'But what for?' she asked, taking up the note.

'Instead of a gowd sovereign,' said Joe. 'They don't make gowd sovereigns any longer.'

MARY J. BYRNE

Tainted

When his mother phoned him, he knew by the tone that this was top-level stuff, although he didn't, at that stage, suspect for a moment the role that was laid out for him. His mother, he often thought, would have made an excellent Reverend Mother, the kind of person who obliged you to do things while carrying on the farce that you wanted to do them yourself, or else that you wanted desperately to do her a favour, and that she saw it as that only.

In the case of his youngest sister, of whom his mother was now speaking – a well-rehearsed speech with a background of worry and concern for the sister which had been brought into sharp focus by the recent falling-off of letters and phone calls from her, especially in the light of the forthcoming Christmas festivities, etc., etc. – this same sister had always proved a trial to his mother, it seemed. Yet he knew, and his sister knew, that the self-same impression had been given to each of them, that in fact the same game had been played with all of them in their childhood. Their mother's worry, intended to mushroom usefully into adult guilt, had somehow done the contrary: it had dissolved, disappeared, been eroded by their mother's endless melodramatic poking at it.

So he listened with one ear, hardly even wondering what the upshot of the phone call would be, although clearly it would be a demand of some kind. He could hardly see what he might be asked to do: the sister was far away, the festivities were rapidly approaching, he had his family to think of and look after as soon as he had put his small business to bed for the week, and that in itself was likely to keep him busy in the coming days. For he had inherited, could not have avoided inheriting, some of his mother's

bossiness as well as her love of manipulating people, so that there
was no aspect of the business into which he did not poke his nose,
no individual who did not feel his initiative sapped and responsibility eroded by his interfering ways. He did not – could not –
realise it, but this, if not doing harm, was certainly not doing him
or his business any good. The only place he did not interfere was
at home: there, his wife was boss, took charge, made decisions
and acted upon them. This had extended into decisions about the
children, their schooling, and ultimately their future.

The thought had struck him, once or twice, that his ceding to
his wife in these matters was somehow related to his early
reactions to his mother and therefore to women in general, or –
by association – that he felt he had no power within the walls of a
house, dwelling, home, and therefore gave himself ultimate
power in his small factory, which was none of these. It was true
that his secretary had organised the small office according to her
liking, and even insisted on serving him a powdered instant coffee
that he hated and gave him heartburn, yet for which he never
reprimanded her. The office was somehow different from the
factory floor; it was smaller and had flowers and air freshener
and toilets and comfortable seats and ashtrays and did, he would
admit, bear some semblance to a home from home.

His mother was still talking and had not yet got to the point.
'Your sister,' she was saying, 'was always headstrong and difficult.' She had fought, he remembered, against their mother, but
in her own female and calculating way. It had been a battle of
wits between them, with him on the sidelines. His sister had, in a
mild way, taken part in the lunacy of the '60s and had – early on
– gone out in miniskirts hidden under sensible dresses which were
later removed in the toilets of discos. Several times he had been
press-ganged into spying for his mother and briefing her with
whatever information he thought would offend the least. This
way he managed to lose the confidence of both sides, neither of
whom understood his desire to be neutral, to avoid trouble, to be
as straight as possible in order not to attract attention.

In his private adult life, he had pretty well succeeded. He was
moderately successful and managed to provide for his wife and

four children. His wife, although she was bossy in the home, maintained a low profile outside it, and the sextet presented the world a pleasant and peaceful exterior and – to anyone interested – interior. His children showed no sign of screwing up and, like his other older siblings, no signs of brilliance either. For all this he was grateful. This, he had often felt, was the problem with his sister. She had been an intellectual, had liked the company of intellectuals. He remembered now how on one occasion she and her friends had spent an evening bending his ear with their interpretation of a selection of pop songs, by the Beatles, the Stones, Bob Dylan. He had found such behaviour a waste of time: only recently he had been pleased to hear, on the car radio, the late John Lennon himself say that he knew as little as anyone about the meaning of some of the songs in question. He had smiled to himself in the car, then looked around quickly to see if anyone had noticed. But of course he had never taken it up with his sister, who had long since gone away and travelled widely, occasionally arriving back to dirty and untidy his wife's impeccable house, mercifully only for short stays. She was now living in North Africa, and his mother was coming to the point.

'I saw a television programme recently,' his mother was saying, 'about Moslems. And I'm not at all happy about her being out there. And then there's this Gadaffi business.' His mind wandered briefly over the American bombing of Tripoli and then to a programme on which Colonel Gadaffi had declared a prominent Irish politician to be a good friend. But it was not politics that had motivated her phone call, it seems, but – and his mind spat the word out – sex. Yes, she was up to her old tricks, enlisting him on the trail of his sister's sexual activities. It was dirty work. He detested it. He wished that she would lose interest and that his sister's activities would cease. That they would both leave him in peace. But they hadn't then, and they wouldn't now.

'I'm worried about these Moslem men,' the voice was saying. 'They have a totally different idea of women and how they should be treated.' He wondered what his mother's ideal treatment would be – something between the Virgin Mary, the Mother Goddess and a raving Amazon? 'And they don't seem to do a scrap of work,' she went on. 'Every time you see the women on TV they're carrying something on their heads or their backs, while the men are doing nothing.' The idea had never bothered him one way or the other, so busy had his life been with keeping out of trouble and seeing that his family did the same. And now his wife was signalling to say that the dinner was ready and would be cold and they all had things to do and could he get rid of his mother please. Sometimes it struck him that his wife's motivation was altogether different from his own.

He didn't know if his wife had flustered him or if his mother had been cleverer than usual, or if the approaching holiday and volume of work had addled his mind, but the fact was that by the time he put the phone down he found that he had agreed to travel to this North African country, whatever it was called, and find out what his sister was up to. He, who hated travelling, who spoke no foreign language and who quite liked spending Christmas in the bosom of his family, had agreed to go to a strange country and look into the mystery. After dinner, as the implications of his trip dawned on him, he came out in a cold sweat. What was he to do when he got there? Why the hell could the whole thing not be sorted out by letter or phone? And what was his place in the affair anyway?

But he knew very well his place was as before, had not changed, and he became angry and sweaty by turns. In addition, he suffered the warming-up of his wife's wrath at what he had agreed to do.

The next day, however, once he had gone through the possibilities of refusing to go, or handling the thing otherwise, he decided to take it in a new vein and treat it as a break, a breather, a visit to a sister he hadn't seen for some time. He got his astonished secretary to make the reservation and send a telegram to his sister. This, he thought, was the least he could do. He didn't telephone, because that would perhaps involve him in crossfire. In a burst of – what? – generosity, lunacy, or plain fear that his wife might decide to come with him (and he knew he had to go through this alone, as they did in the films, if only to save his own face when his sister laughed outright at him), he sent her and their eldest daughter on a week's skiing in Switzerland. To the entire family it seemed things had got dangerously out of hand, and that their father/husband had just about lost the run of himself.

Business kept him on an even keel until the day came for him to leave, which partly managed to convince them that he hadn't gone mad. His wife, for a moment, did think of disappearing business men who resurfaced on TV programmes later, accompanied by young women, but she was reassured by the details she already knew of the mother and sister, and their relationship. Besides, none of them now wanted to lose the advantages gained from the sudden turn of events: holidays for some, freedom from parental supervision for others. A precedent, certain of them hoped, was being created.

The first leg took him to Paris. He could have gone through London, but in a burst of euphoria he'd chosen this alternative. Now he realised that, London or Paris, they were all the same. Airports. Then he was on the second plane, looking around at the motley passengers: a man who was into horse breeding and spent a lot of time on planes and showed polite interest in his own factory and business; a couple of middle-aged tourists who obviously had money; a few North Africans going home for the holidays; a few foreigners married out there; the odd Indian and Middle Eastern business man. There were no clues here to what lay in store for him. He drank and enjoyed Air France's free wine, wanting it to relax him for the meeting with his sister. He wondered if she would be there to meet him or if she would consider it worth her while.

She might, it occurred to him, be extremely annoyed with him. But then, that would depend on what she was up to, if anything. He sighed at the thought of his mother's interference. In a moment's rebellion, he thought she should do her own dirty work. Then the plane landed and he had to think of other things.

He felt lonely and miserable as he went through the multifarious controls, until he realised how friendly people were, and how they spoke English when they found he didn't speak French. At the exit he felt a pang for his family as he saw the happy faces waiting to greet friends and relatives, until he distinguished among them the paler face of his sister, as always dressed in her own distinctive style, and smiling her ironic smile.

'She got you, eh? Even in the days of Christmas,' she said softly as she kissed him on the cheek. She was amused but seemed genuinely glad to see him, and led him out to a small car.

On the way to town he was so busy looking at the people and the animals that the desultory conversation didn't even make him feel uneasy. He was turning to see the face of a woman on a donkey when he heard his sister say, '. . . or have you run away from your wife and those boring kids of yours?' It had never occurred to him to look at the situation from his sister's point of view. He didn't find her interpretation in the least amusing. But he didn't find it insulting either: he just found himself tainted by her suggestion of a problem in his home. He could never envisage a personal problem in his home: his wife would never allow it.

He chuckled to himself. The air must be getting to him, or the flight – something. 'No,' he said simply.

They were arriving in the city now, and he realised that he had never given any thought to the details of life in a country such as this, or even to the appearance of the buildings. Perhaps he had seen too much television – he had a habit of sitting in front of it to avoid having to talk to his family. There was often no other way he could escape: if he went to the bedroom, his wife followed him to enquire if he were ill, and his eldest daughter had occupied the study that he had never used anyway. Perhaps he vaguely knew what a lot of foreign countries looked like, and perhaps that had removed all desire to know more. He had never honed in on details, as his mother did.

'Is it true that Moslems can have *up* to four wives?' he asked, suddenly wanting to know if such a thing were true.

'Oh come on!' His sister sounded exasperated. 'You're not going to trot out that bullshit, are you?'

It occurred to him that she might be living with one of them.

'Are you living with one?' he asked, involuntarily using a phraseology that was really quite foreign to him, the sort of

language he had heard on the shop floor. She might ask him to
get out of the car.

She was smiling. 'No,' she said, looking at him from the corner
of her eye as she turned into a gateway. The smile was enigmatic
and he still felt worried.

As they got his bags and crossed the lawn, he wasn't even
looking at the house or the exotic trees and plants that flourished
even in winter. He was still preoccupied with his mission, with
discovering what made his sister tick, what enabled her to
maintain such a distance from their mother who could have –
should have? – been a nun. If their father had lived, he wondered,
would it have made any real difference? He had often asked
himself the same question, and had a feeling the answer was still
no.

The immediate question now was, what mystery lay inside *this*
house? It drew his attention as she pushed open the door – there
must be somebody there . . . already?

She led him into the hall. He noticed the brass tray and the
warm soft rugs and the wall hangings in the living room and the
huge oak table at one end. To the right he could see her studio
through an open door, and paintings that even from where he
stood looked new and exciting and quite different from what she
had been doing when she lived at home. She had changed: he
could feel it in her whole attitude of body, her relaxed manner,
even though her clothes – the gypsy skirts, the colourful blouses,
the soft boots – were her preferred style, the one that had taken
over where the mini-skirts had stopped. One extreme to another.

But he must concentrate, caught up as he now was in a
curiosity of his own that made him forget that here they were
both far away from their mother, that he could for a moment
think for himself. His curiosity pressed on: who else was here?
Could one just leave doors open here and walk away? Just then he
heard his sister speak to someone in a back room. This is it, he
thought. She was calling him to come into the kitchen, where he
found her standing with a tiny woman in traditional clothes,
shuffling around in bare feet that were painted with some kind of
orange-red dye. She smiled at him now, a smile full of gold teeth,

and bowed to him, kissing her hand and placing it over her heart after she had shyly shaken his with it. He didn't know what to do. His sister was talking to the woman in a language he didn't recognise, and tasting a concoction in a large pot on the cooker. Oh, what he wouldn't give to be at home in his wife's kitchen, sitting down to a real dinner! And he had a week to go before this would end.

Still he couldn't ask the questions, and they sat and chatted and drank some of the whiskey he had brought. Dinner would be later, around eight, his sister said. She took him on a tour of the garden, talked of plants, showed him the vegetable plot, and her latest work, often saying 'we'. There was someone else.

At 6.30 he appeared. He wasn't North African, but spoke English with a heavy accent. He didn't feel like asking, it would emerge where he came from. He felt slightly hostile already as he thought what he was being put through, all because of this guy. His sister was cool and calm, kissing him when he arrived, holding his hand sometimes, or running her hand along his neck as she passed his chair. It was not exactly behaviour that his mother would approve of, but he felt relieved nonetheless. They chatted some more, his sister translating where necessary, and drank some more whiskey.

His mind ran through the names his mother would call her, the cold truths she would apply from a brain unencumbered by the fogs of whiskey. In his mother's eyes she would be nothing better than a whore.

He played with the image and found it didn't work. For him, a whore was someone in thigh boots and a white miniskirt who hung around lampposts in certain parts of town. He could not reconcile this with his friendly sister. He found himself defending her already, defending her against his mother, found that he liked her now, and decided that this was because she had changed considerably; although she was the same troublesome sister she was less intense and more relaxed, and some of this had communicated itself to him. Or was it the whiskey? A mental image of Jane Fonda in the film *Klute* now crossed his mind. His unconscious must be working faster than his conscious mind, he

thought, and vaguely wondered if this was due to the relaxing
effect of the whiskey. He had seen a TV programme which had
said something about one's unconscious being more productive if
one could encourage it, plumb its depths, manage to control it,
calling up associations and ideas at will, thinking of new ways to
do things and solve problems. It struck him, and he knew this was
whiskey-thinking, that his factory needed a little of this kind of
thought, and he wondered if he was up to it or if it was already
too late for him to change. Then the thought flew away like a
swallow in autumn, and was lost among the others that plagued
him. His sister and her friend – what else could he call him? –
were preparing the table for the evening meal. He noticed the
fourth place setting, but just assumed the little woman in the
kitchen would be joining them.

At eight they sat down to dinner and the little woman came,
wearing outdoor garments, to say goodbye. It wasn't her, then.
Good God, there were hardly two women? How did foreigners live
in countries like these? Snippets of ill-read books by and about
Gide, Wilde and others flew about his brain with the other birds of
thought. Get a grip on yourself, he thought, with the flight and
the whiskey you're beginning to ramble. Or maybe you've missed
something that was understood in the several languages that he
couldn't understand at all.

At 8.15 precisely a second young man arrived, and again he
felt relieved. They ate and chatted, and although the food was
heavily spiced, he liked it well enough. He felt closer to reality
once he had eaten, felt he could control the effect of the whiskeys.
The second young man spoke better English that the first, but
occasionally, again, words had to be translated. Everyone made a
great effort on his behalf and he found the whole thing really very
enjoyable. Afterwards they drank cognac and played cards, and
listened to songs in several strange languages, one of which –
Berber – he'd never even heard of. On the bookshelves he
glimpsed books whose titles suggested deep delving into life in
the Maghreb. He would find out soon enough, he supposed, what
the others did for a living.

When the cards were finished they repaired to the easy chairs for one last drink before bed. And it was then that the reality began to slip away from him completely. This time, he knew, it had nothing to do with whiskey, or cognac, or the excellent wine drunk at dinner. This time it was much more serious. It had to do with lives that were so removed from his own that he could not contemplate them. No television programme had prepared him for this: she was sitting on the sofa with the second young man, fondling him playfully as she had done the first. His mind raced. She had perhaps lived with one and was now living with the other? They were good friends? These continentals were different, he had heard . . . No. He couldn't escape it any longer. It was undeniable. But he needed proof.

When all three showed him to his room and headed into the only other bedroom in the house – he could see a huge bed through its open door – he still refused. They were being nice to him, the visitor, the second young man was kipping down on the floor, just while he was here . . .

But he knew, really. This time she had done it for sure. *She was living with both of them.* Making love – oh God – in a Moslem country . . . Phrases that weren't his own flew around his head, lines from sermons by missionary priests at his school. He collapsed onto the bed. His mother's face appeared in the dark before him, and he knew he was doomed. He couldn't even tell her the half of what he had found. He couldn't tell her anything. And he wished fervently that he could die, now, of a surfeit of alcohol. But he knew that his wishes had never been granted, he had never been allowed respite from these two women. And he knew that his sister, even if she didn't know it, was doing it to avenge herself on their mother, his mother too, who had only yesterday spoken to him on the phone, saying how she'd like to have news as soon as possible. He could say she was living with someone, couldn't he? And now he knew he could tell his mother nothing, that she didn't want to hear it, the truth; all she wanted was for his sister to start toeing the line again, and that should he tell it, he would be the one to suffer, to be punished, for whatever little he told, just as in the old days, and his sister would despise him too. And he understood now, in the dark, his sister's enigmatic smile in the car, and he understood too why she was so calm and happy and relaxed: she had finally broken the tie, had had to go this far in order to do so, and it had worked for her.

But what of him? When had they, these two women, thought of him? And where had they now left him? His voyage was a waste, he was stuck here for another six days during which he would have breakfasts and dinners with those three sinners. For that is what they were, in anyone's language. And when the week was over he would fly home with the makings of an ulcer.

And then it hit him: there was no one in whom he could confide. Not even his wife.

He almost cried in the dark room, on the strange bed. He would not even be able to tell his own wife. It would reflect on him too much, would taint him for ever in her eyes, might bring about the divorce his sister had hinted at in the car. And he suddenly saw the value of even confessions, although he had not been to a church for years, and he knew that he had now, in spite of himself and because of a blood tie, been cut off in a new way from his old self, from his wife, from his mother, from anyone who had up to now meant anything to him.

He cursed the day he was born, and fell into a troubled sleep.

Cashmere

Ruth raised an arm. Vertical. Letting gravity drain her blood backwards. The bulging veins flattened. Once again her hand looked smooth and youthful. She pulled it in. The duvet snuggled, moulding itself around her body. This bed was her own virgin territory. No lovers allowed. A fresh white bedcover, sprigged here and there with a blue pattern to admire. No coffee stains. No remnants of a companionable breakfast. Her eye wandered up. The angle where the ceiling met the wall was crooked. Wavy. Hypnotically, it held Ruth's attention, a suitable adjunct to her thoughts. He's not even a relative of mine. She closed her eyes and breathed deeply.

Again, Ruth recited number 20 from the Book of Psalms. Calling God's attention to a Gentile in need. She had prayed for William's death a few days earlier, reciting the Psalms again and again. Repeating his name William *ben* Desmond before each recitation, carefully forming the arcane Hebrew words with her mouth. Ruth had got no response. Perhaps it had been presumptuous of her to suggest a definite outcome to God. Still, she was Jew enough to know that petitioning the Almighty was futile. He had his own indecipherable methods.

The William Ruth had been acquainted with was a grumpy, cantankerous man, not into courting anyone or anything, least of all providence. The clergy had been sent packing long ago. His tufted tan doormat read 'No Welcome Here'. And unhappily, William's wife and son were all too occupied with the daily challenge of watching him go to think of his spiritual demise. Someone, somewhere, needed to remind God of his existence. Age and pain had overtaken him. Hospital was home and he was senseless.

Does it matter whose God? Ruth wondered. Mine serves me well enough. Her mind drifted back to a hot summer's day, the memory of which had faded like an old print carelessly exposed to a daily beam of light. She still had her puppy fat then. 'Look after Mummy for me, won't you? You know . . . if anything happens to me.' 'Don't be silly, Daddy, nothing's going to happen. You'll be fine.' That was all. What would I have said if I had known? What would I say now? Ruth often pondered this question, never taking it anywhere. There he was, beautifully groomed, crisp pyjamas, hair done ready for the attention of 'a nice little Irish nurse'. His heart was in for some repair. But little did she know how much his heart ached. He never said. Her father was leaving her. Had he left already? The hospital said no. She watched as they ordered the soulless machinery to pump more blood through his tired veins. For a moment she closed her eyes and tried to feel his faint vibration. She saw his body pale. Translucent. On that day Ruth willed her father to die and asked for God's assistance.

From her bed Ruth heard the phone ring four times, then click and pause. The machine picked it up. 'Just rang to say two things. Happy Birthday . . . and my father died in the early hours of this morning.' Brian's voice had altered. She recognised the lightness of tone, that moment of transcendence before one becomes weighed down, trashed again by one's own thoughts. Today his voice was gentle, relaxed, kind even. What a novel Birthday gift, Ruth thought, and felt a surge of omnipotence. Maybe she and God were one.

Julia and Brian stood on the step. The light and warmth of Ruth's hospitality shone on their faces as she opened the door.

'Come in quickly, it's so damp tonight.'

'You're so good to have us over again, I'll be bringing my bed soon,' Julia smiled.

'That's a good idea,' Ruth said, looking at Brian.

They were all equal in their fear of soft sympathy. A joke was better than a hanky, they had agreed long before this event. Ruth put the kettle on to make some tea and to keep herself on the move.

'Earl Grey or one of my funny ones?'

'Earl Grey would be lovely,' Brian answered.

The tea went cold rather more quickly than usual. I shouldn't have used my good cups, Ruth thought, the tops are too wide. All show and style, never practical, that's me. There were only a few old plain biscuits to sustain Brian, who was always hungry. He and his mother sat together on the sofa, subdued, and apologised for the lack of small talk. Julia had dressed carefully, in contrast to Brian who looked grubby and dishevelled. Her face was on, framed by a paisley patterned scarf of lavender and pink, which did much to disguise her mood. But every so often the set look of her face relaxed and Brian reached out his hand to settle on her arm.

'I'm sorry we're so unresponsive,' he said.

They don't have much to respond to. Does my silence make them nervous? I don't care. We can all gaze at the fire. I shall cough. Ruth coughed loudly, glad of an excuse to be down.

'Oh shit!' Brian leapt off the sofa. His phone was vibrating. He put it to his ear. 'Hello,' he yelled.

'Go upstairs,' Ruth said. 'You'll get a better signal.'

He ran up, two at a time, clasping the phone. 'Yes, yes,' he yelled. 'I can hardly hear you. Yes, yes, hold on. Mother, what do you want to write on the card for the wreath?'

'We'll write it ourselves,' she called back, indignant at such a suggestion.

'No, we can't,' he pleaded. 'They put it on top of the coffin.'

There was no pause, no hesitation, no waver in her voice. 'Goodbye darling, from Julia and Brian.'

He couldn't say it. His voice, the air, everything, became thick and gluey with his overwhelming emotion.

'I'm sorry, I'm so sorry,' he tried again to speak. 'Goodbye darling . . . Oh I'm so sorry . . . from Brian and Julia, no, no, I mean Julia and Brian. Yes, thank you, thank you so much.'

Brian came down the stairs, his grubby composure wrecked further by a softened face and a red nose. Julia seemed unmoved. Ruth wondered about her 'darling'. She coughed again. Brian produced a well-soaked hanky and blew his nose. His mother remained elegant all the while, not enjoying or engaging in her son's emotional display.

Fuck this, I wish they would go. But Ruth said nothing and gazed again at the happy flames flickering regularly in the grate of her gas fire. Crying men are not very sexy, she thought, and hated herself for being such a cold fish. So easy to say 'I love you', especially during sex. It means nothing . . . a boyfriend somewhere had said that. Since then, she trusted terms of endearment more than that oversung declaration. *How I would love to be called 'darling' so unthinkingly, so naturally, so endearingly. What had William done to deserve that?* she asked herself.

'Is there anything I can do for you both?'

'Oh, please. Would you collect his things from the hospital? I don't think I could face it.' Brian's grateful face appealed.

'Don't be ridiculous, Brian, we can do that ourselves,' Julia said. 'I can do it. Ruth is sick.'

'Oh why can't you accept help from anyone and let me be? I'm the one who has to do it all. You can't go alone. And I'd like Ruth to do it. It needn't be today.' He looked at Ruth again.

Ruth and Julia were silenced by his insensitivity. He couldn't understand the simplicity of a woman who wanted to do one last task for her husband and who needed the silent support of her son to do it. Again they took refuge apart and gazed at the flames.

Brian, if left to his own devices, wanted no funeral, no people viewing his discomfort. 'We should simply toss the ashes over Howth Head,' had been his private suggestion to Ruth. In response to her irritated look he had said, 'We're Low Church, no theatrics.'

Yes, Brian was low all right. That was how Ruth came to collect William's meagre bag of possessions from the hospital a few days after he died.

It was cold outside. Ruth could see her breath. The lights were on, it was after six and the wards were quiet, everyone just fed. Ruth had approached a kindly nurse, on duty, happy to do her bit for the old and infirm. An angel in sensible shoes. 'I was there when he died,' she said.

'I'm only a friend of the family,' Ruth explained quickly, lest the kindly nurse should waste her precious sympathy on nothing.

Ruth found it hard to stay: her mind and her body wanted out of there. The smell of hospitals made her sick. She hovered, trying to fix her feet to the ground, just long enough to complete this odious task. Her mind was not corralled so easily. *He died alone, why pretend, Nursie? His wife and son were tucked up in their respective beds, also alone, not wanting to be tainted with the smell of rotting flesh.* Ruth shivered from her thoughts. Did William care or even see them, or did the sight of their misery complicate his leaving? Who could be sure of anything?

'I think there was a smart leather case, somewhere along the line it must have got exchanged for this one,' Ruth suggested.

'It could be upstairs. Do you know where he last had it? He's been moved around a bit.'

'I'll ring Julia. His wife. Have you got a phone book?'

Another nurse looked over at Ruth suspiciously.

'I know his son's number off by heart, not his wife's,' Ruth explained. Her finger ran along the page and stopped at William's name. She felt uncomfortable. *I shouldn't be here, this is family business.* Ruth began to question her own position. *I want to go . . . Control yourself,* she ordered, as she held the receiver next to her ear and dialled Julia's number.

'Julia, I'm here. Here at the hospital. They can't find the good leather case you put his things in. This one is grey cardboard. What shall I do? I could look upstairs.'

'It doesn't matter, I don't want it,' Julia said. 'What about you, are you all right, you're so good to go out tonight, what about your cough?' Julia, as always, appeared to think of everyone but herself.

'There are no keys.' Ruth was becoming more clipped by the second, not making a whole lot of sense, anxious to get off the phone. She was being watched. *Is our behaviour so strange? What is the standard mode of collection? Am I not gentle enough, sad enough? Too matter-of-fact?* Ruth wondered. She was drained of all comprehension. She signed the form, letting the staff off all responsibility, and left the inferior blue case where it was, and carried out instead a black plastic sack of smalls and pyjamas to her waiting car. The brown envelope containing William's cheap throwaway watch she chucked on the dash. Julia had said it was rubbish. Well, she can throw it out, thought Ruth, as she sped out of the car-park, propelled by her own irritable thoughts. Brian treats me as a wife. When it suits.

Ruth opened the cupboard door. All her clothes were dark. The winter wardrobe was in session. She took a moment to choose. A long chocolate-brown blanket of a coat and black ankle boots. Brown was a little kinder to her complexion than the mandatory black. *They'll be too upset to notice*, Ruth thought. *And I don't even know this man. Did I know my father any better?* She questioned the paradox of her relationships often. Of course I cuddled my old man or he cuddled me, but I don't remember much in the way of conversation. His stomach conversed loudly – after my mother's pickled meat sandwiches. She smiled at the memory . . . and even louder with the pressure of my small head resting on its side . . . I sat on his knee and 'shook the hand that shook the world'. He observed me, admiring, I could see it in his eyes . . . he never felt the need to do any more. Without inhibition, she could remember his fondness for her.

Unlike William, Ruth's father was carried to his final destination on an old cart. Her mind drew back to that antique apparatus, a flat palette with iron wheels, large enough to support the long box. It was guided by a group of bulky wellington-clad men, formidable experts in dark, heavy clothing, who shifted their weight from one black boot to the other as they waited between each ritual movement. No, that she would not forget. She had revived and relived the story often. When transported back, she could feel the damp grit collecting beneath her feet.

She had stood on the women's side of the cold barren building, facing the men. There were many old friends sad at another loss to their dwindling Jewish community, sad for her mother and maybe a little sad for themselves. The sealed-up coffin, elevated on its cart, stood in the middle of the room and formed a division between the two groups. Separating the sexes was taken for granted, so the women had to prop each other up while the men simply stood firm in their place. A few prayers were read before the cart was moved from its position.

I was not ashamed of my tears. So I cried. So what. While the chevrah kaddisha *did their business of pushing the cart out through the large double doors, I cried.* Her father, that day, lay enclosed in a simple unadorned coffin with only his *tallit* tucked in beside him for company. She was powerless in the presence of such well-practised ritual, automatic for everyone but her. Ruth was a new witness. She had never been to the Orthodox Jewish Cemetery before. A child, in a land where children shouldn't have to go. She supposed she would lie beside him when her turn came.

Ruth could feel the fragile weight of her mother resting on her arm. *She needed supporting as much as I did. We followed the coffin together on its journey around the narrow path of the burial ground. The last walk we would ever take with the 'old man'.* New tears seeped out as she visualised the rows and rows of tombstones in neat lines, spaces left, parents waiting for their seed to join them as dust in the earth. No flowers for the dead, just a pebble here or there to mark a visit to a grave, the headstones almost as simple as the coffins, all corpses treated as equal.

Her father's final resting place was neatly carved out of the earth, deep and narrow: from now on his requirements were deemed negligible, a place to fade away. After the coffin was lowered the mourners took it in turns to throw a little earth into the grave, respectfully participating in the act of his burial. It was over quickly. Ruth and her mother walked back to the building and waited for instruction. Others washed their hands at the outside basins, putting thoughts of death and decay behind them, resolving to improve themselves.

Ruth that day was wearing a charcoal-grey cardigan. Her best. All she had that was dark. A new cashmere cardie. Her father had bought it with her – for her. A present to mark her trans-formation. He called her a 'young lady'. Her fingers remembered the scissors tear, just above the top buttonhole. Done with a sharp implement. His comfort to her now completely destroyed. A strange and pointless observance that would remain scorched in

her mind for ever. Her garment was ripped and she was made
ready for the week of *shiv'ah*. The Rabbi read out the ritual prayer
times and the address of their home. Her father was not to be
forgotten, of that she was somehow glad. Ten men were needed to
recite *kaddish* morning and evening.

Mourning she remembered as a complex affair requiring
instruction and assistance from a group of congregants well-
versed in ancient liturgy. Twice a day, through an open hall door,
the men arrived to say prayers. The women set food down on the
kitchen table and provided a little respite for her mother. No one
argued with the Lord's teaching and Ruth's only thought was
God has done my bidding, the suffering is over.

Ruth enveloped herself in the big brown coat and checked her
face in the mirror. She was now ready. Her expression was
appropriately sad.

William was to be cremated; in that Ruth had no say. They
gathered, small in number, at the chapel in the cemetery. Nothing
was said about William except that he would be sadly missed by
Julia and Brian. A few words were read out before he made his way
between the velvet curtains. Ruth's eyes and mind followed the
conveyor belt. She knew he was cold, waiting outside for trans-
portation to the oven. She knew she was not meant to think of
that. *It is not our way to burn a corpse. I am an alien amongst these
people.* The next corpse and family were waiting at the door. Ruth
could hear the noise. *How can one trust ashes? Is the oven cleaned out
each time? I know I'm not meant to think of these things.* In her
prayers, William had become part of her.

Ruth lay awake late into the night with her head familiarly
inclined. Brian's stomach was talking to her. It said, 'I love you. I
love you for being here, in my bed, with me.' She felt content; she
had performed well. She had played the hostess all day, made the
sandwiches, poured the drinks, flirted with the rector and smiled
and been as kind as she could manage. But where was happy?
Brian never called her name, never tried sweetheart, hadn't
heard of darling. Not, that is, until a few days ago.

She longed to wake him up.

CÓILÍN Ó hAODHA

Indian Summer

When it wasn't an island they could free-float on, it was a green, slow slope beach on a coast of bent back trees with no sand. A soft grass strand, then, except where the until-now-hidden rivers bubbled in, where the bog might suddenly bulge up brown, where the boys could paddle on and out forever and never sink in deep enough to swim. Cut off from the mainland of road and railway by a sea of trees – ash and beech and copper beech – the island jutted out into the smooth round bay like a chin, and the rocky drop down into cold saltwater was a stiffened lip. When autumn ends and with it ends the hazy Indian weather, the island will disappear. But even then it was their island only when the weather permitted; even then it was an island only when their parents allowed. And it was to there that they had got, if she had asked the question loud enough, if they had raised their voices loud and safely far enough away to answer back.

Where had they got to now?

On a kitchen-top, one son's dinner steamed warm, then cold, and impulsive ice-cream set aside in the fridge froze to stone in the bowl. In the next-door house, unnoticed until it was too late and it was too far gone, a basket of bread edged slowly away from the last three feet of that year's light, blurring out along the window sill; the sandwiches turned the sun brown once and quietly went stale. And in the last house, half a mile of crows flying away across the fields that separate the two roads that run around the village, nothing happened and there was not a sound, since no one there had managed to make it home on time. A woman wearing an apron and a question mark clicked her tongue. Another mother clipped a cupboard with her skirt on her way out the kitchen door, out with the sun into the evening to try for one last time to force new colours into her fading summer garden. And the last, impractical and angry, fumbled her keys onto the ground when she flopped long-armed into the car, and breathed out one short thought about a dinner party – for four, was it? or five? – forgotten about and for tomorrow night.

Where had they got to now?

They were away above it all, all adrift like clouds in a wooden ship that had been hastily stitched together from a few broken-up pallets and fortunate twigs, some well-spotted – from the ground, and that high up – likely branches. But the ship was strong enough still to weather the changing weather. On a calm day, because that was what it had been, when nothing could have fluttered a butterfly's wing, a storm had head-on hit the elm tree they were sailing in. The waves came swelling and crashing over the blind side of the only tree at the lonely top of the hill. And no matter how quick a man tried to twist away his head or neck or eyes, the waves were like bursts of wind through pioneering leaves, small and sharp and hard. The earlier wind, which had been too soft even to turn a field of long grass silver, was suddenly strong enough to wreck a sky-boat and steal her autumn gold, and sink her.

John, the tallest of them, was standing as near as he could reach and hold to the top of the tree; he was on lookout for the first sight of land. He was also the first among them because he was the eldest, and for having been the only one to allow tobacco smoke to settle on the back of his throat without blinking an eye or scrunching up his cheek. Coughing now into the last puff of a stolen cigarette, he tried to smother the sound and said nothing. The all-hands-on-deck pair on the boards down below him, who listened closely for any word or sign to come from the crow's nest, were so intent on the possibility of a heroic death that they didn't even snigger. Nor when the smoke had cleared did he say anything, until the sun had rolled itself out into a purple stripe along the starboard horizon and showed up the lights of houses, a stretch of road, and even some last people walking home in the tightening dark, from work or the bus-stop or from the shops. Then the call to abandon was made loud and clear and, being as

brave as completely unafraid, the other two clean forgot the
tornado threat to life and limb and immediately obeyed him.

Because they knew as well as John did that when the steady
flap and screech of gulls through a strong breeze began to sound
like a foot tapping out a tune in quick-march time on a tiled
porch, or began to match the rhythm of a fingernail clicked on
the face of a watch, there was nothing coincidental about it. And
they all knew that when white bright wings flashed past in the
night, then somewhere else someone might have switched on an
outside light and just as quickly spread the dark, and wiped a
smile off her annoyed mouth.

'Put out your hand.'

They had to abandon now if night and the ship weren't to go
down with all hands lost. And the way to climb down was all
hands – tight fistfuls of wood and leaves – and just a pair (or two,
or three) of hopeful feet stretched down for a lucky break in the
bark, and not one eye to see.

'Look at me when I'm talking to you, young man.'

Not one of them could bring himself to look down from so high
up, down to where they knew they had to get. And when they
finally made it down again onto dry land, the sea-salt sweat won
with honour and so much effort sneaked off and left just a skin of
dirt, dry and sharp as sand.

'You'll get your death.'

They waded home through the swish of fern and the rustle of
bracken; thick dew clung to their tired legs, and not a word was
spoken. They stopped to split up as usual and say goodbye at the
fork in the road, at the gate that creaked open into a field called
the field of the Judgement Stone. Late as they already were, and
later as they would be still in getting back to back doors and cold
dinners, there was no need for them to pause in doubt or sorrow
about the verdicts handed down in their absence. Guilt may come
late in the day but it never fails to come: they felt guilty now for
their failure to keep good time or to keep faith with their absolute
promises to behave.

'Goodbye' and 'Good night' and 'See you tomorrow'.

The one who drew the line of three to a close, who trailed along

the last as usual, was the youngest. He was the youngest only
by three weeks and he was still young enough then or old enough
now not to mind whether he was called Jimbob or Jimmy or
Jim.

'James,' his mother would say. 'James, you're late. And look at
the cut of your clothes: you're a state.'

He spoke then. He said that it might hold out until the last day.
He meant what they had been waiting for all through the
holidays: good weather. Maybe it would hold out until the last
day, tomorrow – and the ship as well.

But when the last day did dawn and the troubled waters of
three painfully quiet breakfasts had been successfully negotiated,
the ship was long gone. Louis, the middle one – who wore
glasses . . . only to read, and only when no one else was looking
– had cut the anchor loose last thing the night before. And from
where it had been bobbing gently on page sixty-four, he let the
flimsy vessel rock and roll until morning broke and brightened
over where the ship had run aground, somewhere in chapter
twelve, where his eyes had closed. So they were on the island
now, looking for treasure. And they arrived on the very day that
all of them and all of them together had become aware that time
was no longer – and maybe never had been – on their side.

In the beginning, the names given to them by their parents and
the priest's right hand had simple meanings: John was John for
the love of his grandmother's life; Jim was so to make his father
Senior; and Louis was himself because his mother had fallen for
the golden tongue of the King of France. Jim and John and Louis –
for the patron saints of elder brothers and blind prophets and of
kings – their given names had simple meanings. The names they
gave themselves later, on the other hand, were epic: Hercules and
Robinson and Ahab, Zorro and Jesse and Armstrong, Skywalker,
Indiana and Bond. And it was never too late to change them
again or to change them around.

Of course, they had all been on the island before, to travel far and
do battle and to explore. In the back of each boy's mind the place
was well marked out, but their land was not to be found sketched

to scale on any map. No 'X' could be drawn to cross the spot of its location or to show its bounds. Their island of hide-and-seek and war, of red dragons and harmless slaughter, was just this old familiar place or that, a quiet time of the day in the quietest part, then a strange sound or the echo of a sound, and then a mysterious shape or a shadow of a shape. Their eyes lit on the generations of single footprints trampled into a flat thin brown path, and the track worn down and out by the tread of the many gone before them slipped easily into the comfortable pace of their present tense. Even so, they took great care and kept their eyes turned down to search for safe passage around every waiting rock. Six feet followed after the past securely, found the safest tufts of wire-grass to land on and take off from, and let heads and minds lag well behind. They had been there maybe a thousand times before, but never as they were on that day: hungry and sore all over, with nowhere near enough time to reach the end or conquer it all.

It is difficult for somebody to get lost and wander aimless in a place he knows like the back of his hand. And it was impossible for them, in fact: they knew too well the wrist of knobbled fields freckled with bog, the gully-veins that run blue and dark, reed-hairs that stand straight up to where they turn browner and curl down, and the fingernails of soft shoreline bitten into rocks.

Every time John looked up, the grey block of the castle that overlooked the bay and that always gave the sky – in sunshine, clouds or rain – its imperious stare, stood out against the land and the sea, and swelled up. That sight of bold grey made him remember the different face of the man who still lived in the castle's keep, who had travelled a thousand miles under polar ice in the middle of the war, on some courageous mission, and secret too, and totally alone. What he did not always remember then was that the decorated soldier – no rank held lower than captain, with a chestful of medals and pockets full of coins – was now a great age of ordinary old, if the wrinkles on his face did not count like the rings in trees and chopped lumber. The captain was an old man who could only hunch where other people walked and whose words, when any were to be heard at all, all sounded like low sighs, like a storm of waves heard pounding on wet stone walls in the middle of the night.

Any time Jim scratched his nose, and he did that a lot, he always caught sight of the numbers scrawled on the back of his hand, and rubbing off. Was it the phone number of someone he was supposed to ring, or had already rung? Could it be the price or size of some message his mother had tried to make him run? Or, as his hand fell back into his pocket, he would accidentally check the time. And it was twenty-one hours, forty-three minutes and seventeen seconds until the bell of Scoil Naomh Brendán would ring and they would all hear sung in the máistir's voice: *Brostaigí buachaillí agus bígí ciúin!* – over and over and over again.

Louis stopped every once in a while, to squint until the tallest tree in the forest grew back into focus, and to remember all the promises that had been made to him – by his father, by his brother – the promise to tell him how to build, the promise to build a real tree house with planks and six-inch nails and strong plastic, a real tree house that would never give in to rainwater, or slide down and to the side in winter, or rot. And when he made tracks again to make up the distance the other two had left behind them, he was sure that it couldn't ever happen because there just wasn't going to be enough time.

'Which way will we go now?' he wondered aloud as he caught up to the others again; his idle saying was forced into a question when his voice screwed the last word up. Which way would they go now? Some question: as if a dramatic choice of great determination would have to be made to follow the path that carried them so easily along; as if some compromise would have to be wrung from the short shouting distance between three strong-minded friends, or found between the blood-angry rusted gate that was propped up on his right and the thicket of gorse that fell dead away to his left. The other two had stopped, and watched him carefully to see where his thought would end. They were happy enough to listen to him think aloud and to take this part of the action for himself. If anyone knew or was to know which was the way they should follow and go, it had to be him. Although this would never be admitted out loud by any there, it was in the end his game. And as soon as he had turned the track – the footprints of farmers, the hoofprints of sheep and heifers, the pawprints of sheepdogs and terriers – into a dried-out riverbed, the haunt of unseen hunters who crawl ever stealthily forward and of unknown animals in an endless scattering for life, they moved on again and marched in single file. And as suddenly as the sound of their steps broke the silence, the thoughts of ghost Apaches and phantom herds of bison dropped off the edge of his mind and he slipped back into the land of promises, promises as full-grown as the thorns on the gorse they threaded through – and as sharp.

Sharp words were to be heard there too: their island was no paradise. 'We're lost,' barked John. His voice was gruff because the way Jim always silently deferred to the better judgement of *Four eyes, Four eyes* had begun to get under his skin, and needle – and that he did not know where they were going or what was to happen in the end, when he was the eldest, made him nervous as well. But when he began to think that Louis didn't know either – or didn't care? – that he didn't know what treasure they had come to look for or where their search was to begin, the smirk that spread across his face took most of the heat out of his temper. It made him wonder if, with the right face and the right idea, he could work a bit of a fright in.

'Damn' was the word, and then came the sound of a boot sucked out by the ankle from a stumbled puddle of mud and worse. Damn and the sound was Jim. It would serve him just right, wouldn't it? 'I'm dead meat,' he said, as he inspected the damage and ran a finger through the dirt. Blood flooded into his cheeks and cold fingers at the sudden memory of what his mother had said, what his father had done, the last time something like this had happened to him. 'I'll kill you if it ever happens again. Promise me it never will.'

John looked away from the worry and over at Louis. In a better mood, on another day, he would have read a promise there as well, the one of which he had already heard so much tell: of a real tree house that would never, ever fail. At the very least he should have seen the flash of distracted glasses as Louis turned his head back towards the forest; he should have noticed that he was not listening, that he was not interested in joining his conspiracy. But all he did see clearly was the hand reached out instinctively to grasp a branch. He saw the red bubble blow where a thorn pricked in. There was another curse then, but this time it was quieter, smothered, different.

The thought of his own mother's reaction to mud-stained clothes and wet feet struck home to him. 'You'll get your death, darling.' He laughed privately at that – at the *darling* – more privately than the way a sudden burst of laughter could paint over an older, deeper blush of sin. He clipped Jim playfully round the ear – it was all just a game, wasn't it? – and he felt sorry. He was sorry for no particular reason, and for the way things seemed to be going all wrong for them on the last day of freedom, and for being jealous of a book he never thought he would ever want to read. He felt sorry for hoping to frighten Jim. So, for as long as the shame could stay and be remembered clearly, he gathered hand-fuls of loose bracken to wipe the guilty smile from his face and to help get the shoes clean.

When they reached the stile that two-stepped up and down into open land, they decided to separate, to go it alone for an hour, to search out and meet back. It was a simple plan. Everything on the open run of land was laid out flat: a ring fort full of little people – what were the sounds that came from it if not the sounds of feet drumming and hands clapped? – the crooked walls with yellow patches and white blotches, whose vindictive stones looked firm until they were leaned on or climbed over; and the broken-up green of grass and rushes, where deep brown eyes were lowered in and kept close watch. Fanning each way out over the flat, it was a simple plan. Louis had a word for it that began with 'R', but they agreed to just look around until the sun had turned the corner on the distant headland, until they heard a long-practised bird-sound if there was cloud. The word was 'reconnoitre'. Jim was the one who had done all the practising. He had perfected the call-home call of a bird he had never seen or heard sing: a blue crown on a red-bodied bird, with green and yellow wings. The whistle was carefully designed to drive his mother round the twist.

'Sssshhh . . . what is it?'

The other two listened carefully to him now so as not to mix it up with the cooing of a seagull gone soft, a grey crow turned sweet by old age, a cow's cough. And then they were gone, and once it was safely out of sight of uncertain feet, the stile danced – one-step, two-step – the steps of the stile danced back.

Jim was the youngest and the smallest, and took the shortest strides; he disappeared the last, but never quite disappeared out of sight. He could always be seen wandering somewhere along the edge of the view from the gapped wall on the thin hill. Jim was not so fast. He was the sort of slow that works wrinkles into a mother's forehead over years, and sometimes, when there was nothing else to be done, could force a shout or click of her tongue. But all the same, he was quick enough to make a break for it when a back was turned for a minute and fast enough, too, to see the time to move really slow and so be sooner free. And what he was looking at right now was the time to flee.

Standing in under overhanging white thorn and stunted ashes, he could feel the time to run coming. The further he moved into the ring fort, the faster bushes twisted into trees, the thicker nettles and briars sprouted at his ankles and knees. And that was all before the sound: something in the ring fort that older people crossed themselves by was annoyed. Something or someone, or more, was angry at his intrusion on the peace of knitted dark and stitched leaves. What was it in there – voices or hearts or breaths? – what was it in there that could be so angry and annoyed if it wasn't someone or something that stole babies and coloured their eyes green, that could turn milk sour in the fridge, or that woke everyone together in the middle of the night with a vanished scream? His bravery was wearing off now: it rolled off his forehead, down his face and his neck, onto his sleeve. The rustling crawled nearer to him with a breath that smelt of rotten blossoms and the sort of damp soil that sticks. The air stopped, held still long enough to take him off his guard and to send in a love-struck

wasp to distract and frighten him. He flicked it away from his ear.
The first weak brushstroke and an unsteady hand meant that
soon his arms were swinging savagely all around him. To the left:
was that a bent branch or a back turned suddenly away? Had a
face, with a wide mouth, formed in a darkness that his eyes could
not penetrate? Had its one eye really winked? To his right: did he
see thin arms, dark-veined, stretching down to grasp a rock or a
stick, or reaching out for his hot neck?

He couldn't wait to see, and crashed out again into the long
rough grass in a headlong dive for the shifting line where some
sun fell still. Without even one look back into the shade, he fell –
and came to a second later to find himself breathing again. The
time had passed on by. And he, his throat about to burst, was safe
at last, safe and sound in the open field where the only thing with
a cold touch was an imaginary sea. And he was safe at last,
wasn't he?

John moved so fast that he was almost there, where he wanted to
be, before the others had even turned away and left: one foot was
planted up in barren sandy clay while the other slid with pebbles
down the hill in search of grip. The master of all he surveyed was
scrawny then and a little bit pale. It had been a bad summer
whatever way he thought about it: the rain had forced most of
the play indoors, forced the volume of games to stay down, put
dampers on all their fun. The part of the shoreline he was
standing on was still; a pool of sheer water, slabbed stones and
only rumours of fish. The sandbank that ran up into a row of
dwarfed hawthorns was riddled with holes. Sometimes, if he stood
quiet enough he could hear the rabbits dig, catch sight of a cloud
of dust raised, a bobbing of brown-and-white, the pricked ears,
then the brown-and-white scampering away.

One day he could remember now, a day when there had been
no clouds at all and every conversation between mothers had
begun with 'The sky is so blue, the sky is so clear', he had been
standing right there, exactly where he was that day – but not
alone. Louis was standing at his right shoulder, to cover him as
he went forward tentatively into the unknown, into what was

then unknown territory for them. In their silent black-and-white adventure, his friend was committing the whispering sin. They both stopped dead the second they heard the sound. Like the cry of a child, or a high-pitched whine, the sound came from up where the trunks split the dark before the branches strangled in. From in there it came, the wail that shrank their breaths shorter than heartbeats, grew goose pimples and formed a tight film of sweat all over skin. But even when the snouts of two small badgers flickered into a patch of low-flung sunlight, the whisper at his shoulder didn't quieten.

'Careful. Careful, soldier,' it said. 'The mother might be close by and watching us keen. We look like a threat to her, to them. We do, I think.'

Soldier? Careful, soldier? It was 'General' to him. He tried to figure out what could be so threatening about his worn runners, a stick-out shirt, his torn jeans, but nothing came to him – nothing except the shivering whisper that continued on.

'Did you know that she will bite down on your leg, the biggest bone in it? She will bite until she hears the breaking crack. And if you cry out or let a tear drop, she'll go straight, roaring, straight for your neck.'

The teeth would have to clamp down and the jaws would lock until the last breath left his body sorrily and her chasing-tails children were quitened again and safe at home, well fed and asleep. But before any blood ran or cries for help had had to flee, tripping over the rough ground towards the town, the crying had stopped as suddenly as it had begun. The two snouts withdrew into the shade, back in towards the crumbling wall behind the hawthorn, and the shadows on the hedge floor turned back into the more ordinary mysteries of twigs flicked and leaves that waved in a cloudless breeze. They moved on, warier and knowing more now, they moved on – and they were not frightened of anyone or by anything at all.

And there on his own this day, he is not afraid. There is no sound of crying from bird or animal. And the shadows under the hawthorn are motionless, fighting shy, when a spot of sudden blue rounds out the corner of his eye. He scrambles on the dry slope, limps along its sliding surface, walks closer to a white-blue circle and – closer again – he walks closer to a blue-white oval with grey speckles, and wonders to himself if this is it, if this is what they have come to find, the treasure that awaits them on the island. Until, at last – patience, patience now – until at last he is standing right over it on the flat. He hunkers down on the small drop that ends in the quiet sea and all its fishy rumours, and sees what he has found for what it is: an egg. Smooth-shaped and unbroken, the egg lies exactly according to some plan, or maybe abandoned or forgotten or accidentally left behind, in a hollow in the tough clumped grass. How long has it lain there waiting for him? He turns it gently till the hole appears: there is a small black mark pierced once into the shelled dark. He brings it to his ear and listens, holds his breath, but there is nothing inside to hear. What made the hole? Was it tooth or beak? Is the punctured egg a testament to a quick death or to the sharp escape that left the grey silence to wait for him? Perhaps this is the afterbirth of a brilliant bird – bright colours, blue and red and yellow and green, and long feathers – the bird that all three of them have heard, or thought they heard, but none of them has seen.

The sun edges round the headland, throws a few half-hearted beams onto the retreating tide, brushes the small castle's ocean face, and early sunset gleams. It is time to head back to the others but he has time enough to take the egg with him. When it touches cold against his hand and rolls across his palm, he is suddenly afraid – afraid of a thin black line in a zigzag all around, of the chance that the brittle shell might split open and ruin his surprise. He gathers grass into his hands and wraps it well. Carefully, he places it in the deepest pocket of his jacket, in against his breast, and turns back along the shore he followed there. Skittish pebbles make nervous steps and take harder concentration. He makes for the crooked gap and the others where he left them. He wonders if they will be there yet, back before him, because he returns victorious to his men and, if the eggshell can hold out, he returns to them treasure-leaden. The brilliant bird sings insistent from the hill and he hears it clear. He speeds up over the surer ground of grass and nettles, back towards their safe haven.

Louis squatted on his heels below the dead straight tideline of buzzing seaweed, and passed water-smooth stones through his fingers and from one hand to another, back and forth. Letting them rattle to the ground at his feet, he wiped his glasses clean of flecks of sand and the dirt-wind sprinkle. Waves rippled quietly all along the short beach – the herds of white horses were rested, and now grazed lazily over the moving field of green. So lazy was Louis, too, that it took a loud splash and a burst of foam to wake him. The surface settled back and the circles of the splash widened out to nothing, but the trail of swimming bubbles could still be seen and followed. It was a seal; at least one seal, if not more. There was probably just one: a grey-whiskered and forgetful very old bull, or one of his sleek black and inexperienced young. Not many seals came that far into the bay, within thin-eyed view of the beach and the village, or came so close to the shore; and if they did they never came in shoals. Louis waited for the next move. He hoped for the sight of a flipper cutting up into the sky, or of nostrils flared open to gulp fresh air, or of the big lids lifted on wet eyes.

'Do you know?' his older brother had said the last time they had been down there together and talked of eels and seals and sea-lions crowding round and round in choppy water, 'Did you know that seals are blind?'

Seals are almost blind was the correct answer. If the watcher sits or stands still, ignores the ache that begins in his calves and shins, and the cramp that moves steadily up his legs, tightens his chest and makes his hands shake, if the watcher stands or sits and stays still the seals won't see a thing. A man, or a boy, is a rock or a shadow thrown over their poor eyes. But, boy, 'Boy, can they hear.'

The surface of the water is broken again and a round head appears. He says nothing out of place or out loud, nothing out of time, out of present time – and, again, the round head slowly sinks, down it goes and gone. When he does speak, he has chosen all the words he uses carefully.

'Is it true that seals can sing?'

What he means is whether it is really true that sailors jumped ship for the love of sweet-voiced mermaids – for sweet-voiced mermaids with hairy chests and dark pool eyes, with soft mouths and sometimes tusks and always razor teeth. He laughed to himself. He doesn't remember if he asked the question or, if he had, what the answer might have been. Could the answer have been, 'Yes?' He laughed again. The light wind lifted and the sun looked like shining. Vanished bubbles, absent circles, said that the seal had escaped and returned to deeper, friendlier waters, and to the arms of dead men. 'Yes, they can. They did. Well, in those days, the seals could sing.'

Out of the corner of his eye, Louis caught sight of the captain fishing from the end of the jutting pier in front of the castle. The old man was a tattoo of white hair, blue trousers and green waders on the grey bay, a grey sky. The water that licked the foot of the jetty was exactly cold enough for skinny-dipping, that exact dark blue colour, and the lie of the land where the sea slowed and sat still was perfect for spying. What about his days? Who sang or could not sing in the captain's days? What about the nights spent all alone, the many hours he sat in a tin-can submarine under water, in the hissing dark under sheets miles deep of solid ice? What had he to say for all of those long days and nights? Who had he to talk to then, or to answer back with songs? Had he heard the mermaids sing one night, off the port or to the starboard, and lost himself to their charms? Is what stumbles through the village to buy bread and share a gap-toothed smile with every face what left the harbour, or is it only the shell of the one who went away – an empty submarine that floated home by chance and washed up one morning in a spring tide swell?

The captain lived in the keep of the late medieval castle. He walked under a murder hole every time he went to lift and turn the latch on the front door and make the hinges shriek. The wooden door grated open on its iron skeleton, but there was always a smile on his face to greet the waiting children and a few patient words for their harassed teacher. He welcomes another history class trip of mixed motivations and, immediately, the tour begins. Louis followed the nods of the white-haired head to chamber pots and slop buckets, the arms that were leaned against a four-poster bed during a long explanation, the thin fingers as they sketched out a worn crest on a damp wall-hanging, and the ear pressed against the running stone of the castle wall to show the sounds that six feet of granite could make a man miss and make his eyes water. In the few minutes of scurrying time that were left, he took in the arrow-slit windows where seagulls nest. He climbed the sharp spiralled staircase where a stubbed toe or a grazed knee told of the need to watch each step in a way that no one, try as they might – not even the teacher who shouted out for obedience and attention – that no one could ever have said.

But the story was only starting when the door closed softly behind the class and coat hoods and umbrellas were lifted and opened into a lightly falling rain. Louis looked back at the solid door and saw the tongue of a boat's bell hooked to the frame idling in the corner wind. There was no shelter there.

'Children, *ciúnas anois*, this is the last bell from the last ship to set sail, the last boat that left the harbours of the war to brave mission and return home safe.'

The toll of a ship's bell was the comforting sound that had led the weakest children of Israel – the young-old and infirm – through the trapped waters to their promised land. It seemed strange that a short length of frayed rope and a ball of metal could say much more than the quiet, finger-wagging twinkle-eyed man thought his visitors could take. He had spoken on and off for an hour, and yet how much he had passed over in silence: the day a long shark's fin had gone slinking by the bows; the everyday storms that had rolled in to whip the skies dark; the men he had known – the friends – who had given up strength and hope, and fallen in; the way the boom of enemy fire sounds much louder over night water; the night a bruised hull burst and the hold was filling, filling fast; the panic when the rope was grasped and shaken, and the bell rang out over rough waters and the reflections of fire; the way the bell echoed still and would for ever, somewhere in the air and in his ear. But all of this had remained unsaid. And all that it would take is a quick grip and the metal tongue would be loosed free. *Cling! Cling!* The shock of that action by a clueless schoolboy might make the captain speak: 'Come close. Come closer – and I will tell you how I heard the mermaids sing.'

But still he stands, at his familiar distance – that day at the door of the castle, and this day on the pier. Now he is calmly drawing in the line along the reel, to cast it far out to sea again with one quick flick of his wrist.

Caught back to the present by a sudden chill, Louis tried to check the time of the light that slid further down the wet sand with the tide. He could hear Jim whistle birdsong loudly from inland. It was time to go back to the others and leave what is there behind. And it seemed to him, looking back – and looking back again – it seemed that in every movement he made then that he shed something precious, something he couldn't or wasn't allowed to take with him when he went. Even sorrow cannot stay for ever: all it takes is a moment of laughter to break the mind's train – a trail of scattered jewels – and forget. Or the relief he felt when the tension broke and the badgers that were biting at an ivy wall, suckled on the cold stone, fell silent and moved on. Relief came with the silence of their passing, and forgetfulness of momentary terrors. Even fear must disappear as well. And the disappointment when a black shape that darkened the surface near the shore had faded away slowly and gone would wane with the settling of waters. He needed no one to turn around and stare him in the face and say that the game was up: treasure isn't something you can fake. Sometimes treasure – where it can be found or what it might look like to a fresh eye – sometimes treasure isn't even something you can tell.

They met back at the start-off point, sat with their backs pressed against the sweating wall in the shade of a stand of promising trees. Jim, as often then, was fit to burst with talk, and when he spoke, as ever then, he did not weigh his words. The other two shared a lifted eyebrow and a half-felt smirk.

Listen to this. He had gone into the ring fort to look for all the silver and the gold. They knew the circle of stone and brambles he was talking about, the one in the nuns' field, the field with the water tank down beyond the castle gate. They had been there last week, to pick blackberries and watch the moon rise in the middle of the afternoon. But listen to this: halfway in, he had heard the sound of wood breaking and screams sharp enough to send skin and hair flying, so he ran. He ran as fast as he could to where the ground flattened out again and there were stones in easy reach. At least, that was how he would remember it. A hare had burst from a gap in the fort's wall, spun round in a thousand circles, and closed in on the lying boy. Its eyes bulged out and froth poured from its mouth until it hit the ground for the last time and stayed down. What did they think of that, the lads? And what were they to make of it?

John reached down into his breast pocket so slowly that he had enough time to imagine that the zip-clip swinging on his jacket was a drum-roll. The grass was warm by now and slick, and flat and empty. Brought out into sunlight and brushed clean, the egg lay in uneven pieces in the palm of his dirty hand, and smelt stale. He tried to put words on what might have been there. He tried to conjure up the ghost of the talking bird from eight pieces of eggshell. But the evidence of disbelief in their eyes was clear, and briefly unforgiving. The pieces of eight were thrown away.

Louis was humming to himself. He waited for a question like, 'What is that song you can't sing?' but it never came. He was thinking about all they had to show and tell for a day of treasure hunting: one dead animal, a smithereens shell, and the soundless ring of an old ship's bell.

They dropped out onto the grass, worn out by the morning of fruitless search – and for a few minutes of wet foreheads and sticky backs they wished for rain.

What was supposed to happen next? The boys followed the bed of a nearly dried-up stream. One skimmed stones: some rattled through the grass along the banks, some were sucked into mud, some found water and made a splash. Then the great idea struck him and he remembered it still. Why, why had he not thought of it before this?

'Let's build a dam to keep the sea out and the river in.'

They had reached the shore. The stream they had navigated leaked out into a tiny bay of careless seaweed rocks scattered on a bed of scum. Someone had built a fence across the mouth of the cove, had strung barbed wire loosely around rough crosses, around and over. The place to build a dam is right there – just before the banks of the river drop further and harder, where the stream runs faster to the noise of the ocean, where the water runs shallow and clear.

It was winter in the middle of the river. The sun was shining and the sky was blue. The grass where it could still grow was green, and the river ran as cold and as rapid as melted snow. The river knows of neither time nor season, nor cares. They took off their shoes without untying the laces, and time was measured on the rolls turned in the legs of trousers and in their cries of *Freezing–O!* In the beginning, cold snapped at their ankles and knocked knees, bit at noses to spite faces and to flush them red. The river saw the danger reflected in the stones and handfuls of mud passed from hand to hand and pushed carefully onto a rising line, and rushed on. The wall rose higher and higher, and the frightened water rose behind it still. On the horizon, the tide flipped around the long grey line under the sky, and the tops of swelling waves flaked and whitened.

Clouds built up all that quick afternoon, gradually blotted out the blue jigsaw pieces and made the earlier sunburn light settle for a purple and orange glow. The unshaped stones and the soft mud meant to bind them solid together slipped all the time, and the river trickled through. But the dam began to hold, and held; the stream was held back like their breaths, like blown cheeks and the tips of tongues between determined teeth. The top of the dam had just broken the surface of the running water when the first shout came to them and was heard.

'Ho!'

A figure in black approached, crying as he came. 'Ho.' It was a man with hands hard enough and arms strong enough to string

barbed wire and nail crosses. But at first, in the distance, he was a
fly at the corner of an eye. As he came closer, he was a dog and
then a bull, and then a giant. When he stood still for a moment
and leaned on his walking stick, he was a lone tree bent back into
the wind. But in full sight of the boys hard at work on his land, he
felt himself become the kind of man he never thought he would be
– an old man, old and angry and shrill.

The boys who stared at him were to get out of his water and to
get off his land. He wanted to know their names and the houses
where they lived. And he watched them as they jumped away,
and scrambled to pick up shoes and coats and to get out of there.
He wanted them to scatter and to leave his island in peace. The
old man's last desire for a peaceful island would have echoed in
the ears of the tearaway boys, if it hadn't been imagined – or
imagined still.

There was nothing to do during the holy hours of late Sunday
afternoon but wait. So the old man waited for as long as he could
take. The championship was over for another year. It had ended
with no cups won, and no training of the team to come until
March and the chance of lighter winds and a weak sun. But they
had broken their backs in this past season, and himself along with
the best of them. They had run at all hours and in all directions
and at his command, and caught fast and turned faster and
plucked the *sliothar* from the *bas* and gone in hard. He was sure
that they would not stop their lives to count their losses or to
bemoan their lack of medals; the reward of private honours and
local cheers would be enough for them, or would have to be. And
the tourist season was over: no more strangers wandered into his
pub and clicked their way around the stone floor to talk about the
beauty of the open grate as if he had made a work of art, or about
the smell of turf smoke and how it should be for ever remembered,
or of the state and craft of thatch. Born behind the bar, he had
worked there all his life and when he was not working in behind
he stood out in front of the counter with the others and downed it
like the man he was – the man he always had been. He never
married. He said, though no one there would ask, he said that he

was never a man for all that. And some among those who listened to him, in the haze of alcohol or a spirit of gentle misunderstanding, had never asked him what he meant by *that*, and had politely nodded heads or shrugged their shoulders to agree. He was happy the way he was and no one should begrudge him a little peace.

But there was something about the silence of a Sunday afternoon that nearly killed him. And in later years, his ill feeling for the Lord's day deepened. No one walked down the street or leaned on a gate or shared a cigarette while they waited for the blinds to run up and the key to turn, while they waited for the time when lips and throats could be wetted with the powerful stuff and tobacco smoke breathed indoors again. At home for the long day, the men would talk politics, or put the parish in the right order of sport and generations: what cousins once removed and the teams they played on and their ordinary aunts and uncles. The boys fought the battles, or the matches, that their fathers had not won, and wandered out of the house without a word said about where they thought they were going. Daughters of all ages spent hours on the telephone, and the hush of devotion after a roasted dinner was left to the company of women alone. At least, that was what he had gleaned from half-heard conversations and complaints. It must be as simple as that, and as awful; it had to be as simple as he had heard and still believed. Some soft talk of what he did not love could not be begrudged to him, or by him.

In later years, when Sunday afternoons had lengthened and when sometimes they didn't end until Wednesday and it seemed as if nothing could ever break them, he went back to the land. Five acres of poor soil and a few thin cattle went to prove that he was local and established, that his roots went deep down and were well watered. He took his endless time to walk it as slowly as his age and the weather would allow. He loosened hay from bales and a few times a year he tried to spread seaweed over the ground from the back of a borrowed tractor. He thought of it as he walked, and talked aloud; he imagined what the land might have been if he had given it more time when his arms were younger.

But there was very little that could be done now – just think. Just thinking would have to be enough.

There was not a lot to think about: the land was his, and it was there. His father had not owned and worked and loved the land all his life to leave the five acres of bog and sand for his son to own and work and love, in his turn, as a debt of honour. He had not won the few poor fields from another man in a game of cards, nor in a gamble on a horse race where the favourite might have fallen four full fences from the last. It was neither his just reward for due legal process nor stolen goods, nor stolen goods returned to their rightful owner, him. The plot of poor land he owned had no history that went deeper than the blunt knife of relentless weather or the endless ebb and flow of the Atlantic along its shore could reach. All he knew was that the land was his and it was there, and that for most of his long life he had not cared. But when his life became a month of Sundays, a few fields between the village and the sea began to feel more like home to him than any pub lounge or back room. On the island, as it was sometimes called, his loneliness was not a fraction in the grim calculus of providence or an accident of fortune. The island that he crosses to and walks is the place where his loneliness is a calling: a lone blackthorn tree in the corner of a field can hold all four seasons of weather in its branches, and not stir one; one bird can crow long and low over a swoop of the bay and be heard by all.

He lit another cigarette, coughed loudly and shifted the stick he always carried in his grip. He spits. The burning in his chest was getting worse but he wouldn't let it worry him a bit. The shudder of the cough passed quickly and he settled into his long stride again to wait for the next fit. He was on his way back now, hurrying his walk a little. He did not wear a watch and hurried in case he arrived back to find a crowd gathered round and beating on the door. Or worse still, in case he passed an open door on his way home where the hum had already begun and the fire was lit and one drink after another was being poured.

That was when he saw them: the three heads ducking up and down over the bank of the river. He moved closer. What did they think they were doing? What were they doing here? He was surprised that all he felt was anger – and that he bawled them out of it. He saw them run and their panic calmed him down. He didn't understand why they had not heard him coming sooner, and escaped quicker. He could never have guessed that they had bigger things on their minds, that they wanted to hold the river up and hold back the tide. He saw mick-acting but no danger, and that was what would so confuse him later. Why all the shouting and the waved stick? Why his anger? He hadn't been afraid. He knew who they were and they knew him. He wasn't scared but still he had felt threatened. Maybe that was what had brought him running across the field on old legs, the thought that this was his place alone and not to be tampered with – not to be played with or changed or conquered by others. Or at least, not until he was long gone – and maybe not even then either. In the long afternoons of thinking that will come later, the worst thing will be when he remembers his exact words and the ring of truth to their tone, the worst thing will be to know that his words had said exactly what they were supposed to mean: Leave an old man alone and leave his land in peace.

He sighed as he recalled the day, flicked a dead butt into the grate and lit another, opened a fresh bottle of rum and shuffled himself in closer to the fire. It was three o'clock in the morning and another Sunday afternoon was almost over. The glasses had all been cleared away and cleaned, the floor was swept and sloshed with water, and sleep seemed possible. He might sleep for an hour – and then another.

And then morning broke straight into Sunday afternoon again and another cock crowed.

The boys had headed straight for home. Their first panic gave way to an out-of-breath relief and a happy explanation: the old man had gone mad, and nothing else needed to be said. Something under the liver-spotted skin had twisted and he had lost the head. Still, it had been a good day almost up until the end – and the further away they got, the further out of sight of the man and the river and the island, the more the day changed for the better. The dam was nearly finished; it leaked through a few cracks here and there. Maybe they would have time – some afternoon after school, on a long weekend – maybe they would have time to get back and seal the gaps where the river found a way through yet. But they never did. They split up at the bend for home and turned to shout and wave. Their last unclouded night of freedom fell.

Winter ate up the rest of autumn that year and when snow fell, for the first time in ten years and for three full days, they had already long forgotten all about the madman and the leaking dam and a chest-load of treasure that had never been lost or found. The three boys never went back to the island. School started the day after the building of the dam and it was a very long way to Friday. Over the long weekend in October, they made their first successful landing on the moon. Come Halloween, they staked out and killed off the four worst vampires from among their classmates with a silver mixture of eggs and flour; they lit bangers and hid and ran, and threw rolls of toilet paper up around all the telegraph wires in the town. By the middle of November, they were on the hunt for whales through the long wet grass in the field behind the school. But a spate of vicious squalls at Christmas put an end to the whaling and scattered the whole crew; the great sea beasts dove deep under and made off fast for warmer, calmer waters. Long planned and well provisioned though it was, the second moon landing failed in April – and nothing was the same again. They did not go back to the island after that last September. By the time the skies had cleared some space for blue behind the grey, the river was too small for them and so was the bay. And by the time summer came round again, Indian or cowboy, the boys had bigger fish to fry and there were more serious battles to be waged and won. The island sank out of all sight and lay on the seabed somewhere, waiting to be discovered.

It is true that the field where the road split in two to snake around the village and where the boys broke for home was called the field of the Judgement Stone. And true it was, too, that the seat of judgement spoken of was a dolmen made of limestone. But the great slab of grey on a small rise in the dead centre of a field just

outside the town was much more down to earth and wild
weather than could ever be a guilty plea or a harsh sentence or
a man-made law. Rain could rough and pit the surface of the rock
but – even after years and years of green growth and fall – it wore
no wig of straggling lichen, no flat black cap of soil. The certainty
of its final verdict was less eloquent than words, and was spoken
lower.

A year before the last summer ever of the three boys, a team of
archaeologists paid by the anxious local council had spent six
months camped on the site of the ancient grave, digging for gold.
They pitched their tent in one corner, laid lines in a grid of perfect
squares, started work along the outer edge and moved gradually,
by turns of trowel and brush, closer. One of the men who spent
the winter there, who wore blue boots and half-moon glasses and
who spoke in the fits and starts of never-ending thoughts, told the
curious who gathered that teeth turned up in broken ground are
the seeds of skeletons; that a speck of alien pollen could be a sign
of something or other; that a tiny shard of pottery in the heavy
clay would be a prize hard won.

There is a true story about how the dolmen became known as
the Judgement Stone. One day, a judge whose name has been
forgotten – but whose face and frame have not been erased by
time or talk: he had pointed ears and laughing eyes and a lazy
walk – the judge was on his way to a sitting in the town of the
District Court. A case due to be presented from the list that
morning was troubling his mind. As he passed through the tiny
village built about the walls of a castle that was in those days five
crooked miles from granite justice, he saw three small boys
gathered in the field around the dolmen. He reined in short,
leapt without looking from the saddle of his bay horse, and
greeted the boys. They were too engrossed in the game they
played to notice the gallop of his arrival or the horse's snort.
When they did turn their attention to him, they said: 'Silence. We
are holding court.' And so the shrewd judge decided to lay his
painful case before them.

Two men out at sea were fishing from their boat. The man who
could not swim fell over the side into the water. The other, afraid

that his friend might be dragged under, threw his fishing line in the direction of the drowning man. He was saved by hanging on with both hands to catgut – but the unseen hook snagged on and took out his right eye. Now the half-blind man demands just compensation for his grievous loss from the saviour of the day, and from the law. The three listeners deliberated for a moment, before the smallest among them spoke: 'Let the one-eyed man be rowed out to sea in the same boat, and cast overboard again at the same distance from the shore. If he can save his own life, he must be paid the due award.'

There is some dispute about the case. Some say that the soft-voiced judge asked the boys to adjudicate in a quarrel over the division of an inheritance of land. And it was the tallest boy who spoke, not the smallest: 'Let one brother divide the land as he desires, and let the other then choose his portion.' There is some dispute about the case – but none about the field or the judge-ment or the stone. Everybody is agreed that peace was restored to the mind of the nameless judge, that he thanked the boys with silver (or gold) and mounted his bay mare once more to journey on and to dispense his wisdom to the amazement of the court.

Many years later and only a few shorter years ago, in exactly the same place would stand the three late sailors, all still reeling from the wreck of their ship of elm, their failure to discover buried treasure or to build a dam across a snow-water river – all at the end of their Indian summer. To them, the place where they stood and said 'Goodbye' and 'Good night' and 'See you tomorrow' was neither in the shadow of the dolmen nor under the eye of judging stone. In the growing dark of that last night, they heard no spirit voices and they saw no ghosts. To them, the bend for home where they split up was only the first step on an invisible bridge that spanned from home and school to the island, arched high over an ocean of ash and beech and muddy water. Nevertheless, some decision was taken silently in the field beyond them, a decision that would not be revoked.

By the time the weak sun was pierced by the rounded turret of the castle the next morning, the bridge was gone. A giant, summoned from the restless deeps by some forgotten formula of secret and terrible magic, had reared his head through the tranquil surface of night water. By the light of the moon and the power of his great claws he had ripped out each foot of the crossing way – and carried out a sentence of nature to the very last letter of its law.

Goodbye and good night and see you tomorrow.

*   *   *

It will be seven years before three women gather in the long grass corner where gardens taper in and hedges meet to overgrow. They talk all together: one about her decision to give up in the end and to dead-head the wilting roses; another of the accidental flick of the wrist that has let cakes of bread rise faster and higher, and softened the flesh beneath the crust; the last is worried about varicose veins in high heels and the crush in elevators. There is a pause for breath before one of them says:

'Have you heard the news?'

The woman still struggling to get out of a crowded lift and ease the agony in her feet has not heard that he is dead. A black rosette has been seen unravelling down along the grimy pane of the shut pub's window. The ink on the pinned note was running in the rain but its directions were clear. The details were, as always, the same: the removal would take place from the funeral parlour on the evening after and there would be a morning burial in the seaside graveyard after Mass at eleven in the local. When they have all commented on this, and have rested the poor man's soul on God's right side, the women return to what they know best and love most, and talk as if nothing has changed in all the time that has gone by.

Where have they got to now?

Although the events of this story did not take place long ago, long ago, and even though the characters that act and speak are as real as characters can be, it still comes as a surprise to hear and say that the truth is often stranger than any made-up history. But this is true: the doctors and nurses hard at overwork in the college hospital in the city had turned an old pub owner into a candle. The patient had presented, involuntarily, at midnight, with burns to both his feet. And if the truth is to be wholly told, the old man himself had kick-started the course of pain and treatment. He said that he had dropped off in front of the fire and neither felt nor smelt the burning in his sleep. One way or another, a doctor from Libya and two nurses from a town down the country admitted a patient with sharp and recurrent chest pains and feet scorched to just above the ankles. They found the black spot on his lungs on the third day, and had turned him into a wax doll by the end of the same week. At no time did the man show fear. Through his mother's pride and a groundless fear of his father's hand, he knew his catechism off by heart: God had created him, and redeemed – and he was saved at the very moment when drink and the devil seemed to have done for him.

Goodbye and good night, the pub owner said, and see you all tomorrow.

Sometimes even now, when the wind is changing and the light is fading, one of the island boys goes home to a funeral, to study the old man's face. The skin is tallow, the colour of February primroses from his mother's garden, and there are neither shaving nicks nor the trace of veins. Smooth and pale and cold is the candleman laid out before them. In the shuddering light of a shuffling night – when all hands were held tight to the sides, each head straight up and shoulders back in the slowly moving line – all that the old man would have needed was a cigarette wick and Major incense to make the scene of his conversion look complete. But the candleman can rest in peace – the same peace of an island of tall trees and moody weather left undisturbed by a trio of treasure-seekers and dam-builders, and unconquered; the peace that might come from knowing that of the three who fled his voice that day, two have grown far enough away to forget that it exists.

The one who stealthily returned – once, twice, and since then, often – has grown too old to believe in the stories his mother told them then to wipe sorrow from the face of any funeral. The candleman was not specially selected from out of all the many people in the world to herd cattle and sheep in heaven, to tame camels and apes in hell. God had need of no man to train hurlers with ever-fresh legs, 'Run, Michael, run would you, for God's sake!' He would not be called upon to marshal all the angels who danced upon a pinhead into shape. No. Even then the boy was too old to be lied to, and too proud. And now, though older yet, he knows that he has not grown old enough to believe in nothing at all, to think that all losses can be explained. A sharp wind came swinging in through the open door into the dark, and its sudden gusts put the candles set at each corner of the coffin out. Lit again, the heat that rises from four weak flames made the boy's sight (and memory) of the night blur for a moment, before it settled.

During his long lifetime, the old man had lit up neither faces nor eyes. From the sidelines or after hours in the bar, he could cause cheeks to burn with rage or shame, and made mouths fry in the curses that they spat or swallowed the second his back was turned away from them. The women at the funeral were more generous to him. The twenty (or thirty or forty) women in the mortuary chapel, who would never have married him – no, not for all the whisky in Scotland – linked arms in the fight for their man, and let the rosary rattle from their lips like a devotional can-can. If some of them had loved him once, sneaked looks at him from under veiled eyes or from behind books, why had he not returned their love, or the love of one? Had he really believed everything that was said in the pub by the men who stood at the chapel door that night, lighting up again and talking down – that they envied him his solitude and just the dreams of love? Maybe they never thought – or ever hoped – that the faithfulness of animals and the warmth of drink would be enough.

The captain filed in at the head of all the other men, patted the pressed wax hands as he passed. His pause was gentle, and his look, and the momentary touch: he was like a man who slipped into a darkened room to check that his child lay fast asleep, and was well tucked. A half-smile and not a word aloud was all he gave but, then and later, it seemed enough. The crowd heaved forward again and settled back. The island boy watched him move away, noted the awkward gait of which everybody spoke under his breath: from an early age and then for ever the captain had kicked with the wrong foot. He limped quietly out and away before the hearse left, back to where he could always hear the sea and breathe salt air. He could have answered any question the boy might have asked him, if he spoke.

What lies hidden in the dead man's chest?

But, then or later, he did not ask the question.

The lid was screwed on to the tune of the litany, and a chorus of matches struck along the tinders. The glow of cigarettes and candles made the boy remember a story once told to him of new lights suddenly discovered in the dead of night. It was the tale told of the man who spent all the riches of his life in search of greater treasure. He abandoned his beautiful and noble wife, a white-haired boy and raven-haired daughter. He travelled a hundred years of miles, and many miles more, over land and over water. He begged and he borrowed and he stole. His sight faded and his strength failed as he grew old. In the last days of light and of his life, in the last corner of the last cave on the last continent, he stumbled on the long-lost treasure trove. But when he broke the rusted lock and lifted the lid off the ancient sea-chest – all with his greatest effort – a whirl of dark air rushed in and sifted the jewels through to the wooden bottom: it sucked the blood-red heart from rubies, blew the blue-green soul from emeralds, burnt amber to cinders and made ashes of all the gold. The last the poor man saw before his sight winked out for ever was the cold light pour from a constellation of new stars.

The three boys went their separate ways at the turn for home on the last evening before school began again, and the game was over for good. John was busy for six days out of seven for all the next summer holidays. At work in a fruit shop, he weighed oranges and bagged lemons and clanged the till – and when he fell in love, it spelled the end of him, and of them. At the time, the jealousy of his friends made them think that the understanding of first love would be easy. Things change really. By the end of the summer, Jim was taking the bus every morning to go to school in the city. He started to use words that didn't count the others in – 'Isn't that right, *guys?*' – and played sports that all three of them had always agreed were for women. But nothing could hold him back, and nothing did.

So, there was no one there that day – not even the one who never really left the place. He wasn't there on the day when a keystone slipped and the river sensed a weakness in the wall that held it back in, and drove harder, and won. The loosed water brought everything with it through the dam: the reflection of the old man's face and the prints of feet on the run away. And although the speed of the stream dropped quickly from its first rush down to an even level, it carried still earlier things with it as it went: the wreck of a pirate ship, the racing heartbeat of a brown-and-white hare, a golden egg, and all belief in treasure. Out went they all into the smooth round bay where white horses graze and play. For a time it seemed certain that the memory of a white-haired fisherman would be lost at sea as well, along with the boys that they were then.

But some stones stayed. The biggest at the bottom held firm and were not swayed by the waves. The onward run of the river is relentless but the tide turns on the ocean bed as it must and does. Some of the flotsam was drawn back in towards the shore by the current, and washed up. And if he could be as certain this day as he was once upon a time when he was young, the boy would promise to guard it with his life and keep it safe. But the only thing that remains with him now exactly as it was in those days is his regret, the regret that not one of them was there, that he wasn't there himself. No one was there, that morning or that afternoon or that evening, no one was there at the very moment when a day-long years-high dam came tumbling down.

PAUL GRIMES

Singing the Blues

Steve Galvin parked at the rear of the Coach and Horses and looked out at the pub. At four storeys high and the same distance wide it looked as though it had once been something special. A coaching inn maybe, servicing the main route north out of London. Now the paint was peeling on the drainpipes and the wood around the windows was bare and buckled.

Steve left his car and made his way into the pub. Half a dozen customers were scattered around the large room. A young woman lounged behind the bar. The carpet had been patched in places by black masking tape and the whole place smelt of stale beer and tobacco. At the far end of the room he could see the stage. A metal chair stood by itself on wooden boards beneath a bare light bulb. He turned to the bar. He needed a drink.

The woman looked up from her *Evening Standard* and then dragged herself across to where Steve was standing.

'A Blackbushe and ice,' Steve said.

The woman turned and searched the bottles behind her. Steve watched her pour the drink. 'Is Mrs Griffin about?'

'She's upstairs.'

'Can you let her know Steve Galvin's here.'

'What's it about?'

'I'm the entertainment tonight.'

The woman lifted her head and looked at Steve and then turned to the telephone. 'She said you're to go up, it's that door behind you.'

Steve drank his whiskey and then climbed the stairs behind the door. At the top of the stairs he found a small office and a woman sitting at a bureau.

'Come in, Mr Galvin. I'm Sandra Griffin.'

She had a hard, well-worn look. Her bright red lipstick matched the unnaturally bright red of her hair. She looked late forties or early fifties, but was probably older.

'Where's the other one?' she said as Steve came into the room.

'Sorry?'

'There's supposed to be two of you.'

'He hasn't arrived yet.'

'You're due to go on in ten minutes.'

'Yes,' said Steve.

'I was listening to your tape today. Not my kind of music, but you sound competent. I'll tell you the kind of music you should do. We get a lot of Irish in, they like Country and Western.'

'We don't work like that.'

'What do you mean?'

'We don't play a set; we're much looser.'

'Now look, lovey, I was in the business myself. I was a singer. Still do a bit. And if there's one thing I know, everybody has a set.'

'We have a lot of material. What we play depends on our mood.'

'Well, I'm telling you, the mood here is Country and Western. You play anything too way out and they won't like it.'

'I'll see what we can do.' Steve itched to be away from the woman.

Downstairs in the bar Steve looked around for Dave, but there were still just the half dozen or so people. He walked over to the bar.

'Can I have another Blackbushe, a double, with ice. And a pint of Directors,' he said to the woman, and then turned away to go back out to his car.

There was no sign of Dave's Granada in the car park. Steve looked at his watch; it was almost eight. Dave was not usually late; he was the punctual one. A whisper of concern rose within him. He didn't have a good feeling about this gig and he did not want to be doing it on his own.

Back in the bar Steve found his whiskey and beer waiting. He drank the whiskey quickly and took the pint away from the bar to a table. As he sipped at the beer he noticed that a few more people were beginning to arrive. His audience had almost doubled.

Steve was halfway through his pint when Sandra Griffin came into the bar and walked over to his table. She looked pointedly at her watch.

'You're supposed to be starting at eight.'

'There's hardly a crowd here.'

'And where's the other one?'

'Looks like he didn't make it. I'll do it on my own.'

'I'm paying for two.'

Steve could feel the mellow mood that the alcohol had been building begin to crumble. 'What do you want to do, cancel it?'

'No, you've been advertised. You'll just have to go on as you are, but I'm not happy about it.'

Join the club, thought Steve.

It took five minutes to connect his guitar pickup to the PA and fix the levels for the guitar and the mike. When he was satisfied with the sound Steve reached into his bag and took out his harmonica rack and fixed a G harp into it. He tuned the guitar to the harp and then played a D chord and blew the harp against it. Blowing low down on the harp, he made it sound like a train pulling slowly away from a station. He built a rhythm on the harp and then started to play guitar. He closed his eyes and lost himself in the sound as he worked the harmony of the two instruments.

Steve played like that for nearly five minutes and then brought the tune to an end and opened his eyes. The crowd had doubled again: now there were thirty or so people in the bar. Some were talking amongst themselves and some were watching him. He reached up to the harmonica rack and released it so that it came down against his chest. He needed to change the mood. He hit an E chord hard so that the full depth of the guitar rose up from the speakers and then he started chugging into a fast twelve bar.

Steve played for thirty minutes before he stopped. By that time the crowd had grown again. Some of the people had moved closer to the stage and were enjoying the music, but these people were in the minority. The rest of the crowd seemed to be hardly aware that he existed.

'I'm going to stop for a few minutes and wet my whistle,' said Steve and put his guitar down on the stage.

At the bar he ordered another Blackbushe and Directors. As he drank the beer he noticed a woman at the other end of the bar looking at him. He caught her glance and threw her a smile. She had one of those almost pretty but sensible faces and short dark brown hair cut in a fringe over her eyes. Steve couldn't tell if she was on her own. He picked up his drinks and walked towards her.

'Are you enjoying the show?'

'Yes, you're very good.'

'Thanks. Are you on your own?'

'No, I'm with a friend. He's the reason I'm here, he's a fan of yours,' said the woman and looked past Steve to smile at somebody.

Steve looked around to see a man approaching. He was about the same age as Steve, but taller by four or five inches. He was wearing casual clothes, so clean and crisp they were almost a uniform.

The woman reached out her hand to draw him closer. 'This is Mark and I'm Gill.'

'Gill tells me you're a fan.'

Mark's blue eyes lit up. 'Yes, I saw you a few times when you were with Blue Monday.'

Steve grinned at the memory of those times.

'Can we get you a drink?' said Mark.

'That's very good of you, a Blackbushe and ice, please.'

Mark turned to the bar and Steve turned his attention back to Gill. 'So what do you think of the blues?'

'I don't know. It's all very sad.'

Steve looked carefully into Gill's eyes. Gill held his gaze for a moment longer than necessary and then turned quickly to her friend.

'Mark, how are those drinks coming?'

Mark turned around from the bar and handed Gill and Steve their drinks.

'Mark has your album.'

'I don't believe it.'

'He was going to bring it along and get you to autograph it.'

'You should have. It must be years since I've seen a copy.'

'I saw you at Hull University in 1972. You were brilliant. I bought the album the next day.'

'Christ, ten years. A lifetime ago.'

Steve watched Gill as she took a drink and studied him from over the rim of the glass. He could feel some kind of electricity in the moment and was wondering how to exploit it when he became aware of another figure approaching him. It was Sandra Griffin.

'How long do you normally take for your break?' she said as she came up to Steve.

'It all depends.'

'People don't normally take a break until they have done at least an hour.'

'I was thirsty.'

'I can see.'

'I'll be going back on in a minute.'

'And another thing, people aren't enjoying your music.'

'That's hardly my fault.'

'Whose fault is it then?'

'You booked me.'

'I didn't book you, I booked a group. I thought we were getting celebrities.'

Steve picked up his beer and slowly drained the glass.

'Are we going to get something more lively?'

'Well, actually, that was the lively stuff, it gets more depressing from now on.'

Sandra Griffin's eyes burned for a second and then she turned and walked away. Steve turned back to Gill. 'Your good health,' he said and swallowed his whiskey in one go.

'She doesn't seem pleased.'

'Not one of my greatest fans.' Steve moved closer to Gill. 'Can I get you a drink? I need to get myself another one to take up on stage.'

Gill drew back towards Mark. 'We're fine, we've only just started these.'

Back on stage Steve saw that the pub had started to fill out. The tables in front of the stage, which had been empty for the first part of his set, were now full. Steve put down his drinks and plugged his guitar back in and tapped on the mike.

'Good evening ladies and gentlemen, and welcome back. I have had a few requests from the audience. Some of you found the first part of my set too lively so I'm going to slow it up a little. This is a Sleepy John Estes song which is guaranteed to bring you right down, it's called "Working Man Blues".'

Steve began to play the opening chords of the song and then closed his eyes.

Fuck you, Sandra Griffin, he thought.

Following the song Steve hitched his harmonica rack up to his mouth and played a few notes against the guitar. He was still reasonably in tune. He reached down for his pint and took a long pull.

'This is a Jimmy Reed song called, "Honest I do",' he said. 'Honest I do,' he repeated, and laughed.

Steve took the song very slow, playing extended guitar parts and long harmonica solos. He could sense some restlessness coming from the audience, but he was way past giving a shit. When he finished the song he reached down for his pint and took another long haul of the beer.

'Jimmy Reed was a Chicago blues player,' said Steve. 'But we are a long way from Chicago. A long way from anywhere, really, when you think about it. I'd like to welcome you, ladies and gentlemen, to the Coach and Horses. A sophisticated establishment and purveyor of fine wines and good music.'

Steve laughed to himself and played a chord on the guitar and then ran it up the neck and played a little blues run. 'Yes siree, ladies and gentlemen, the blues.'

He reached down and picked up his beer. He knew that it was getting messy but he was past being concerned. He played another half dozen songs before he decided he could no longer be bothered. His second set had lasted just over thirty minutes.

He finished off the last dregs of his beer and began to pack his guitar and other equipment away. Somebody switched the juke-box back on and a Johnny Cash song started playing.

'Johnny Cash is not bad,' thought Steve. 'Johnny Cash is OK.'

Back in the office, behind the door marked Private, Steve faced Sandra Griffin again. He watched her as she glared back at him.

'In all my years. In all my years of booking acts. In all my years in show business, I have never seen anything like what you did tonight.'

'I'm sorry if you don't like my music.'

'That wasn't music. That was just some drunk. I shouldn't pay you nothing. I'd be perfectly entitled to. I'm certainly not going to pay you what was agreed. I booked a partnership. So by rights you should only get half. But you don't even deserve that.'

'How much do I deserve then, just pay me what you want to. Frankly, madam, I do not give a damn,' said Steve, and laughed.

Sandra Griffin threw three ten-pound notes onto the table. 'There we are.'

Steve picked up the money. 'Thank you so much.'

'You make me laugh, people like you. Call yourself a star. You don't know the meaning of the word. A star would have got up on that stage tonight and delivered. You're nothing. You had yourself a hit record once and now you're nothing. A has-been. A washed up has-been.'

Steve put the money in his pocket and looked at Sandra Griffin's face. The eyes were red and glazed with anger. Her sausage-fat fingers gripped the edge of the table. She was braced for confrontation. Steve was ready to say something but then realised he didn't care. Even if she was right, he didn't care. The moment was not that important. He breathed out hard and then turned and walked away.

Down in the bar Steve was debating with himself whether to have another drink. He was going to be driving home drunk anyway, so what the hell. He ordered a double Blackbushe and looked

around for Gill. He was wondering if he could somehow separate
her from Mark.

'It has been done before,' he thought. 'In the old days, when I
was a king.'

He couldn't see Gill or Mark. There didn't seem to be any other
possibilities. He wasn't even sure if he wanted to be with a
woman. He was a strange mixture made up from the elation of
performance, the bitterness of the confrontation with Sandra
Griffin, and the heady indifference of alcohol. He needed to get
away from the pub. He finished off his whiskey and turned away
from the bar.

As he walked towards the back of the pub the jukebox was
changing records. Kenny Rogers was giving way to Elvis Presley.
He pushed open the door and looked out into the darkness of the
unlit car park and the night sky. Stars struggled for life in the
thick darkness of the clouds as he looked around for the moon.
Way back and low down in the sky he found it, pale and thin
against the lights of London.

'Not blue,' he thought. 'Not blue, but definitely not one
hundred per cent.'

CLAIRE KEEGAN

Close to the Water's Edge

Tonight he is out on the balcony, his dark tan stunning against the white of his dress shirt. Many days have passed since he left Cambridge, Massachusetts, to spend time at his mother's penthouse on the coast. He does not care for these rooms, with the vicious swordfish mounted on the walls and all these mirrors that make it impossible to do even the simplest thing without seeing his reflection.

He stays out on the beach and through his shades watches the bathers, the procession of young men with washboard bellies walking the strand. Women turn over on their deck chairs browning themselves evenly on all sides. They come here with their summer books and sunhats, reaching into their coolers for beer and Coppertone. In the afternoons when the heat becomes unbearable, he swims out to the sandbar, a good half mile from the shore. He can see it now, the strip of angry waves breaking in the shallows. Now the tide is advancing, erasing the white, well-trodden sands. A brown pelican, a small piece of the past, floats by on the Texas wind. Joggers stay close to the water's edge, their shadows fastened like guardians at their sides.

Inside, his mother is arguing with his stepfather, the millionaire who owns these condominiums. After his parents divorced, his mother said that people have no control over who they fall in love with, and soon afterwards married the millionaire. Now he can hear them talking, their enraged whispers gathering speed on the slope of their argument. It is an old story.

'I'm warning you, Richard, don't bring it up!'

'Who brought it up? Who?'

'It's his birthday, for Christ's sake!'

'Who said anything?'

The young man looks down. At the hot tub, a mother braces herself and enters the steamy waters. Screams from racing children pierce the air. He feels the same trepidation he always feels at these family occasions, and wonders why he came back here when he could be in Cambridge in his T-shirt and shorts, drinking his Australian beer, playing chess on the computer. He takes the cufflinks from his pocket, a gift his grandmother gave him shortly before she died. They are gold-plated cufflinks whose gold is slowly wearing off, revealing the steel underneath.

When his grandmother first married, she begged her husband to take her to the ocean. They were country people, pig farmers from Tennessee. His grandmother said she had never laid eyes on the Atlantic. She said if she saw the ocean, she could settle down. It wasn't anything she could explain. But each time she asked her husband, his response was the same.

'Who'll feed the pigs?'

'We could ask the neighbours—'

'You can't trust anybody. That's our livelihood out there.'

Months passed; she grew heavy with child and finally gave up asking to see the ocean. Then one Sunday her husband shook her awake.

'Pack a bag, Marcie,' he said, 'we're going to the coast.'

It wasn't yet light when they got into the car. They drove all that day, across the hills of Tennessee towards Florida. The landscape changed from green, hilly farmland to dry acres with tall palms and pampas grass. The sun was going down when they arrived. She got out and gasped at the Atlantic, whose end she could not see. It looked green in the evening sun. It wasn't what she expected. It seemed a lonely, infertile place to her, with the stink of seaweed and the gulls fighting for leftovers in the sand.

Then her husband took out his pocket watch.

'One hour, Marcie. I'll give you one hour,' he said. 'If you're not back by then, you can find your own way home.'

She walked for half an hour with her bare feet in the frothy edge of the sea, then turned back along the cliff path, and from the shelter of some trees, watched her husband, at five minutes

CLOSE TO THE WATER'S EDGE

past the appointed hour, slam the car door and turn the ignition. Just as he was gathering speed, she jumped into the road and stopped the car. Then she climbed in and spent the rest of her life with a man who would have gone home without her.

His nineteenth birthday is marked by a dinner at Leonardo's, the fancy seafood restaurant overlooking the bay. His mother, dressed in a white pants suit with a rhinestone belt, joins him on the balcony.

'I'm so proud of you, honey.'

'Mom,' he says and embraces her. She's a small woman with a hot temper. She gazes out at the water.

'Will you fix my tie?' he asks. 'I never could do this right.'

She knots the silk into an unnecessarily tight bow.

'There,' she says. 'You'll be the belle of the ball. How many mothers can say, "My boy's going to Harvard University?" I'm a pig farmer's daughter from Tennessee, and my boy is going to Harvard. When I'm low, I always remember that, and it cheers me up no end.'

'Mom!'

'You play your cards right and this could all be yours some-day,' she says. 'He's got no kids. You wonder why I married him, but I was thinking of you all along.'

Just then the millionaire comes out with a lighted cigar and blows a mouthful of smoke into the night. He's an ordinary-looking man with the whitest teeth money can buy. 'You-all ready? I could eat a small child,' he says.

The restaurant owner greets the millionaire, escorts them to the table. A wooden board of crab claws is brought out. The millionaire eats them with his bare hands and clicks his fingers for the waiter, who pops a champagne cork. He always drinks champagne.

'Did you hear about this guy Clinton? Says if he's elected president, he's gonna let queers into the military,' he says. 'What do you think of that, Harvard?'

'Richard,' his mother says.

'It's okay, Mom. Well, I don't think—'

'What's next? Lesbians coaching the swim team, running for the Senate?'

'Richard!'

'What kind of defence would that be? A bunch of queers! We didn't win two world wars that way. I don't know what this country is turning into.'

Smells of horseradish and dill spill out from the kitchen. A lobster has got loose in the tank, but the waiter dips a net into the water and traps him.

'No more politics,' his mother says. 'It's my boy's night. He got a 3.75 grade point average last semester. Now what do you think of that, Richard?'

'3.75? Not bad.'

'Not bad? Well, I should say not! He's top of his class at Harvard!'

'Mom.'

'No, I won't be hushed up this time! He's top of the class, and he's nineteen years old today! A grown man, almost. Let's have a toast.'

'Now, there's an idea,' says the millionaire. He refills the champagne flutes. 'Here's to the brightest young man in the whole state of Florida,' he says. (They are smiling now, suddenly at ease. There is a chance that this dinner will not be like the others.) '. . . and to not having queers in the military!'

The mother's smile capsizes. 'Goddamn, Richard!'

'What's the matter? It's just a little joke. Doesn't anybody around here know how to take a joke any more?'

The waiter arrives with a steel tray and the entrées. Turbot for the lady, salmon for the young man, and lobster for the millionaire. The millionaire wants more champagne.

'There must be some fine women up there at Harvard,' he says. 'Some real knockouts.'

'They accept us on the basis of intelligence, not looks.'

'Even so. The best and the brightest. How come you never bring a girl down?' The millionaire ties a napkin around his neck, takes the pincers and breaks a claw open, picks out the meat. 'They must be all around you like flies,' he says, 'a young man like you. Why, when I was your age I had a different woman every weekend.'

'These olives!' the mother says. 'Taste these olives!'

They eat in silence for the rest of the meal, as the millionaire likes to concentrate on his food. Afterwards, the *maître d'* comes by and whispers a few words into the millionaire's ear. The lights around their table are doused, and a lighted cake is carried from the kitchen by a nervous Mexican waiter singing 'Happy Birthday'. It is a pink cake, the pinkest cake the young man has ever seen, like a cake you'd have at a christening party for twin girls. The millionaire is grinning.

'Make a wish, honey!' his mother says.

The young man closes his eyes and makes a wish, then blows hard, extinguishing the candles. The millionaire takes the knife and carves it into uneven pieces, like a pie chart. The young man stuffs a piece into his mouth, licks the frosting. The millionaire reaches for his mother's hand, clasps her jewelled fingers.

'Happy birthday, son,' the mother says and kisses him on the mouth. He tastes lipstick, stands, and hears himself thanking them for a pleasant birthday. He hears his mother calling his name, the waiter saying, 'Good evening, sir,' at the doorway. He is crossing the highway now, finding a space between the speeding cars. Other college kids are drinking beer on the promenade, watching the bungee jumpers throwing themselves into midair, screaming.

Down at the deserted beach, the tide has reclaimed the strand. The water is rough in the night wind. He loosens the knot at his throat and walks on and on, losing track of time. Up at the pier, yachts with roped-in sails stand trembling on the water. He thinks of his grandmother coming to the ocean. She said if she had her life to live again, she would never have climbed back into that car. She'd have stayed behind and turned into a streetwalker sooner than go home. Nine children she bore him. When her grandson asked what made her get back in, her answer was, 'Those were the times I lived in. That's what I believed. I thought I didn't have a choice.'

His grandmother, with whom he lived while his parents broke

up, the woman who embraced him so tight she bruised him, is dead now. Not a day has passed when he has not felt her absence. She is dead, but he is nineteen years old, and alive and inhabiting space on the earth, getting A's at Harvard, walking on a beach in the moonlight without any time constriction. He will never marry; he knows that now. The water looks like liquid pewter. He kicks his shoes off and, barefooted, enters the salty waters. The white waves that mark the sandbar are clearly visible in the darkness. He feels dirty, smells the cigar smoke on his clothes. He strips naked, placing the cufflinks safely in his pants pocket, and leaves his clothes on the strand. When he wades into the big white-fringed waves, the water is a cold surprise. He swims, feels clean again. Perhaps he will leave tomorrow, call the airline, change his flight, go back to Cambridge.

When he reaches the white waves, he is relieved. The water is deeper, the waves angrier now that it is night. He can rest here before the return swim to the shore. He lowers his feet to feel the sand. Waves thrash over his head, knocking him back into the deep water. He cannot find solid ground. His heart is beating fast, he swallows water, goes farther out to find the shallowest place. He never meant to drink all that champagne. He never meant to go swimming in the first place. All he wanted was to wash the evening off him. He struggles for the longest time, goes under-water, believing it will be easier if he comes up only for air. He sees the lighted condominiums on the shore. Out of nowhere comes the thought of his grandmother, who after coming all that way, and with only an hour to spend, would not get into the water, even though she was a strong river swimmer. When he asked her why, she said she just didn't know how deep it was. Where the deep started, or where it ended. The young man floats on the surface, then slowly makes his way back to the lighted condominiums on the shore. It is a long way off, but the pent-house lights are clear against the sky. When he reaches the shallow water, he crawls on his belly and collapses on the sand. He is breathing hard and looking around for his clothes, but the tide has taken them away. He imagines the first species that crawled out of the sea, the amount of courage it took to sustain life on land. He thinks of the young men in Cambridge, his stepfather saying Harvard, like Harvard is his name, his mother's diamonds winking like fake stars, and his wish for an ordinary life.

DERMOT SOMERS

The Fight

That old man was built to last. He was at least seventy, maybe more, the oldest herder there. Short and broad, he had a mane of silver wire on his blunt skull, copper skin, blazing eyes and full-fleshed Arctic features. He was a bit drunk already when I reached the square at eleven in the morning.

The sleds had arrived the previous day, skidding in from the tundra in convoys. The reindeer trotted briskly as far as the outlying houses where the streets of packed ice began; they got nervous, skittish, tossed their dehorned heads, pulled right and left. Women, children, wrapped and hooded in reindeer-skin, clung to their sacks of produce – frozen fish and deer-meat. The drivers yelled and lashed the rawhide reins, prodded with birch-wood poles. By nightfall the streets were lined with patient teams still hitched to sleds outside shops, shebeens, shanties.

In the morning, the clapboard houses, faded greens and blues, stood slumped and buckled along the Siberian streets as if the weight of snow on the tin roofs had grown too much to bear. A bronze Lenin, in a light jacket, painted silver, looked as if he had frozen to death.

The competitions were underway when I reached the square; rope-throwing, tests of strength, a little singing. A corner between two blank gable-ends was cordoned off for wrestling. Rough green canvas lay stretched on the ground. Old snow banked up against the walls had been stamped into a terrace where the hardcore spectators and the fighters gathered: intent young men, oblivious to the cold, with a sprinkling of fathers, trainers, mentors – people from the vast spaces beyond the town, dressed in rawhide tunics and deerskin boots that came up the thighs for wading snow. They were awkward on the streets, rolling and striding like strange sailors.

The referee and the umpires were a different breed, squat Russian pros hired in from the city, all bone and muscle with scarred, grizzled skulls. Green canvas was their country. There were Russian spectators too; Ukrainians, Georgians, Muscovites, clad in every fur and pelt available, bar reindeer-skin. They were the settlers, the colonists, sent north to exploit the natural resources, oil and gas. For them, the herders were the spectacle. Distorted music, machine-gun rhythms, blared from speakers. Bunting shivered against the sky. A Russian organiser barked through a megaphone, calling the fighters, warning the crowd. He was in a state of official anger, the megaphone locked to his mouth. Arguments broke out, the victims attempting to answer through the broad end of the tube, growing desperate as they were shouted down.

The crowds on the street, in the sun, were festive, last night's vodka still in the veins, firing up again at the sight of a bottle. For once, I felt no temptation at all – more like disgust. For the first time in years I sensed release, like an early flush of spring. Not many reach my age here – late fifties; they die of hardship. The abuse in town, among settlers and herders alike, was so casual, so wanton, that it was easy to feel superior. I had seen it before – at horse-fairs, cattle-marts, on dying islands, diseased continents.

I spotted the old man straight away, because he had to be noticed. He gave off a sense of compressed force that even the powerful referee couldn't match. He was heavy with age, the chest and waist dragging the shoulders down in slopes, but it was old muscle stacked away, not fat. He sat on the snow with the older men, the way they sat on the tundra, their backs straight, legs stuck out in front, toes in the air, the rawhide under their arses impervious to damp or cold.

He was bawling advice, encouragement, quarrelling with the megaphone. A bottle circulated among his cronies and he took his slug in turn, but he was apart. His grey tunic, huge and simple, was cut from something like sailcloth sewn over hide. I guessed it was the fabric that shielded the airplane from the cold at night – the ancient *Andwa* that had brought me to the edge of town.

The wrestling was the main event. The herders fought because it was traditional on the tundra and a source of prestige among the clans. The proudest definition of a man was his record as a sportsman. There were scores of bouts to be got through – each fight a single round, one fall only, both shoulders on the canvas; the referee rummaged under the loser, knuckle-rapped the victor and the men untangled promptly, as if the posture were indecent once the fighting stopped. Pairs would continue to be matched till they whittled down to a champion.

The old man sprang to his feet between rounds. He strode on and off the canvas as of natural right and rallied the crowd. The man with the megaphone would turn away, blaring into the face of some hapless herder who had missed his fight because he didn't recognise his name in Russian. Embarrassing to watch the nomads in their outlandish garb attempt to argue with the funnel, hanging their heads like children in confusion.

The old man saw decline and decadence about him on a grander scale. He shook his head in anger at the standard of the sport, the level of involvement from the crowd. He coached them in the ancient war-cry of the tribes, the deep and threatening *Haw! Haw! Haw!* His barrel-chest boomed like a mammoth-horn. Silver hair streamed in the wind, his face turned berry-red. I ducked behind a stranger's shoulder each time I photographed him, but whenever he wheeled around he seemed to seize my eye and I would turn away as if it were pure accident.

After a feeble bout when a man was floored in thirty seconds and staggered off with a froth of blood on trembling lips, the old man reached the canvas in a long stride. Like a tent lifting in a storm his tunic came off. It fell on the snow, collapsed on itself, billowing resistance. He wore a grey shirt and shapeless trousers. Heaving enormous shoulders, he challenged the crowd to take him on – all of them, together. He was stable on his trunk-like legs. The professionals kept their backs discreetly turned, studying lists of names. I kept my head down.

A figure bobbed at my elbow. A wrinkled face, ruddy like a winter-apple. He wore a Brezhnev hat – a closet-communist – a Nikon, old as mine, around his neck. I'd seen him stalk the action at a distance. There was a young photographer too, with a Canon, dressed like a war correspondent, down on his belly with the wrestlers. But the man beside me would be the local pro. Half his shots were dummies: looking busy without wasting film. He too kept up a running commentary, his voice weaving in and out of the megaphone and the war-cries. Everybody knew him; character instead of stature. He was at my elbow now.

'*Zdrast!*' he saluted. 'American? English?'

I lied, from force of habit. It's easy to lie in Russian. The round face, the stubble, the mouth full of steel and a little gold were comic, but the round bloodshot eyes were shrewd. '*Journalista?*' he probed.

I lied again. He pumped my hand in welcome. 'Aaah, *collegi* . . . !' His fist was tiny. He pulled a hip-flask from the pocket of his sealskin coat, raised it between us. Antique silver, the lid gone, replaced by a blackened cork.

Even as I shook my head, he was reading my eyes, grinning in recognition. He tilted it into his mouth. The scratched silver glinted like ice. My jaw gritted – the steel teeth, cold silver, the spirit like raw electric current. Close up, I felt the jolt of vodka. He sized me up with a sly grin. Everyone in this town belonged here – we both knew that. Except for the herders; they came in for supplies, for the wrestling, to get drunk. Everybody else belonged, including me.

'What do you think of our fighters?' The teeth glittered with good-humoured malice, daring me to be honest. Two young men stood on the canvas, their faces heavy, almost stupid: the town-expression. They didn't look like that on the tundra.

'I wouldn't like to fall out with them.'

He shrugged dismissively, 'They're only herders.'

I was stung by the typical Russian sneer. 'What's wrong with herders? They're extraordinary people.'

'I didn't say there was anything wrong with them.' Delighted with himself. 'My father was a herder. My brothers are herders.

All my family are herders . . .' He spread his arms till the greasy old coat creaked. The spectators had switched from the fight to our encounter.

'And now you're a photographer –' I said, trying for irony in bad Russian, '– the imitation of life.' He laughed loud and long; the best of both worlds.

'Not a photographer –' He pounded one tiny fist in the other for emphasis, threw out his chest. 'A journalist! Like you. *Collegi!*' He looked like he was about to embrace me with professional enthusiasm. In a minute he would pull out his card and expect mine. The curse of the new Russia – the business-card.

Volodya was his name; he didn't give the Arctic version. He was a stringer for a city paper. He made up stories, he said, bursting with the sly humour of it, and sold them to Russian papers from time to time. That was journalism! There were a couple of native papers in the old tongue, he shook his head – he edited one himself, as dismissive of his work as he was proud of his scams. I recognised the joke, the inverted humour of the colony.

The old man was on the canvas again, his tunic back on. '*Haw! Haw! Haw!*' he bellowed. The response was weak.

'Who *is* he?' I asked.

'The Old Champion?' Volodya said, 'He's seventy-two.'

I paused in respect. 'Champion of what?'

'Hey, old man,' Volodya shouted, in high good humour, jerking his thumb at me, 'what were you champion of?' The brick-red face returned a stony glare. He said something about me that made the crowd laugh. Volodya strutted across in his black sealskin, his commissar-hat, fur-lined boots, and slapped the muscled shoulder, the way a jockey slaps a horse, grinning back at me the while.

'Wrestling,' he said when he returned. He had grown serious after his little journey, as if something of the canvas had rubbed off on him. His chin was out, his chest proud. 'When I was a boy, Sergei was the "Champion of the World". Kids like me didn't know his real name. We didn't know he had one.'

I looked across at the old man, puzzled. In his wizened way the photographer looked as old. 'When was this?'

'He was Champion the year I was born. I'm fifty now –' A sharp glance, as if I might dispute it. 'He fought every wrestler in the North, all the Russian pros – he never lost a fight. He was Champion for twenty years without a break.'

'What happened?'

'What happened? A guy threw him. Then another guy. It was over.' He mimed the throw, elaborately, in miniature, as if he had had a hand in it himself. 'A long time ago.'

The old man was watching.

'What does he do now?'

'What do you want him to do? All his generation are gone. He's too stubborn to die.' Around us, they were nodding, turning away. 'Hey!' he taunted the old man, raising the Nikon as if to take a picture, 'You're too stubborn, isn't that it?'

The huge fists rose in salute and a scowl creased the old face. He had all his teeth.

The bouts continued for another hour. I would have left, except I was Volodya's celebrity and it would be a betrayal. When others spoke to me in Russian, he switched us into English. He kept me briefed on developments.

The same faces recurred on the canvas – the quarter-finals. They were better matched; the standard improved. The clan leaders watched from the sidelines, seated on the snow – hard, mature men with moustaches and sharp eyes. Authority sat naturally on them. They smoked like everybody else, but they didn't drink in public. Money changed hands, discreetly.

In the semi-finals two young men stood out, one in each bout, one in blue, the other in brown. Their round Arctic skulls were hooded in crow-black hair. The eyes were ice-blue, brilliant, as if Scandinavian blood had tempered them.

'Yes, yes, they're brothers . . .' Volodya was impatient. Of course they were.

They met in the final. The crowd, in their tunics and deerskin coats, rugged faces intent, looked like an audience in an ancient arena. They were used to myth. They expected it.

The young men stood on the canvas, gripped each other by the belt and sleeve. Woven from coloured wool, the belt was wrapped twice around the waist and knotted at the side, long tails trailing vivid tassels. It was as strong as a canvas strap and crucial to the grip. They came apart, dissatisfied, and the referee stepped in. The belts came off. Each man in turn hitched up his heavy tunic like a cassock and his brother tied the belt around him, knotting it with savage tension. They never caught each other's eyes. The referee tested them with powerful heaves and stepped aside.

Nothing happened for a while; long moments stalled in quivering tension, matched perfectly; then bursts of motion when they cartwheeled on the canvas as if it were a trampoline. No move seemed carried out by force; each tumble was a sudden yield that heeled into a wheeling throw, was followed through and countered into a set of flowing rolls, as if the pair were flogged together by some external force. I felt its rhythm in my feet, whipping the canvas against the snow. Volodya yelled their story in my ear – there was a woman in it. In this world of ice and snow, of sleds and sliding motion where it mattered little that the wheel had been invented, they were like twin wheels striving to break the axle.

One slipped. Falling, he twisted on his hip and shoulder. The crowd hissed. The other fell on him with a vengeful lunge, gripped his body savagely and thrust with all his weight, forcing the shoulder towards the canvas. The referee's hand probed. And still they wheeled, crabwise, scraping broken circles on the canvas. The trapped man was struggling for life. His brother summoned sudden strength. Legs braced for leverage, he smashed down with his chest and shoulders, once, twice. Rigid as a club, he went on hammering as if to drive his enemy through the canvas into the ice.

The loser shouldered past me in a stench of sweat and shame. The referee raised the winner's hand and I watched the Old Champion rising to his feet, eyes blazing. These were the shots I wanted. He had stepped sideways and was directly opposite me now, all the available light on his face – as if my instinct had revived.

The winner stood, arm raised. The old man lumbered towards him, reaching with a champion's handshake. He was already speaking. The youth looked through him without a hint of recognition, and turned his back. Through the lens I saw the old man stumble, as if he had crashed into solid ice. But he recovered and kept going, following his outstretched hand.

I lowered the camera. In the throng of bodies I couldn't move aside. Close up, eyes glazed, he looked ancient, the skin hard and cold as if he had been dug out of the snow. Volodya thrust my arm out in a greeting. The old hand was huge and hard, like a piece of bone or timber in a museum. The stare was fixed on me; the left hand moved inside the tunic, dragged the bottle out. His thumb flicked; the cork fell out of sight between our feet. He tipped his head back, swallowed, his eyes still holding mine. The gaze was cold and mottled as old glass. I struggled to free my hand, but his grip was fixed, forgotten. He lowered the bottle, thrust it at me.

SEAN COFFEY

Home Run

I'm one of these women who know nothing about sport. I don't understand it. That is to say, I don't understand why people watch it, talk about it, get emotional about it. I come into the TV room and when I ask who's playing, my two sons just turn and look at me pityingly. 'Ireland!' they say, or 'Man United!' or whatever it happens to be. Mike doesn't even respond. There was a time he found my ignorance on matters sporting an endearing eccentricity. He'd try to convert me. He doesn't try to convert me any more. He won't attempt the conversion, like they say in rugby. It gets into you, the sporting terminology, when you live in a house of men.

The boys love sport. They dress in football shirts. Man United for John, Juventus for Kieran. I think I'm a bit disappointed about Kieran. He's the younger one. I always thought he was more like me. I thought he might be different somehow. When he was younger he used to ask me how I was feeling. I'd ask him how he was and he'd tell me. I suppose you could say that he was sensitive. But that would imply that his brother, John, is insensitive, which he isn't. It's just that the question would never have occurred to him. They're both nice boys. A credit to us, as our friends say.

We're a popular couple. Mike is great fun. I play the quiet, witty foil to him. It's usually dinner parties. Most of our friends are late parents, still stuck in the baby-sitting situation. We go to their houses, invite them to ours. Sometimes me playing the foil to Mike gets a bit out of hand and we row in front of them. I don't think they mind. In fact I think it probably reassures them. Reassures them that there is life after kids, that some spark can survive it all. Or maybe we just reassure them how good their own relationships are by comparison. You never can tell. Even with friends.

We don't communicate, Mike and I. When I bring something up that's important to me, he acts like he's being ambushed. He gets defensive. Yesterday I said to him, 'We don't talk any more.' His answer was, "Talk, then,' which stung a bit, but I still persevered. I told him I felt sad all the time. I told him I was lonely. 'Lonely?' he says, puzzled, 'sure haven't you got me and the boys?' I mean, what can you say to that? The guy can't even get to first base when it comes to emotions. There you go – another sporting metaphor. I read in a problem page once that men need something to talk about because they can't talk about themselves. That's why sport is so important to them. In my experience this is exactly right. Some of these problem pages can be spot-on. I read quite a few of them. Probably because I can't depend on my friends for reassurance.

I'm equally guilty, I suppose. Mike has an excuse, he's not able to express how he feels. I am. I could try harder. I could set it up for him, set up the shots and he could pot them. He'd think it was his own doing. It wouldn't be, but that wouldn't matter. I could frame the whole thing in such a way that he couldn't miss. Well, I could if I had the energy. Which I don't. Bloody snooker. Bloody sport. Of course, I suppose that's what I should really be using on him – sports lingo. Tell him that we have to dig deeper, that we've hit The Wall, that we're at the wrong end of a two-goal deficit and deep into injury time. That life is slipping past us on the blind-side, wherever the hell the blind-side might be.

It annoys the hell out of me, sport. The amount of human time, money, energy that gets devoted to it astounds me. Transfer fees, TV rights, pay-per-view, I hear them talk about it all. Such a waste. As far as I'm concerned, sport is a huge confidence trick perpetrated on the world's populace. The rich world's populace, that is. It's the new opium of the people. Mind you, it has to be said that I was never any bloody good at it myself. Quite useless, in fact. I played hockey at school – for the C-team. If there'd been a D-team I would've been on that. You had to play. There was no choice. I hated all sport. Except maybe rounders in primary school.

We played rounders in primary school. Mixed teams – boys and girls together. There was a boy, he always picked me on his team. I'd whack the ball and start running, running hard, trying to get everybody home. 'Run, Anna, run,' he'd shout, and I ran. Ran like I've never run since. Running for him. And for me too, I suppose. He was an outsider – arrived into our school in fourth class. His parents had moved back from England. We became an item, an innocent, pre-pubescent sort of an item, but an item nevertheless. He lived down our road and we walked to and from school together. We talked. He was nice. Sometimes he'd turn around in class just to smile at me. It was this that gave us away in the end – one of his mates copped on. When the next break came they gave us a really hard time. Him more than me. It was the cardinal sin, after all, for a lad to be found consorting with girls. But he didn't give them an inch. He didn't deny anything, he simply turned the whole thing back on them. He faced them down. I suppose it helped that he had an aunt teaching in the school, but it was more than that. He had a winning sort of way about him. From that day on things in our class were different: there was no segregation in play, there was no teasing. We could be friends, boys and girls. That was in fourth class. I sometimes think that those last few years of primary school were the happiest years of my life. 'Run Anna, run,' he'd shout, and I ran. Trying for a home run, with all the bases loaded. Like they say in baseball.

I know all the jargon. And maybe sport isn't bad as a metaphor. Because sometimes when I lose it with Mike, it's like I'm running again. Except it's with words that I'm running and it's not a ball I've whacked away, it's some moment of pointless banality that Mike's way of being has forced me into. I lash it away from me and just go for it, head down, tearing into him with words, words that keep coming. Tearing through his complacency, past first base, him surprised and confused, past second base, him hurt and angry, past third, him angrier still. Running with the words. Running for myself. Running until eventually I run beyond his coherence. Then he hits me. Just the once usually. On the shoulder or in the ribs, never the face. He hits me and I know then that I've got through, gone all the way. Scored a home run, I suppose. It doesn't happen often. Usually I stall at second or third base. But every once in a while I have to go all the way. It's the aim of the game, after all, isn't it?

GERARD DONOVAN

Glass

When I was young I thought my mother was a loose woman. I think it was because of what happened to my dad. He was killed working on a dark morning in February while digging a trench for underground phone cables. A car veered onto the hard shoulder, catapulting him into the air, and after that happened I stopped talking for a while. My mother cried for a week. To make up for my silence, she said.

Another week went by and three more and the silence stayed nested in my mouth. I followed my mother's hand into a creamy building with greenish tiles in it. A man talked to her and then to me and then to her. Might take months or weeks or tomorrow, he said. I wanted to talk but the words couldn't come out, as if blocked by a door or a table or something. Then my mother said she had to get something and left me alone with the professional man.

'And now, Paul – your name is Paul, isn't it?'

I swung my legs. His tweed jacket smelt of cigarettes. He had more questions.

'Think of words as little breaths of air. You can breathe, can't you? Breathe for me, Paul. Let's try it together.' He stood up and exaggerated a big breath, pulling his shoulders back, letting it out in a long sigh as he slipped his brown fingertips inside his pockets. He did this for some time. I looked past him to the lawn outside his window where a cloud froze in the blue sky. I thought my words could just as easily be spit too. Then I could spit on him. When my mother came back she asked me to wait outside and then she brought me home and didn't say a word the entire way.

She took a part-time job in the local pub so that she could get out of the house, and, I think now, away from me. We lived in Drumford, a small village in the west of Ireland, and the pub served tourists, mostly Germans and Americans who stopped for sandwiches and tea on their way to the Connemara mountains or salmon fishing on the Corrib River. It was at this time I thought she was loose for seeing another man, because that's when she met John.

Mr John Higgins made up for what I could not say. He made up for my silence right from the first day he appeared at the house and shook my hand: I was fourteen, it was 1974. My mother told me that he worked as a signalman at the railway station in Galway City. He visited our house twice a week after that, driving late in the evenings in his Escort after the last train he had to service came in from Dublin, his jacket shoved up around his neck, the distant mountains framing him as he took the last steps to our door and knocked. It didn't take me long to dislike him, and I disliked him all the way through spring and all the way through summer in that big silence the professional man could not penetrate with his tricks. John never stopped talking.

Higgins was loud and twitchy. He fed cigarettes into his mouth for quick puffs and he was everywhere in the house at the same time, darting from living room to kitchen for coffee, to the front door if someone knocked, to the toilet, where he talked to himself. He sucked up all the space around him. My mother wandered around the house whispering like a ghost; I often wondered if she knew he was there.

Sometimes John and my mother went out for dinner and a local big band, and when they got back to the bungalow I'd hear them knock over the pots and plates and laugh. I could see them too, if my bedroom door was open, touching each other at any opportunity.

'Put on the Mr Sinatra, Carmel. I love Frank, I do,' John said. He took her hand and twirled, his green scarf flowing off his shoulder, looking a real professor of the floorboards. He said, 'I sang at the Skeff last week for my brother's birthday. He claimed I sounded like Tom Jones.'

'You do in a way,' my mother said, and sipped from her

whiskey before hugging him with her free hand. He swung away from her, loosened his shirt and winced a song into a pretend microphone.

'The summer wind . . .'

And she laughed. John made her laugh.

One night they came back and moved the furniture so that the floor was clear for another dancing session. John set two Brendan Boyer singles to repeat on the turntable and they jived. He grabbed the ribbon from her hair and ran behind the couch, waving it above his head. She ran after him, shouting, 'Give it back!'

'Try taking it from me. Go on!'

'I spent a fortune on that ribbon,' she said, leaning across the sofa, stretching her fingers as her figure pressed against the cotton of her dress.

'Sixpence if it was a penny,' John laughed.

'More than that, you bas . . . you bastard!' she giggled, and fell limply against him, and he held her straight although I could see that she didn't need the support at all.

Then they played slow music. Then they sat on the couch and he put his arm around her. 'You're a fine girl, all right.' His sweat glistened across his smile, his white shirt wet from the armpits. He kissed her cheek, but my mother turned her lips to his. He stroked her hair and she lay back, pulling him down onto her. I lay in bed, the pillow pressed to my ear even though I couldn't shut anything out.

Next weekend, another night of dancing and drinking. They stumbled into the house, chattering wildly at the tail end of some topic. This time John did all the singing and my mother twined red and yellow ribbons through her hair. Then she asked him to turn off the music. He lifted the needle and extinguished the melody.

'I want to tell you something, John.'

'Yeah, oh yeah?'

'I want to get married again.'

Without moving, he placed the needle back to the vinyl and started to sing even before the music started.

'I'm serious!' she shouted into the noise.

'We barely know each other yet,' he said.

'Will you turn that down?'

'I need my space,' he shouted back. 'I'm not ready, Carmel. Aren't we having fun? Don't you like me?' He danced to her in little dips of his knees, trying to grab her hand.

She turned away, folded her arms. 'Will you turn that off?'

He shook his head, laughing, dancing, singing into his fist.

'I'm not going to take that away from you,' she said. 'I just want to have you around enough that we can get used to each other.'

He moved around, trying to get her to swing with him. He turned the music up. She snapped. 'Get out!' she screamed. 'Get out, get out!' Even with the record in the background, I shook.

'Carmel, I'm only –'

'Just get out.'

He took his jacket and left in the dead of night. She cried herself to sleep while the record turned under the needle. A few days passed and he reappeared, and it started all over again. Music, drinking, arguing. I was angry to hear him refuse her, glad that he did.

My mother knew that I had heard them arguing.

'He has a problem with drinking, I think,' she said. 'You should be more forgiving, Paul. I know you don't like him. He needs time. When are you going to say something to me? Just to me?'

I wanted to talk to her even less now. Soon her wrists started to swell and she had to give up her part-time job, and her outings fell to a night or two a week at bingo. She took pills she didn't think I saw, the ones she kept hidden with the wine bottles she also didn't think I saw. Her eyes darkened and grew hollows, and her hair was a pegged-up bunch of grey. She looked a hundred years older than thirty-seven.

As I lay on my bed listening to my mother and her new flame dance and then fight, I wished that my dad would come back for a visit and, with the strong arms that held me as a child, beat the tar out of John Higgins, beat him all the way back to Galway City,

call him a waster, and kick his arse a few times more after that. I
wanted this even if it meant my father would have to return to his
grave at such a late hour. And when the furniture started moving
to the edges of the room and the couple pounded the floor with
their shoes, I wanted my ancestors to stir from the ground and
join my father. I wanted the earliest traces of our family to move
from the ground of the Russian Steppes or the Spanish south and
give the dancemaster Mr Higgins, Esq. the drubbing of the
century until all that was left of him was a whimper. I played
out the scene like a film I'd watch in the Town Hall cinema: after
taking care of Mr Higgins, my father returns to the house and has
tea with my mother and me, tells us how he feels and where he is,
and I ask if he knows whether we'll all be together again since he
has the inside track now that he's in the afterlife. My dad listens,
scratching his chin, which he does when he's thinking but can't
find the words. I imagined our conversation: *Dad, give me a sign
that you can see me*, and he says that yes he will, *You'll see*. And on
those dark nights I fell asleep playing that scene over and over
and woke up to a world made of only my mother and me, a world
that limped on without him, wearing its bravest face.

The summer slipped by, the leaves stiffened and disintegrated,
and by mid-autumn John had lost his job as signalman. His manager told him they were cutting back on the Dublin–Galway
service until the spring. John started drinking and lost his car to
the bank; so now he cycled out to the house evenings, his scarf
blowing, his light a needle in the long road.

   He and my mother spent more time together, and soon they
were arguing again into the night hours. She said she was tired of
asking him to move in, and he said she was only asking out of
pity now because he'd lost his job. Pity or not, John Higgins soon
began leaning his bicycle against the wall of the house earlier
most days, letting himself in with an 'I'm back!' and putting his
six-pack and sandwich in the fridge. My mother never said
anything to him about it, even when she came back from a long
walk and found him sleeping on the couch. Then he stopped
bringing anything and helped himself to what we had, watching

television with his right leg hopping. I never acknowledged him. One day I walked through the living room and he turned to follow me with a stare from his dark face, his lips set, his fingers tight around a beer.

'If you're this angry now, what will you be like when you're my age?' he asked.

I stopped, unsure whether to keep going or turn around. He leaned forward and poked a finger at me.

'Take it easy and don't be so morose all the time. Life is living for the day, Corpus Deum, that's what I say.'

I decided that I could not wait for my father to come back from the grave for Christmas. I'd have to do Higgins in myself. He stood up, furious that I didn't respond.

'Talk, can't you? Open your bloody mouth and say something, you little git. You make me nervous, like I'm never alone.' He shouted now, his whole body spastic.

'Go out and play. Go on!' He put the bottle down and took a step toward me. I left quickly, kicked a stone around the yard, then beat it high into the air with a stick.

At the end of November my mother sat me down and told me that I wouldn't be seeing John again. 'I hope you're not disappointed, Paul,' she said. 'I like him, but John's afraid of me. You'll understand when you're older.'

She laughed and caressed my hair, and I pulled back a little, embarrassed at her affection. We had never been a close family; my father had been a quiet, somewhat lonely man, and I was not used to her touch, even though she was a kind woman. As winter came and deepened, John faded from my thoughts. He is the type who slips easily out of memory, and only his shrill talk or a vinyl record can bring him back now.

An Arctic winter spell comes once every few years to Ireland. The weekend forecast for the middle of December was for heavy snow. By late Thursday, clouds hung over the village.

I lay under a woollen blanket dotted with red donkeys. We were saving oil. The cold made my feet feel like blocks. I had taken off my trousers and draped them around my head for warmth. As

I tried to sleep I saw the snowflakes twisting under the street lamp and over a deep frost serrated across the window. After an hour lying still in bed I was still shivering.

My mother closed her bedroom door. I squeezed my eyes shut until colours lit up my eyelids. One by one the house lights went off in our neighbourhood. At one o'clock it seemed I was the only person awake in the village as the snow flung itself against the window, piling into the sill. I rolled over but couldn't relax. My ear sank against the pillow and I heard the blood roar inside me.

A shadow slapped the bright reflection of the street lamp off my face for an instant. I kicked off the covers and ran to the glass, rubbing a circle in the frozen film with my breath. A machine moved under my window. I cupped my hand and peered as the outline went by, gouging out an arc of snow. The JCB with a plough on the front passed under the street lamp and then into the black, waving its white shawl across the silence between light and dark. The cabin glass made the driver look like an insect in biology class at school.

Morning came, and the sun was a pale yellow circle pressed like a fingertip against the ice on the bedroom window. I glanced at the road and saw where the machine had cleared a line for cars. My mother was reading the newspaper at the breakfast table.

'Richard and Stephen are coming tomorrow for a few days,' she said at the sound of my footsteps. 'They'll have to stay in your room.'

I had met them before. They were her sister's two sons. My mother watched me pour my tea and smiled. 'Their mother and father need some time alone. Make your room tidy, would you?'

I guessed the boys' parents were fighting. I hadn't seen Richard and Stephen in years; they were a year and two younger than I, and that's most of what I remembered about them. But other matters occupied us that day. By eleven o'clock the snow was falling so hard that forecasters called it the heaviest snowfall in Ireland since the Second World War. The lake beside our house froze, and that night's weather was the worst on record, though we weren't as badly hit as the rest of the country. The army trucks moved out of their barracks in the midlands where drifts buried the roads in some of the smaller towns. Up north, gale force winds cut off outlying islands.

By the time the two boys arrived next day on the early afternoon train and took the bus out to our village, the storm had blown itself out. After they had rested for a couple of hours, we traipsed across the frozen lake since the sky was clearing. It must have been well after six in the evening when the moon floated from a patch of cloud, bright at the edges, its yellow gauze spread across the white ice like butter. I careened on the bike over the ice as the other two stepped cautiously.

My mother called, 'Remember, the lake is still dangerous even if it's shallow!'

'Okay,' they said, and moved even slower. I cycled off into the middle of the ice and ignored them. A while later, I noticed the brothers gathered about, looking down at the ice. I cycled over.

'Jesus, we thought you'd never come,' Richard said, and he pointed at something. I let the bike drop and joined them.

'There's someone in the ice,' Stephen said. 'Someone's in the ice.'

I knelt down, but clouds covered the moon. We waited in the pitch dark until the moon moved out into the stars again and lit up a face that stared at us from under the ice.

'Jesus,' Richard said.

My nose touched the cold sheet. A boy, maybe seventeen, dressed in a tuxedo, his hands raised to his shoulders, palms facing us, leaning against the dirty glass, as if asking us to let him in, to let him back. His face shone handsome and clear.

'We'd better call the police,' Stephen said.

I nodded, aware of how calm the lads were and of a strange detachment in me, and I thought that maybe they'd seen things at home that might have seemed worse to them. I motioned with digging actions that we could cut the ice and drag him clear.

'No, you idiot,' said Richard. 'We'll fall in ourselves.'

They skidded back to the house, but I waited with the boy. I brought my face close to his until all that separated our skins was the ice. I put my hands to match his and felt them stick to the surface.

He was silent too.

After Richard and Stephen reached the house my mother ran to the edge of the lake, screaming at me, her words garbled. I left my bike beside the drowned boy in the tuxedo and ran to her. She grabbed me as if from a raging river, hugged me too tightly and too long.

The police came in black coats filled with pencils and note-books, and they told my mother the boy went missing after a party Thursday night. He was last seen running off with a champagne bottle, they said, shouting something about swim-ming in the lake. My mother wept into a hanky as she poured the policemen their tea. 'The poor boy,' she kept saying. 'His poor mother.'

In the living room the television said more weather was on the way, and snow was falling again as we went to bed. Richard wanted to sleep on the floor, even though it was too cold and hard for him. Stephen fell asleep as soon as I had put out the light; I lay beside him as the moon swung around the roof, thinking about everything and nothing. I knew my mother was worried by everything. It was as if the world had heaped its concerns on her forehead. I slept until the beating of an engine pulled me from the bed and to the window.

Two large wheels rotated into the glare of the street light, followed by a short steel frame from which snow blew in a curving wave of dirty white crystals. I looked for a driver but saw only the shape of the JCB and its solitary play against the yellow of the streetlights as it cleared the snowdrifts and mumbled away into the distance. I thought of my father. I wished I knew why he had left without warning and where in the big night he was now, and if he was alone like the man in the machine or the fellow under the ice. I had once dreamt I met him on a street: we faced each other, trying to talk, but neither of us could get a word past what seemed like glass between us.

I leaned my head against the window and sleep drifted against my forehead.

A noise outside the window woke me to more snow. Then there it was: a shape flitted past the window up to the roof. I looked around: the brothers were buried in their blankets.

'Wake up,' I said. But the words hadn't a sound to them.

Richard shouted in fright when I shook his shoulder. He twisted into a sitting position.

'Wake up,' I said. 'We're going outside.' Nothing.

'Jesus, you're trying to talk!' he said.

Stephen was breathless. 'Paul is almost talking again. It's a bloody miracle!'

'Are you both deaf?' I asked. Silence. I'd surely never speak again.

Richard looked at me with his mouth hung open as he dragged his trousers along the floor and up his legs.

I said, 'I heard a noise outside' and pointed to the window because that's all I could do.

Stephen wrapped his scarf tight around his neck and clapped me on the back. 'Good man! You lost your voice and now you'll find it. Keep looking!'

We crept in single file past my mother's room and the drone of her television to the top of the staircase. The television clicked off, boards creaked across her room, and my mother waltzed to the bathroom a couple of inches from where we crouched. She sang to herself, and the smell of drink harmonised the tune on her breath.

We tiptoed down the stairs and out the front door into the bone-cold air. Stephen's red hair flew around his orange cashmere scarf. We tried to run to the pavement, but our steps sank knee-high. We beat our chests for warmth.

I motioned for them to stand still.

A timid voice floated from the roof, a voice I recognised. I wasn't surprised. In recent weeks, word had it that things had not gone well for John Higgins. Word of trouble with another woman and her husband, and Higgins having to leave town for a month to let things settle.

I said, 'I know who you are.' And I heard my words float onto the crisp air.

One side of my face was absent from numbness. We all moved together, our eyes fixed to the figure on the roof, our shoulders touching. I stared until I swayed. Richard and Stephen were probably too interested in the stranger to realise that I had just said something. The mound of snow perched on the roof seemed to oscillate, and an arm lifted a bottle to the head. A chunk of snow fell from his forehead.

'Can you get down?' Richard asked.

I watched the bottle fall with a thud into the snow. I thought how much John could see from the roof: the lake, the fields stretched ghost-white to the sea, the lighthouse.

He grunted and caught hold of the drainpipe. I couldn't tell if he'd heard me. He kicked at the wall of the house, probably trying to get the blood flowing in his legs before shimmying down.

Stephen turned to me. 'If we climb up to help him, we'll hang by our arms until we freeze too. They'll have to cut us down like cardboard.'

The light went on in my mother's bedroom. The window opened and she leaned out. She looked at John as he swayed to her right. Then she looked down at us and back to him and called in a clear voice: 'You'll have to let go, John. Go on. Push yourself away from the wall and let go.'

'I can't.'

'Push yourself off the wall, John.'

'I can't stop drinking. I love you, Carmel.'

'I know, John. Let go of the pipe.'

'I'm letting go, Carmel.'

John fell awkwardly. We struggled through the snow to him.

'He's puking,' Stephen said.

We dragged him into the house by the shoulders and positioned him on the couch while my mother scurried about in the bright kitchen making chicken soup. Richard took off John's shoes and socks while I undid the shirt. The smell of whiskey was cold on John's lips. Stephen started a fire with wet logs. He crouched down and blew until a flame crept around the sizzling timber.

I helped my mother pour the soup. She looked at me. 'Don't be angry with him, Paul. He's lonely, but I won't waste any more time on him, if that's what worries you.'

'I'm not worried.'

She gasped. 'You're talking again! Oh Paul!' She hugged me, her chest heaving.

'I heard a noise outside,' I said.

'It must have been the fright, then. Thank God for that. Thank God for John Higgins. My little boy has found his voice!'

After Higgins fell asleep and the two boys went to bed, I made her a cup of tea in the kitchen. She talked and talked about me talking. Then she took a small mirror from her purse and traced the lines on her forehead with a fingertip. She met my gaze unflinchingly.

'I'm not getting any younger, don't you see? But a lot of men would like to meet a widow who lives in a clean house. I'm going back to that pub. I'm going to meet a nice man on his holidays. I miss your father, Paul. But I'm lonely. And now you're better. Now I can be better too.'

I nodded. I had never heard her use that word, *widow*, as if my talking had loosened a truth in her, that spoke to her, finally told her she was alone. I returned to my room, undressed, turned out the light, and listened to the silent white storm heave against the window.

LORCAN BYRNE

Delivery

On Thursdays, after the last delivery of the long day to the mad Kennedy woman, Charlie Blue was allowed to keep the van for the night. He could head home to his mother, proud behind the wheel of the yellow Hiace, waving to any of the fellas from the old schooldays he might happen to see in their long gardens, playing with their kids or mowing their midsummer grass. The arrangement suited his mother. She would have the dinner ready and then, after watching *Coronation Street* together, he would drive her into town to Horan's Hotel for her weekly game of bridge. Tommy Horan also owned the grocery store and she thought he was a great man altogether, a generous man to let her son have the van so that she should get to her game of bridge. Charlie said nothing but knew Tommy Horan to be a bit of a bollocks, with his limp lettuce and soft tomatoes and yoghurts past their sell-by date. He said nothing because his mother could turn as nasty as the twelve-year-old Jack Russell she kept on her lap and fed with the better bits of meat from her dinner-plate.

A sparkling drizzle made Charlie Blue turn on the windscreen wipers. The sun came out properly again and the road shone blackly, and the smells of fresh-cut grass and warm earth rose from the fields and hedges and in through the open window of the van. The wipers squeaked and Charlie turned them off, mid-swipe. With one hand he extracted a cigarette from a packet of Silk Cut and lit it with his Horan's Hotel cigarette lighter. He chewed the smoke before gulping it into his lungs. The slipstream reddened the cigarette-tip and sprinkled grey flecks of ash onto the dashboard and delivery-books. Charlie Blue smiled. He felt lucky. Lucky to have his driver's licence, lucky to have his mother still alive, lucky to be working for Tommy Horan, even if he was an old bollocks. A wisp of smoke brought tears to his right eye.

August 20
  A month already. A day just as lovely, the clouds low over the Slieve Blooms. Light balls of dandelion seed drifting across the land like a first snow. And I resent this beauty because Bobby cannot see it. I paint it but I resent it. The swallows slice the landscape open and I delight in seeing it bleed. From my window I can see the gate and the wallflowers staining the stones with their blood. At night, the shrieks of the hunted comfort me. I am not the only one in pain. In the morning I cannot bear to dress and prefer to let the shadows clothe me. I go to each of my fifteen windows and decide which will frame that day's work. I might eat, if my body lets me, and then I bring the easel and the piano-stool to my chosen window and start to paint.

Charlie took it handy around the last turn before Kennedy's. It was a year to the day, he realised, since poor old Foley lost control of his tractor and trailer on this very turn and killed Mrs Kennedy's young son. Bobby was his name, only four or five years of age. They were planting flowers at the base of the big stone pillars when around the corner came Foley, shouting about the brakes, the trailer already up on the grass verge, throwing huge lumps of grass and earth into the sky, the front of the tractor rearing up like a crazed horse. Mikey Tuohy, from Trasna, saw the whole thing from his field above the road, gave a detailed account to the gardaí and drank many free pints on the strength of it for a long time afterwards. He said the screams of the mother nearly stopped his heart. She picked up the body of the boy before Tuohy could get down to the road, and she ran the whole length of the long driveway up to the big house, screaming the whole time as the boy's head flopped lifelessly against her arm and shoulder. Poor old Foley sat in the ditch and took off his cap and didn't even recognise Tuohy when he arrived down beside him. Tuohy said he shouldn't have been allowed on a bike, let alone a tractor, because the old fella was half-blind.

LORCAN BYRNE

September 3

Horan's got somebody new to deliver the groceries. I recognised him: Charles Cullen. He knocked and stood on the porch and stared out for ages, out beyond the fields. At what, I don't know. He stretched his arms out wide like Christ crucified, as if to embrace the earth. Then he yawned and knocked again. He lifted his shirt and scratched his stomach. With his toe he shifted the box in nearer the wall and left slowly, looking back every so often at the door. While I was emptying the groceries afterwards I discovered a box of chocolates I hadn't asked for. I must remember not to pay for that.

The land is bled dry and colours are slowly ebbing back to brown. My nipples harden in the cooler air that moves against my skin like long grass. At dusk, when the night enters the house, I look for Bobby. I want to run a bath and squeeze warm water over his small, smooth back. I want to turn back his soft sheet and lift him into bed and bring the edge of the sheet to his chin. I want to kiss his eyelids as he sleeps. Instead, the darkness gnaws at my own.

Once, last autumn, at dusk, Charlie saw an owl standing on the right pillar of Kennedy's gate. It didn't move as Charlie edged the van past the rubble of the left pillar and then past the gate still on its side since the accident, gripped by a hinge in the shape of a huge clenched fist. At first, he thought it was a shadow, but could not figure out what cast the shadow. He had drawn alongside and quietly rolled down the window when the top of the squat, dark shape swivelled. From the centre of two wide discs two eyes stared evenly at him, appraising him, daring him to move and then with two or three beats of its surprisingly wide wings it slowly, disdainfully, flew off low over the field towards the trees. Charlie remembered feeling uncomfortable, judged somehow.

October 9

Charles still brings the groceries. For the same reason, I both hate and love him being on my porch each week. He reminds me of a better life. I so clearly recall Charles in class, tall and clumsy in his desk. I had to let him stand in the end. He was freer that way. And the day I decided he had a gift, it comes back so clearly. (I detest this clarity that

*precedes Bobby and Bobby's death!) He brought me up his finished
painting and at first I was disappointed: 'A Beach in Summer' it was
called, but everything in Charles's painting was a different shade of
blue, not just the sea: blue sand, blue hills, blue boat, and what I
thought was a blue sun. I asked Charles why he hadn't used colours
and he said in that scared way he had, 'Well, Miss, it's a beach at
night-time, you see.' Charlie Blue they called him after that. Maybe he
still paints. I hope so.*

When the guards arrived Mrs Kennedy wouldn't let them into the
house, Tuohy said. Nor the parish priest neither. In the end
Sergeant O'Reilly had to break a pane of glass and reach in to
release the catch. They found her upstairs washing the child in
the bath. The blood-stained water went everywhere, over the
walls, the mirror, drenching Fr Seery and Dr Murphy as they
forced the dead boy out of her arms. Dr Murphy waited until after
midnight and then phoned his wife, who came over and stayed.
Mrs Kennedy didn't come out of the bathroom until the next
morning. She came downstairs still covered in blood and told Mrs
Murphy to kindly leave her house. Hasn't been seen outside the
grounds of her house since the funeral. From the high field Tuohy
says he sometimes sees her sitting all day at one of her windows.
Or walking naked to the woodshed or throwing scraps out to her
cats. As Charlie drove up the weed-invaded driveway he kept his
eyes peeled as always. He threw his cigarette butt out the
window, thinking to himself that he had only two cigarettes left
and that the old bollocks wouldn't be paying him until tomorrow
evening. He'd better spare them. He peered up at the high field
behind the Kennedy house and reckoned that Tuohy was probably spending a lot more time up there than he needed to.

December 25
   *I found a packet of mince pies I hadn't ordered in the box of groceries
yesterday.*
   *Every so often a man comes to the gate and stands there staring up
at the house. Who is he? I wonder. He was there last week and again
today.*

I feel Bobby's presence strongly today. I fetched the Christmas tree from the attic and put it in the front room where I decorated it. I write in its shifting red and blue and green light. I have wrapped his favourite toys and placed them under the tree. I close my eyes and he is there, lying full-length on the rug in the winking light, opening his presents, turning his blond head around to smile up at me, not minding a bit that they're the same presents as last year. I drink my wine and eat a mince pie. Too rich for you, Bobby, too rich.

Charlie couldn't imagine his former art teacher naked. Every other woman in town had spent time naked in his open-mouthed dreams, even heavily made-up Mrs Simpson, the Englishwoman who ran the post office. Mrs Kennedy was older but not by a million years, she could only be forty or so, and she had had a good shape back then during his time in the Vocational School even if it was concealed by long dresses and colourful knitted cardigans. He had liked her. She hadn't written him off as stupid. She had tacked up a painting he had done of a beach at night-time, right up beside the board where everyone could see it. That was good. It was worth being called Charlie Blue for that.

February 18

This week Charlie hid a couple of tangerines in the box. I love him for these small gestures, the only kisses I receive.

Today, the stranger walked up the driveway to the door. I saw him clearly through the glass, tall, blond-haired, blue-eyed. Serious. He just stood there, for ages, unmoving. One of the cats scraped the kitchen window and I looked away for an instant. When I looked back, he was gone.

Snow fell again today but a hard sun made it retreat into the hungry grass.

Charlie felt sorry for the grey mother cat with her matted fur. She came up to him as he pulled back the side door of the van. He reached down to scratch her head and she arched her back in response and rubbed her length across the leg of his jeans. You've no life, Charlie said, not like you used to, anyway.

He was halfway to the porch when he saw last week's box exactly where he had left it beside the old iron mud-scraper. A busy line of black ants led from the box to a gap between the front wall of the house and the concrete floor of the porch. Confused, he walked up and down for a while, looking at the front door and windows. He put the box he was carrying back into the van, lifted his T-shirt and scratched his stomach. Underneath the beech hedging that ran at right angles from the corner of the house he saw a torn egg-box and a scatter of clean chicken bones.

April 28

I feel so heavy. As the world outside grows lighter and fills with tender hope I become heavier. My paintings are still in winter, almost monochromatic. I paint from one window now, from Bobby's room, which provides the best perspective on the gate.

My handsome stranger is making good progress. He began by laying out the stones in rows and chalking numbers on them. Every so often he stood and looked back up at me, serious as always, his blond hair barely visible from where I sit. The wall is finished. All that remains are the pillar and the gate.

Charlie smoked a cigarette, then knocked on the door for the first time since he began deliveries to Mrs Kennedy nearly a year before. Just leave the box on the porch and she'll bring them in herself, Horan had said. But he couldn't just drop the new box down beside the old one and let the ants crawl all over it. The door swayed open under pressure from his knuckles.

'Mrs Kennedy?' he called into the shadowy hallway.

May 21

Charlie still leaves his small offerings. Yesterday it was a packet of fig rolls. I cannot eat them but am nourished by the gratitude I feel.

I heard the owl call again last night. Closer this time. I pictured his long brown swoop, the talons, the terrified writhing of his prey, the beating rise into the night-time trees.

The pillar is almost finished. The gate lies on its side on the grass, its big hinges hanging loose, like God's amputated fists.

Charlie felt cold. These thick-walled country houses were impossible to heat, from a single range anyway. His eyes adjusted to
the gloom. A silver blur materialised into a bunch of keys
hanging from antlers mounted on the wall.

'Mrs Kennedy?' he called again. He turned a round brass door-
handle. The front room. A painting on an easel. Others stacked
against a florid wallpapered wall. An untidy pile of silver knives
and forks on the rug. He closed the door and moved towards the
back of the house, towards the kitchen, he presumed. This door
was open. He flicked the light switch because the venetian blinds
were down. A fridge hummed in the corner. Three bananas
blackened in a glass bowl. There was mouse dirt everywhere, on
the table, the breadboard, even in the butter and sprinkled across
the cold plaques of the range. Teeth marks scored a bar of pink
soap in a chipped enamel dish. Charlie went back out into the
hallway and stood at the bottom of the stairs. He shivered.

'Mrs Kennedy?' he called and started up the steps.

June 20

*The days are like children, reluctant to come in from their play, and
tonight the sky is a gentle purple, taut as the skin of an aubergine.*

*I have washed all my brushes for the last time. Each one released its
own history of colour into the lather in the palm of my hand. Each
shining sable as fine and pointed as ever, russet-tipped. I emptied the
wooden cutlery-box and put them into it along with my palette and
tubes. My gift to you, Charlie Blue.*

Tomorrow I will walk through the gate.

The smell of white spirit lingers.

While Charlie waited for Sergeant O'Reilly and the doctor he
smoked his last cigarette leaning against the side of the van,
looking out over the trees to the distant, darkening Slieve Blooms.
Bats flitted in and out of the yellow light that spilled from the open
doorway and upstairs window of the house. He had just ground
the cigarette butt under his heel when Sergeant O'Reilly walked
over and handed him a rectangular wooden box, then told him to
go on home, that the ambulance could take over an hour to get

from Ballinasloe and that there was no point in waiting. He'd see him tomorrow. Ambulances never hurry for the already dead.

Charlie drove back into town and parked outside Horan's Hotel. The bollocks could keep his van. Through one of the hotel windows he could see the bridge players intent on their cards. His mother was there too, at a table to the left, serious and resourceful, a tall glass of mineral water at her elbow and the Jack Russell at her feet. She must have phoned a neighbour, he supposed. The dog sensed his presence, looked out but did not move.

He reached into the van and took Mrs Kennedy's box of brushes and paints from the passenger seat. Slamming the door with his shoulder, he put her gift under his arm and walked on, out past the last lights of the town and into the blue shadows of the moonlit countryside, feeling nervous but welcomed, like a stranger at home in what was once a foreign land.

MARY MORRISSY

While You Wait

'Clutch,' he yelled, 'clutch!'

The green Zodiac came to a shuddering halt. In its gleaming bonnet Edel could see convex reflections of the over-hanging trees.

'I can't,' she wailed, 'I can't do this!'

'Don't be silly, Del,' Victor said, 'of course you can.'

The unpaved road stretched ahead, a lush aisle of grass down its centre. Edel knew every stone, every bend of it. She knew the whitethorn and the fuchsia, the oak tree at the abandoned house with its rusting collapsed gate attached by baler twine to the posts so that it had to be lifted open. But sitting behind the wheel of a car made it all threatening. The landmarks became obstacles, the serpentine turns ambushed her, the potholes mocked.

'Well,' Victor said finally, laughing, 'we can't just sit here. Let's try again. And remember . . . the clutch.'

Damn him, she thought. This had all been his idea anyway. Teaching her to drive. Edel suspected that it was boredom; they were into their second week at Edel's mother's and in this setting Victor had seemed ill at ease, his jocular manner a handicap in the face of the busy disapproval of the Forristal household. It was the haymaking season, so the house was empty for the long hot afternoons and Victor was at a loose end. He had offered to help but Ned, Edel's brother, had considered this, as he did Victor's presence, as something preposterous. He was a city boy; what would he know about such things? He might as well have been a woman, as far as Ned was concerned. The car was Victor's only trump card. It conferred on him a status he would not otherwise have enjoyed. He ran Edel's mother into town to do the shopping; he drove Ned to the creamery. Ridiculous and all as they thought it, this large sugared lozenge of a car, the colour of lime sherbet, the Forristal family found it – and Victor – useful.

Edel had never told anyone how they had met. She was ashamed of it because it had not been a lucky accident. She had seen him and wanted him; the direct line between wanting and having had never been so clear to her. He had been sitting at the heel bar. It was the latest innovation at Hamilton's department store, an American idea. There was a high counter like a saloon bar and a row of tubular stools with red leatherette cushions, fixed to the floor with bolts. A neon light flashed on and off overhead which read 'While U Wait'. It was a Monday, mid-morning, quiet. Edel had already twice tidied all the little compartments on the electrical counter where she worked, sorting the miniature bulbs and the fairy lights, standing the squat white fuses upright, marrying the two-pronged plugs, male and female. She was loading coin into the till when she saw him halt at the counter opposite. She busied herself – Hamilton's biggest boast was 'our staff are never idle'. She stacked batteries while she watched him heave himself up onto one of the high stools at the heel bar and unlace his shoes. He deposited them on the counter top and she heard him say 'heels and soles'. He had a newspaper folded into his jacket pocket and he fished it out and began to read. There was something absurd and defenceless about him sitting there in his stockinged feet. The heels of his socks were worn thin and she could see the dull rose of skin through them. There was a hole in the big toe. It put him at a disadvantage, she thought, as she eyed him surreptitiously. His dark hair was cut jauntily and slicked down with hair oil which gleamed under the store lights. He had a fleshy face, scrubbed and babyish-looking. He wore heavy-framed spectacles. Oh dear, she thought, they'll have to go. He was smartly dressed, a tweed sports jacket (no elbow patches, thank God) and a shirt and tie. There was a noticeable crease in his dark pants – a mother's touch, she hoped. A clerk, she guessed, taking his elevenses out of the office. The shoemaker set to on the shoes. It was a noisy machine with a belt drive that whined like a dentist's drill. The heel bar seemed to Edel like a

pocket of heavy industry in the midst of household linens,
electricals and cosmetics. It had the funny smell of a factory and
the clattery serious air of male business. The regular customers
were nearly all men; the women who used the heel bar were
usually limping and in distress, bearing a stricken stiletto or a
single shoe with an amputated heel.

Heels and soles took less than ten minutes, Edel knew. She
would have to move quickly. She was alone at the counter and
shouldn't leave. Vi (no, she corrected herself, Miss Hunter –
Hamilton's policy forbade staff to use one another's Christian
names, too familiar) would not be back from her break for
another fifteen minutes, and the shoemaker was already on to
the left shoe. The neon sign tantalised. The shoes were being
handed over now. Money was changing hands. There was the
sharp ring of the till. Edel watched as he bent over to tie his laces.
Then he eased himself down from his high perch. He flexed his
feet in his newly-minted shoes, then he turned on his fresh rubber
heels and walked away. And then she noticed that he had left his
newspaper behind. She darted out from behind the counter across
the aisle, whipped the paper and ran after him. She caught up
with him at the main entrance. Cold blasts of air came in through
the revolving doors meeting the dry heat of the store. She tugged
gently at his sleeve. He wheeled around.

'Your newspaper,' she said, 'sir.' (More of Hamilton's policy.)

He smiled, at first surprised, then gratified. 'Why, thank you,
ma'am,' he said.

She saw a flicker of appraisal. Her move. 'Why don't you ask
me out?' Edel asked boldly. The revolving doors gasped hot, then
cold.

'Why don't I?' He smiled cheekily, then stashing the paper
under his arm he was swept away in the cool carousel of the
glassy doors. A week later, Victor Elworthy came back and
bought a two-pronged plug at the electrical counter and asked
Edel Forristal to a matinee at the Savoy.

Edel felt she had come a long way. She felt it particularly when
she visited home. And contrary to her expectations it was not a

pleasant sensation. She had been so homesick in the city at first,
staying in a damp bedsitter on the Ring Road where the bulbs
were always blowing and the distant coin box in the hallway was
always ringing – but not for her. She spent weeks waiting for
someone to shout up into the well of the landing, 'Call for
Number 4.' She felt rebuked by the gay chatter of the girls in
Number 3, their stifled laughter on the landing on their way back
from a late night, their sleepy early morning conversation. She
lived near the cattle mart then. She remembered the loneliness of
those drear November mornings, watching the cattle being
shipped in, their wild eyes visible through the slats of the trucks,
their caked tails waving feebly, their plaintive howling audible
over the hissing of tyres, the jangle of bicycle bells, the drone of
buses. It made her feel doubly desolate. The bellowing cattle
reminded her not only of home, but of the loneliness of home, the
suffocating sadness of a place that already felt abandoned even
before she had left it.

Then she met Babs, who worked in Hosiery. They moved into a
cheerier flat. Granted there was still green mould growing in the
shared bathroom down the hall and the electricity meter was
greedy as an infant. Suddenly in the midst of cooking dinner the
last coin would drop down and the bubbling of potatoes, or the
chops hissing on the pan, would quietly subside like the stealthy
withdrawal of affection. The hothouse glow of the two-bar fire
would fade slowly to black while plumes of steam from their damp
washing, straddled over the backs of the kitchen chairs, gloomily
exhaled. When Edel looked back on it, everything in this world
seemed metered, monitored, rationed. Oranges were a luxury; the
war a live memory. But after six lonely months Edel felt she had
arrived. The city became, thanks to Babs, a place of possibility.
Babs knew where to go – picnics in the Botanic Gardens,
afternoon tea at the Metropole where you could easily whip a
second iced fancy from the cake tray if you took the precaution of
sharing a table. Edel would remember this time as a kind of
courtship. A courtship with the city itself, in which the crowded
tram rides to the sea and the smogged rough and tumble of the
municipal baths were like shyly offered gifts. She liked the city's

mix of serious grandeur – the pot-bellied parliament, the flint-
faced university, the declamatory statues of patriots – and the
slatternly charm of the streets with their fruit sellers, their littered
pavements, the garish fluorescence of ice-cream parlours. It was
just such a mixture, gravity and contingency, that she wanted in
a man.

Victor worked nights. He was a Linotype operator on the *Daily*.
Later in their courtship he had taken her on a tour of the works
one Sunday morning when the caseroom was idle. He proudly
showed her his keyboard, which to Edel looked for all the world
like her mother's treadle sewing machine. Bigger, certainly, more
masculine, the heavy ingots of lead hanging on pulleys hinting at
a more weighty purpose. But what was he, really? Only an
industrial typist, Edel thought, refusing to be visibly impressed.
Another evening he took her to see the presses run. They stood in
the loading bay, a smell of ink in the air as the press thundered
and rattled. Only then could Edel begin to understand Vic's
urgent pride in his work – the hugeness of the press, the pulse
and noise like the roar of war. Oil-begrimed men clambered on
the platforms of the vast machine beneath the feathery wave of
the newspapers as they reared and dipped overhead with the
crazy motion of a rollercoaster. Other men sorted and bundled the
copies as deftly as if they were large decks of cards. Then, packed
and smacked, the papers juddered down rollered chutes into the
black gape of the delivery vans. All in the dead of night, as if
secretly.
    Saturday was the only evening they could meet, and even then
Victor was wide awake and buoyant at midnight when Edel was
ready for bed. She tried not to dwell on this mismatching too
much; it brought her back to the manner of their meeting. By
rights, she should have waited. Waited for the right man to come
along. Trusted to chance.

Edel had no real desire to learn to drive. She had been quite happy
to sit back and be a passenger. But Victor was penny-bright in his
insistence.

'Come on,' he said, 'there's nothing to it.'

When she sat behind the wheel she felt it intrinsically wrong. She should not be in charge of something so large and powerful. And she wasn't in charge of it. Even switching the key in the ignition made her fear the car would suddenly leap into life.

'Not until you put her into gear,' Victor said, snorting with laughter.

They inched around the back yard, Edel nosing the car tentatively around the perimeter, past the black doorways of the outhouses, circling the water pump on its altar of concrete, the rusting mangle in its bed of nettles. These things seemed grounded and necessary, while she sat in a candyfloss car, playing.

She did not feel so bleakly inauthentic in the city with Vic. In fact he was considered quite a catch, a man with a job and a car, good-looking in a neat, presentable way, smart, keen. Keen at first, Edel thought. Lately she had noticed a certain creeping reserve; she wasn't sure whether it was her own nervousness about losing him, or a cooling on his part. Some reserve of her own prevented her from asking. The nerve she had used to attract him, the bold subterfuge of it, deserted her at close quarters. She had begun to brood about what a young man with a car and a salesman's good looks could get up to on sunny afternoons when he was free to wander in the city alone. She felt acutely the need for something definitive to happen. Perhaps that was why she had asked him to come home with her.

After a few days Victor took her out on the open road. Strangely, it was easier away from familiar sights and Ned's reproachful looks when he returned to the house in the evening to find Edel stranded in the yard with Victor, helpless with laughter, as the car juddered and stalled. Her mother considered the whole driving business unseemly. She just about tolerated being driven about by her daughter's young man. She suffered Victor's eager offers of transport with a mute embarrassment. But to see Edel behind the wheel was another thing altogether. It just wasn't proper. Pretty soon, Mrs Forristal reasoned, she'd be smoking cigarettes and going into lounge bars.

Away from the prying eyes of home, and out on the empty tarred road, Edel could build up some speed. She wanted to succeed at driving, not for her own sake, but for Victor's. Particularly if he was having doubts about her. The fortnight together in the country had been a forlorn kind of success. Vic regarded it as a holiday, though for Edel it was the rallying season when extra help was needed around the house. Ned had made his own of Victor in the way that men did. They had found their common ground and traded information about cars and tractor parts, engines and horse power. But her mother had been more resistant. Victor was the first man Edel had ever talked about, let alone brought home. Mrs Forristal understood what Edel was saying by this defiant show of hospitality. This man is going to be my husband.

Edel had never been so conscious of her background before. But seeing the way her mother and Ned lived through Victor's eyes made her feel anxious. Ned's mud-caked wellingtons standing splay-footed on the brush mat inside the back door, the crude washboards and tin bath they used for the laundry, the chipped crockery, even the scummy top on the milk carried in an enamel jug straight from the dairy, spoke of a dour futility. The constant feeding of the range, the endless hauling and carrying, the grinding impoverished repetition of their routine began to oppress Edel.

'You're getting to be a bit of a speed merchant,' Victor said, interrupting her thoughts. 'Fifty m.p.h., no less!'

She braked immediately.

'No, no,' he said, 'don't do that. You're really getting the hang of it now. You have to feel comfortable.'

Alone here with him, she did, upholstered in leather in his capsule of modernity, gliding through the dappled countryside in the late glinting sunlight. She rounded a bend and almost collided with a herd of cows.

'Whoa,' Victor said, as if it were he who were driving the animals.

Edel geared down and applied the brakes gently. All she could see ahead were the black and white rumps of a dozen beasts lazily swaying while a young lad with a stick hollered at them.

'Great,' Victor muttered under his breath, 'we could be behind this lot for hours.'

'They won't have far to go,' Edel said, 'probably the next house along.'

She was happy to chug along behind the chequered cows, watching their flaky flanks and skeetering hooves on the tar, and keeping a safe distance. They were in no hurry, after all.

'Come on, come on,' Vic urged. The slow patience of the countryside irritated him.

After about half a mile, the young boy swung open a gate on their right and urged the cattle in off the road, threatening and cajoling by turns. He stopped as Edel eased the car by and stood almost in salute as they passed. He had heavy straw-coloured hair, a knotted little face, small contemptuous eyes. He stood for several minutes looking after them. Edel watched him in the rear-view mirror, a small, defiant figure standing at a gate. The sun was very low now and they were driving due west. A mile further on, they veered around another bend in the road into the full glare of the setting sun. Victor leaned over to pull down the visor to shield Edel's eyes. As he did, something solid and heavy blundered across her vision. Everything seemed to go dark, as if a large rain cloud had plunged the sky into stormy relief. But this thing, a corpulent shadow, kept moving. Edel braked, the car slewed dangerously and she came face to face with the petrified eye of a Friesian just as the bonnet of the car ploughed into its mud-caked flank. There was a soft, cushioned thud as the car glanced off the animal and spun wildly, skidding headlong towards the ditch.

'Jesus!' Victor yelled as they came to a jolting halt on the rough camber, and the engine cut out. He peered out the passenger window at the felled cow lying on its side and thrashing in-effectually, a sharp gash on its belly full of matted blood, a sticky pool oozing onto the tar. Edel, lifting her head from between her hands which were still gripping the steering wheel, saw only the cow's eye watching her with mute, terrified appeal. Then the animal bellowed.

'Let's get out of here,' Victor said.

'What?'

'I said let's get out of here.'

She hesitated. She knew exactly what should be done. She should get out of the car, run back to the youngster who had been driving the cattle, get him to call his father with a shotgun, and put the beast out of its misery.

'Shouldn't we . . . ?'

'Ignition,' he commanded, and for the first time behind the wheel she was swift and decisive, as if all the hours of instruction had been for this moment. She did as she was bid, turning the key, feeling the power surge up through the accelerator as the car righted itself and moved confidently forward. But by the time the power had reached her fingertips it had been reduced to a faint but pervasive trembling.

They pulled in at a shady crossroads. The sun had gone down. Victor got out slowly and went to examine the front of the car. There was a large dent in the radiator and a blood-flecked hollow in the left wing where metal had met flesh.

'Thirty quids' worth at least,' he said, coming round to her side and opening the driver's door.

She dragged herself over to the passenger side. Her limbs felt like lead.

They hid the car in a barn close to the house, its nose burrowed in a thicket of hay. They told the Forristals they'd run out of petrol.

'Typical,' Ned said. 'Women!'

Victor left first thing in the morning to take the car back to the city. Edel was left to make excuses for him.

'Took fright, did he?' her mother asked.

She and Victor would never talk of it again, not then, nor after they were married. What was it, only a dead cow, Edel would tell herself. Or a dying cow, dead now one way or another. But in her nightmares it would resurface. She would awake aghast in the wounded dawn (Victor beside her, still on nights, newly asleep) a windscreen image of the scene seared on her brain. The beast's bewildered eye, its baffled pain, the bloodied haunch of the sugar plum car and Victor hissing at her to put her foot down. She it was who had taken fright.

The Moon Shines Clear, the Horseman's Here

The house is a holiday house, one of dozens dotting the landscape around here, each one perched in its own scrap of field, overlooking its own septic tank. Polly can seen the chunks of thick white pipe sticking up from hers, her tank for the moment. The pipes are the main feature of the field or garden or patch of lawn or whatever it might be called which surrounds the house. The other feature is the well, a concrete block with black pipes emerging from it and snaking across the grass to a hole in the wall of the kitchen.

Polly lived at home in this valley until she was almost eighteen. Her father was a teacher in the village school, and her mother a stay-at-home mother. She baked, milked cows, scrubbed the house, and was very particular about her religious duties, although not, thought Polly (not called Polly then, but Poilín), very seriously religious. Anyway she made fun of the ladies who became ex officio keepers of the church, arranging the altar flowers and pandering to the priest and his every need, although she must have known that such women were found everywhere, were essential to the efficient running of the parish. Without them there would certainly have been no flowers, no choirs, no special ceremonies on local feast days. Without them the priest would have provided the bare necessities, Mass on Sunday, confession once a week, no frills. 'My New Curate', Polly's mother called the local women who provided all that decorative trimming of song and flower and special extra prayers. However, she would never have missed Mass herself on Sunday; wearing a showy hat and white gloves she and Polly sat with Polly's father in the first row of seats. This was the time when men and women sat on different sides of the church, but Polly's mother protested, she sat on the men's side. It was not a blow for gender equality but quite the opposite. She sat there to proclaim her superiority to all the other women, in their headscarves and dark old coats, or their trousers and anoraks. In the parish, she felt like royalty, and Mass was the appropriate context in which to give public expression to this attitude.

The family observed other essential religious formalities, some seemingly private in themselves but linked by invisible threads to the social and cultural web that enmeshed everybody. For instance they said the Rosary every night after tea, praying for the souls of the departed dead and also for living souls to whom they were closely related or who had power and prestige. They prayed for their cousins, the Lynches and O'Sullivans, in Cork and Tipperary, and for Éamon and Bean De Valera, and they prayed for the Taoiseach, and they prayed for the Archbishop of Dublin and the Bishop of their diocese. They prayed for the Inspectors of Education who would descend on the school once a year and ask the pupils insultingly silly questions, and for the county football team. It seemed to Polly that this praying strengthened their connections to these people; it seemed to her that she had some role, for instance, when the county won the All Ireland Final in Croke Park. She might have been a cheerleader, not that she knew the word then. She was a silent supporter speeding her team to victory, and she had a hand too in the running of the country. Then sometime in the late sixties, the Rosary stopped. It seemed all Irish families reached some communal decision overnight, or as if someone in a position of authority had issued an edict and all the Catholics of Ireland obeyed it. Could there have been some sort of referendum? Anyway, it stopped.

Polly's mother was different from the other mothers in the valley. Polly would have found it difficult to pinpoint in what this difference resided, but if pushed to select one word would have said 'old-fashioned'. Her mother did not like to wear make-up, indeed she never even owned a lipstick. Her clothes were slightly out of date – excessively elegant white lace blouses and long skirts – when other younger mothers had slacks with straps under the insteps and tight polo neck jumpers. She never wore trousers,

even though a lot of her work was out of doors, with the cattle
and in her garden. At night she liked to do embroidery, executing
tiny white flowers on white table runners, broderie anglaise,
although she called it Mountmellick Lace.

Polly's mother was snobbish. She was not a native of the
valley, but of a big town, where her family had been leading lights
in the Irish language movement. It was thanks to this that she
had come to the valley to learn its dialect, and there met Polly's
father. Now she lived in a simple way, but she still considered
herself and her family a wide cut above most of the neighbours,
and this sense of difference coloured every single aspect of her life.
That was probably why she did not wear lipstick or mascara, or
jeans, and it is definitely why she did not go to bingo on
Thursdays with all the other women. Polly accepted her mother's
self-assessment, and believed that she was more ladylike, more
refined, more valuable, than other people's mothers, although
she often felt more comfortable in those other people's kitchens
than she did in her own.

The view is sublime. That's what Polly was told, all the time she
was growing up. That she lived in the most beautiful place in
Ireland was drummed into her along with tables and catechism
and alphabet. She believed it as certainly as she believed that God
made the world, or that Ireland un-united could never be at
peace, or that Gaelic was the one true language of Ireland and
eventually would be spoken by every Irish citizen. In fact she
probably believed in the beauty more profoundly than in any of
those other tenets of the local faith. It seemed verifiable. The
crashing waves, the grey cliffs, the purple mountains: did these
not, in their awesome wild grandeur, constitute perfect beauty?
But even then she felt drawn to nature in its more intimate
manifestations: a tern breaking the surface of the sea, a seal
poking its shiny nose above the black water, hares boxing among
the rushes at Easter. The little flowers that bloomed from May to
November in a relentless routine of colours. Primroses, violets,
orchids. Saxifrage, the colour of bloodshot eyes. Eyebright, self
heal. But she was not enjoined to admire such details. They were

taken for granted, like the hidden natural resources, the still unpolluted wells, the little farms that kept the valley humming in tune with the seasons. Somehow she deduced that all of this minor nature was commonplace, perhaps occurred in places which were not the most beautiful place in Ireland, perhaps in places not in Ireland at all.

There are no flowers in the fields now, because it is December. Rushes sprout like porcupines among the tussocks, and the rusty tendrils of montbretia spread themselves here and there, in limp abandon. Otherwise nothing. What a month to choose for a dramatic return! Polly turns from the window and decides to light a fire, the traditional antidote to the gloom outside. When the briquettes are blazing in the grate and she is sitting in front of it, with a glass of red wine in her fist, she feels happier. Unlike its garden, the house is attractive, designed according to some international template for country cottages, with wooden roof beams, rough white walls, a slate floor. The fire makes it perfectly cosy.

When she was twelve Polly went to secondary school in the nearby town, travelling by bus every morning and evening. The bus was a new idea; until recently anyone who could afford to go to secondary school from this area would have had to board, and Polly's mother wanted her to go away, as she had, to a convent in the middle of Ireland, where she would learn to recognise how superior she was to her neighbours. But her father opposed this; he wished to encourage his pupils to avail themselves of the new educational opportunities. Polly had to set an example. She had to use the free bus. Her mother agreed reluctantly. If she had had the faintest idea of what went on on the bus her resistance would have been stauncher. It was much more vulgar than a bingo hall. It was worse than the pub, to which her mother never went; it was as bad as the disco that was held in a hotel outside the town on Saturday nights. Boys on the bus teased, cursed, and swore. Girls huddled in the girls' section and either pretended not to pay any attention to the barrage of insults and mock endearments which was constantly fired at them from the boys' section, or else they encouraged the boys, subtly by glancing at them in a knowing, sly way, or overtly by joining in and giving as good as they got. Give us a kiss. Have you got your Aunt Fanny? Fancy a carrot? Try this one for size.

There were two kinds of girls on the bus, slags and swots. The slags wore thick beige make-up over their acne, and had long spiky eyelashes, a sort of badge of slagdom for all the world to see. Their hair was usually artificially coloured or streaked, or looked as if it was, although one might wonder why this should be since they were aged between twelve and eighteen. But maybe they coloured their hair as they coloured their eyes, just to show the world who they were, just to show that they were defiantly, proudly sexual, just to show that they were not like the swots. The swots wore no make-up, and their hair was usually left severely alone and tied back from their faces with bands or ribbons. Or it was short, although that became more and more unusual as the decade, the sixties, dragged to a close. On the bus, the swots sat together at the top of the bus, quietly chatting among themselves about teachers and homework and ignoring what was going on around them. The slags chewed gum ostentatiously, with the slow long chews slags specialised in, and cast their sidelong odalisque looks at the boys. The looks were also slow, slowness being one of the chief slag characteristics. What's the rush, their sauntering swagger seemed to say, arrogantly. Time belonged to them and they had lots of it.

Sometimes a boy and a slag, who were going together, tried to share a seat and hug and kiss *en route*, but this was not allowed by the bus driver. Girls and boys were not supposed to sit together. The bus driver was a man aged about sixty, Micky the Bus, who though old was sharp as a razor. He tolerated almost everything, except sitting together and canoodling. If he caught a couple breaking his one rule he threw them off the bus. It was against the rules of the Department of Education, but that didn't bother Micky. He knew, quite rightly, that the Department would never find out what he had done. He knew that his word was law on this bus. This was before the days of litigation and before the days when children or teenagers were aware that they had any rights at all. Nobody would have dreamed of questioning Micky's

THE MOON SHINES CLEAR, THE HORSEMAN'S HERE   139

absolute authority on his own bus, not even the beigest blondest
slag.

Once in town, boys and girls separated, going to their gender-
specific schools, girls to the nuns and boys to the Christian
brothers. They never really understood what went on in the
different schools, and this mystery about how the other half
actually spent their day added spice to their lives. Polly, long
before she was interested in any specific boy, felt it, when they got
out of the bus at the bank and the blue-clad boys all walked off in
one direction, gaining dignity when revealed in their full height,
their long thin blue and grey bodies moving purposefully up the
hill to the grey castellated structure which looked like a fortress or
a prison. She found them interesting then, and intriguing, as they
disappeared into the secrets of their days.

There was a loneliness about going in the other direction, with
the flock of girls in brown skirts and blazers, to a place as ordinary
as a bowl of cornflakes. Polly felt that where she was going lacked
importance, although as soon as she got there everything that
transpired seemed important enough, and challenging. She was a
good student.

A good student. She had to be, to satisfy her mother and her
father. And it was not easy to keep it up. Not because she was not
clever, or interested in her work, but because her friends did not
approve of academic achievement. Polly was in danger of going
too far, which would have pleased her parents but outraged the
girls in her class. So when she found herself speeding up – finding
that she could enjoy reading history, or botany, derive a pleasure
from learning and understanding which was true satisfaction,
not just the fulfilment of an urge to please some adult – she sensed
some sort of danger. She held back. It was not so hard to do, and
involved nothing more onerous than not reading as much as she
was supposed to, half-doing her homework instead of doing it
properly. Doing well was easy, it was a habit she could see her
way into clearly, as if doing well were a clean, shining river down
which she could sail effortlessly once she caught the wind. But
not doing well was even easier. All she had to do was fail to hoist
her sail, slide along under the work instead of gliding on top of it.

She espoused the mediocrity which was what girls in that school, at that time, aspired to, even the best of them: her friends Katherine and Siobhan, both of whom had been her closest friends since she was four years old and to whom she was bound by ties of eternal loyalty.

Polly has a week to spend in Ireland, and during that time she is going to face the devil. She has read somewhere that in everyone's life are seven devils, and only when you meet them and overcome your fear of them can you find your guardian angel. (It was a novel about Chile, that she read in Danish; devils, angels, saints and sinners have lead roles in Chilean folk belief, according to this novel.) Her mother. That is one of her devils, the one she is going to meet and talk to, regale with the story of her life, Polly's version. Until Polly tells this story to her mother she will be unfree, ununited, unwhole. She is not acting under psychiatric instructions. She doesn't need a psychiatrist to tell her this elemental truth. There is unfinished business between herself and her mother, between herself and this valley, and time is running out.

But there are distractions. She takes time settling in. She has to find her bearings. She has to find the shops. It is easy to fill the time with routine tasks when you are in a strange place, even if it was once a place called home. The first days she spends trying to heat the house, and organise the water supply. The water is cloudy, white like lemon squash, full of clay or lime or something worse, and the central heating doesn't function. Men in caps come and mutter darkly in Irish to one another and hammer at the pipes, and Polly has to be at home to let them in.

Then it's desirable to explore her old haunts. She goes for a long walk to the hill at the back of the cottage. A road winding up past other bungalows, a few with grey smoke trailing up from their chimneys and most seeming empty, closed up like her house had been. After the last bungalow, a gate and then heather, sheep, sky for a mile, until you come on something surprising: a cobbled street, an old cottage and schoolhouse, looking out of place on the hilltop in the middle of nowhere. It is not the usual place for a school, exposed and far from where anyone lived. A film set, that is what it is, Polly remembers suddenly, a chink opening like a trapdoor in her head. There it is, something she has not thought about in thirty years: the commotion when the film had been made in the valley, the trucks trundling up the hill, the star-spotting, the jobs for extras. Everyone had been an extra. Katherine and Siobhan had been schoolgirls in the classroom scenes. All the other people had been villagers, or men drinking beer from funny tin mugs in the pub, or country folk at the market. Even the animals got parts: Siobhan's mother had hired out her hens for a pound apiece per day. But Polly had not participated. Her mother would not allow it, disapproving as she did of the film which, although the word was not used, focused on a passionate adulterous affair, conducted in a range of scenic Irish settings. How Polly's mother discovered this was a mystery. Nobody else knew what the film was about. It was impossible for the extras to follow its plot, such being the nature of filming. But Polly's mother had her sources. And unlike most of her neighbours she did not need whatever extra money she could lay her hands on. She did not need to prostitute herself or her daughter to Hollywood. The film had been a disappointing experience, an experience of total exclusion, for Polly. No wonder she had forgotten all about it.

Polly kicks the filmset cobbles with her walking boot, and continues to the crest of the hill. The sun is still shining, low and strong, but the joy has gone out of the day. She can feel night falling already, the afternoon is sinking into a silvery grey dusk although it is only four o'clock. The sheep bleat on the bare hillside. Polly feels a huge longing for her home in Copenhagen; she longs to be there, in her old house, with the bustle of the city ten minutes away on the electric train. She longs to go to the opera at a moment's notice, as she often does, or to meet one of her woman friends and drink some wine in a warm pub, with the lovely Danish Christmas decorations up, the sense of a long simple tradition of paper hearts and straw goats and tiny flickering candles everywhere, in every window, on every table. Copenhagen celebrates light in the deep midwinter, glows with optimism and hope.

Back in the cottage, she pulls the tweedy curtains to shut out
the bleakness and throws a few sods of turf on the fire, then
phones Lia, one of her friends, and tells her how she is feeling. Lia
says 'Come home if you want to,' which is what Polly knew she
would say. And Polly says, inevitably, 'I don't really want to. Not
yet.' 'You don't have to do any of this if you don't feel like it, you
know,' Lia goes on. 'And you are allowed to change your mind.' 'I
know, I know. I will in a day or two if I decide that,' says Polly,
laughing. This is the sort of conversation she always has with Lia,
long meandering sentences full of pauses, and words like 'feel'
and 'decide' and 'maybe', phrases like 'well wait and see' or 'it'll
probably be OK.' They are so different from the sort of conversations that Polly has with Karl, which are to the point,
conducted in short complete sentences, verging on the terse. He
is practical and decisive, and it has taken him a long time to
understand Polly's meandering ever-changing mind.

Paddy Mullins sat with the rough element on the bus, smoking
hand-rolled cigarettes and slagging people. A lot of the time these
boys were laughing as they pushed one another and exchanged
insults. 'Done your sums, Smelly?' 'Yes Fat-arse, but I'm not
showing them to you.' 'Surprised you had time. Seeing as how
you were cleaning the pigsty again most of the night.' 'Shut up
Fat-arse, don't pick on him 'cos his daddy's a farmer.' 'Farmer?
Tax dodger.' The language of the bus was English, although the
language of home and of school was Irish, and some of the
children, especially those from Polly's valley, did not know
English very well. But they had to speak it anyway. English was
trendy, the language of pop singers and films, the universal
language of teenagers. Only the most prim or the most childish,
the most excluded, would persist with Irish in this context. The
slags had a name for people like that: Ireeshians. Polly knew the
rule of the bus and spoke English on it but she was called an
Ireeshian anyway, because her father was a teacher and her
mother was a snob and generally disliked.
    She was also called 'Lick'. All teachers' children were called
'Lickarse'; 'Lick' was its derivative, used by the girls, who

eschewed strong language. Farmers' children were given the epithet 'Smelly', Paddy was called 'Mackerel' because his father was a fisherman. He answered to the name, and gave as good as he got in these bouts of slagging, most of the time. But there were occasions when for no discernible reason he would fall out of the teasing loop. He would fall silent, and stare into space, thoughtful, enigmatic. Most of the boys did that. They had quiet moments, moments when they seemed to withdraw from the hullabaloo of a schoolboy's life and think deeply about something for five whole minutes at a time. What were they thinking, when they did this? Polly did not know. But she would have liked to find out, although as yet she had no inkling of how she could do this. Inside a boy's head was as impenetrable as inside a boys' school, somewhere she assumed she could simply never go.

Paddy would sit on his bus seat, gazing ahead of him, not necessarily out the window. Gazing at nothing. Then anyone could get a good look at him. Not that he was anything special. Indeed until this week Polly had considered that, whereas the girls on the bus all looked different, the boys all looked alike. There were smaller ones and taller ones, of course, with one unfortunate individual at either extreme. And there were a few fair-haired ones, with pale complexions and gentle manners – they tended to be short-sighted and wear glasses – who were not rough boys but good boys, and who sat near the girls, consulting their books or more often chatting to girls. Their fair, feminine looks seemed to give them an advantage when it came to making friends with the latter, as if they were less threatening in their less blatant masculinity. And of course they were not as aggressive as the bulk of the boys, that band of brown-haired barbarians, who exuded maleness like a herd of bullocks and couldn't sit still. Dark, large-boned, stubble-chinned, too big for almost all the spaces they were obliged to inhabit, too big for the bus or the school, for the houses they lived in, these were boys whose true element was not a classroom or a school bus, but the high seas, or a meadow or a bog on the side of the mountain. A battlefield. Most of them were good footballers. Their school won the All Ireland schools championship nearly every year.

Paddy was on the team but was the keeper, a position regarded with mockery by the girls and the fair-haired boys, although his team mates appeared to respect it well enough. Polly was accumulating information about him, almost without knowing what she was doing. He was a keeper, he was good at maths and chemistry, he was planning to be a scientist. He had once danced with a girl from the next parish for a whole summer but the relationship had fizzled out. He had been to Dublin many times with the team but never on a holiday to anywhere. His father was a fisherman, they did not own even a small farm, just a house and a field, and he lived about ten miles from Polly's home – he had not gone to her primary school, she did not know his family. They did not speak Irish in his house. There was some anomaly about his mother. Like Polly's, she was not from the district. Some people said she was English.

School finished at three thirty and at four o'clock the bus collected pupils from both schools and ferried them home. So that meant almost half an hour in the town, if you were very efficient about leaving your class. Usually this half hour was spent looking in the shops, or getting chips if you were lucky enough to have a shilling. People with a boy- or girlfriend found other ways to use the time – walking hand in hand on the pier, or chatting in the town park.

Paddy and Polly bumped into each other at the corner of the main street, one day in May. This was about a month after she had begun to look at him. By now she knew the contours of his head, the line of his eyebrows, the set of his shoulders, better than she knew her own. But she did not know how he felt about her, although Siobhan had said once, in her most serious tone, 'I think Paddy Mullins likes you.' So now Polly muttered hello, and averted her eyes, preparing to move quickly on. Even as she let his face slide from her view, to be replaced with a view of the pavement, she felt angry and frustrated, because she knew he would not have the *savoir faire* to initiate any sort of conversation; one of the svelte fair boys could do that, but not a boy like Paddy, one of the bullocks, the goalkeeper. He would not be able to talk even if he wanted to as much as she did. Also, she knew in that second that he did want to. His surprise, his pleasure, when they met like that, told her everything she needed to know.

She was wrong about his *savoir faire*.

'Poilin,' he was saying. She stepped back and looked at him, astonished at her good luck, their good luck, that he was able to say the necessary words. 'I'm going down to look at the boats. Do you want to come?'

It was as if he had been doing this sort of thing all his life.

They got through the town as quickly as they could, and then strolled down the pier. The sea was choppy, but a choppy dark blue trimmed with snowy white, and the sun was shining on the fishing fleet, on the clustering red and blue and white boats: the *Star of the Sea* and the *Mary Elizabeth*, the *Ballyheigue Maiden* and the *Silver Mermaid*. The air was full of energy.

'That's the one I go out on,' he pointed at the *Silver Mermaid*. It was a large white fishing smack with lobster pots on deck, and heaps of green seine nets piled on the pier in front of it.

Polly had not known he was a fisherman as well as a keeper and a would-be scientist. 'Do you do that often?'

'Weekends when they're out and I don't have a match.' He smiled. His smile was stunning; it lit up the day and gave his face a sweet expression which it didn't normally have. Usually he looked rather worried, as if he were carrying some burden.

'Do you like it out there?' Polly realised that although she saw fishermen around every day, she hadn't a clue what they experienced, out in those boats in the middle of the night, hauling in fish which disappeared into the new fish plant down the street. She could see it now, a grey block on the edge of the harbour, and in front the bay with the low hills on the other side, and the blue bar in the middle distance, beyond the great ocean. 'What's it like?' Out there, she meant, on the sea.

'OK.' He looked out, then at the *Silver Mermaid*, then out again. He reflected and seemed to come to a decision, to say more. Possibly he had never described the experience before. 'It's dark, and usually cold, and usually wet as well. We let down the nets over the side, five or six of us. Then we wait. That's the best part, waiting, gripping the net, wondering what happens next. Sometimes we talk or someone sings or we all sing. But usually we're just quiet. Standing there, waiting, in the night.' He paused and Polly wondered if she should say something, contribute some question or comment. But she couldn't think of anything. 'When we haul in the nets there are all kinds of fishes in them. Lots we have to throw back. Catfish, dogfish, cuttlefish. The cuttlefish are interesting. They have big brains, for fish. Once I kept one in a jar.'

'For a pet?'

'No. To dissect in the lab.'

'Did you?'

'I didn't use enough alcohol and it rotted. It exploded. Very smelly!' He held his nose and laughed. Polly laughed too, looking at the sea, crisp as a sailor suit, and trying to imagine the smell of exploded cuttlefish. In a minute Paddy said 'It's time to get the bus.'

This was May. It was a glorious month, as it often could be in that part of the world. Long sunny days, some so warm you would feel like swimming, although the water would still be freezing. Swallows were flying high over the meadows, and larks twittered constantly, tiny dots so far away that they could have been daytime stars. Polly's mother was busy in her garden, one of the very few gardens in the valley. She raised bedding plants from seed in trays which all through March and April had been placed under the windows of the house. Now she was raking beds, planting out nasturtiums and antirrhinums and Sweet William, nicotiana, stocks. She was feeding roses and weeding the rockery. She was setting her long rows of lettuce and onions, carrots and parsnip, her beds of herbs.

When Polly came home from school, at five o'clock, she would still be in the garden, her gardening apron over her summer dress, her red rubber gloves sticking out of the pocket. She would greet her with 'You could get an hour in before tea!' Meaning an hour of study. Then she could get three or four hours in after tea. Polly was doing the Leaving Cert in a month's time, in June, and her mother expected her to do well. What she meant by 'well' was quite specific. Polly would win a scholarship, a medal proclaiming her to be the best student in the county. At least that.

Polly had studied hard in secret for the last few months. To Siobhan and Katherine she said, 'I'm hopeless. I'm way behind!' But at home she realised she was way ahead. She could feel her progress, and it astonished her that progress was actually possible, even now, even after her years of calculated dawdling: that by concentrated attention, careful effort, an improvement was discernible even to her, even without the endorsement of good marks or teachers' comments. She had never felt so in control of her work before.

The change in her relationship with Paddy did not alter this. After the walk on the pier, she knew something had happened to her. She had thought about Paddy quite a lot before, but in an idle, controlled way: she could daydream about him at will, when she had nothing better to do, almost as if he were a book she could open when her day's work was done, and close again as soon as more urgent considerations beckoned. Now she found herself filled with a glow of emotion no matter where she was or what she was doing; a pleasurable excitement simmered not far under the surface of every single thing she was doing, bubbled in her veins, as if her blood had been injected with some lightening, fizzy substance, as if the air she breathed were transformed. Light, bubble, crystal. These were the words for what was happening to her. Walking on air, people said. And she felt light as air, translucent as one of the new green leaves in the hedges. Since the whole of nature seemed to share in this lightness and newness, the fresh-looking waves and the new crop of grass, the tiny bright leaves on the brown fuchsia bushes, she felt that she was part of the world around her, the world of nature, as she had never felt before. She could have been a leaf, or a blade of grass, or a calf or a bird or a lamb. Even a fish, swirling in the cold blue ocean.

She worked as hard as before. But sometimes she could not keep herself seated. Her physical energy got the better of her, rushed through her like an electric shock and forced her to abandon her sedentary ways and go for a run along the lanes. Her mother watched these bouts with some foreboding, but said, 'I suppose you need some exercise.' Often she added 'as long as it doesn't interfere too much.' Polly smiled. She smiled at everyone now, even her mother, and couldn't care less what anyone said to her. She transcended it all. She was superior, blessed, different, special, and none of the trivial irritants of life had the slightest influence on her.

The Leaving would be fine. She knew it. There was less than a month to go. If she did not open a book from now till the exam, she would probably still do very well.

Paddy and she met every day after school. They walked on the pier or they walked on the streets. Within days the entire school population within a thirty-mile radius knew they were 'going together'. That meant it was a matter of a few more days till the adults got wind of it; some blabbing girl would be sure to mention it to her mother. But it did not mean that Polly's parents would find out, unless some malicious person, some mischief-maker, decided that they should. In this community all normal adults would know that the last thing Polly's parents wanted was that their daughter should be having a relationship with a boy, especially a boy like Paddy. All normal adults would protect Polly and Paddy, and leave her parents, who were not popular, in the dark.

This is what happened.

After about a week of walking on the pier, in a state of increasing physical excitement, Paddy steered Polly to the town park, the known courting spot for schoolchildren. It was a walled park, secreted in the middle of the town, behind rows of houses and shops on all sides, and had a sheltered, enclosed atmosphere very unusual in this place of exposed bare coasts, windy hills. Also it was full of high trees, sycamores and elms and flowering cherries; the sheltering town allowed them to thrive here, whereas in the valley where Polly lived hardly a single tree would grow. They sat under an elm in the corner of the park and kissed, their first long kiss, so longed for that it stunned both of them. Paddy apparently had not kissed the girl he had been connected with the previous summer – Polly did not think he could have, because his experience of this seemed to match hers so exactly. That is, he was surprised by the powerfulness of the experience, by the delight it gave him, and at the same time it seemed the most natural thing in the world. He and she kissed as if they had never done anything else. You had to learn how to do almost everything else, even the most basic physical functions, but sex, apparently, you did not have to learn. Your body knew precisely what to do, without having had a single lesson. At least it did if you were like Polly and Paddy: in love.

Time passes quickly when you are in love and kissing. They had not realised that. They seemed to kiss for a few minutes. But when Polly looked at her watch two hours had gone by.

They had missed the bus. Every single child on that bus would know precisely why they had missed it.

Polly was OK. She had a phone in her house, and her father had a car. She telephoned from the kiosk on the square; for once the old phone was not out of order. She told her father she had been delayed in the science lab, finishing an experiment, and he came to pick her up. Paddy had to set out on foot, hoping he would manage to hitch a lift.

From then on they had to be careful about time.

The Leaving started. Polly sat in the school hall, at a brown desk, and read the pink examination papers. Nothing in them was a surprise; the traps they had been told to watch for had not been set, as far as she could see. The predictability of the whole examination was the most surprising thing, and it was also vaguely disappointing. She had been given dire warnings. You must read the entire course. You never know what will come up. But when it came to the crunch you did know. She felt cheated.

Paddy did not. In the boys' school, the examination technique was more refined. They knew exactly how much they had to do, and did not do a jot more. After every paper Paddy was able to calculate exactly what marks he had got – A in Irish, C in English, A in chemistry. Polly breathed deeply, superstitious. How could he be so sure? Wasn't he tempting fate? The results were, according to her way of thinking, as mysterious and unforeseeable as any aspect of the future. That there was a direct link between the work she had done and the results, she was afraid to believe now, although she must have believed it when she was studying. She wanted the exam to be a lottery. That was the attitude of the girls in the girls' school, whereas the boys regarded it as something much less like a game of bingo and much more like a field to be ploughed. Such a sense of control was essential for schoolboys whose main ambition and duty was to win football matches. Pretending the Leaving was some mystical rite of passage, a mysterious test of intellectual prowess, was a luxury they could not afford.

Polly never found out if Paddy's calculations were correct. But she won the lottery. Straight A's. Three separate scholarships. Money flung at her from the County Council, the Department, the University. Her mother must have been so pleased.

But no, she was not. She could not have cared less.

Her mother is sitting in front of the television watching a soap when Polly comes into the room. She has not bothered to get up, to open the door, but the door was open. It is still safe to leave the door on the latch then, in this place. Polly walks in and says, 'Hello! Hello!' There is no response whatsoever. Her mother continues to watch TV and does not even turn around.

She tries again. 'Hello,' Polly says. 'It's me, Polly.' She speaks Irish; although she has not spoken it in thirty years, as soon as she set foot in the valley it emerged from her mouth, automatically. She repeats her greeting and calls herself 'Poilín', which does seem unnatural.

Nothing happens. So Polly goes and puts her hand on her mother's shoulder. Her mother turns. She does not seem at all surprised. Her poise has not deserted her. She smiles, so that her whole face lights up. She reaches towards Polly and Polly prepares for an embrace. But it doesn't come. Instead her mother shakes her hand. She shakes hands and Polly feels a sudden giggle rising in her throat. The gesture seems so ridiculous. Her mother's hand, though, is very warm and Polly remembers that they were always like that; to feel those hands on your hand, on your forehead, had always been an intense comfort and a pleasure.

'Poilín!' she says. 'Poilín!'

She is deaf. Suddenly Polly realises this. She is deaf and

apparently her sight is poor also: thick glasses occlude her eyes.

'I decided to come back,' Polly says slowly, looking closely at her mother. She has aged terribly. Of course. Her hair is white and sparse, she is wearing those horrible goggle-like glasses, her face is wrinkled with deep shadowy ridges, the kind black-and-white photographers love, like the cracks of a river delta. But when she smiles, her face is still recognisably her face, whatever the essence of it was – its sweetness, its primness – has not changed one iota. That same expression of polite surprise, the head tilted in a manner both coquettish and disapproving, the same poise. The same superiority.

The surroundings have not changed at all, in one sense, and in another the house looks totally unfamiliar.

Polly had regarded their bungalow, which was the very first bungalow in this valley, as an extension of her mother, elegant and superior, better than any other house for miles around. But now she sees that it is shoddy and lacks any vestige of style, as the old, derided houses do not. The floor is covered with green linoleum, with brown-grey patches in front of the range and near the door. The cupboards are painted cream, the table her mother is sitting at is red formica. There is a kitchen cabinet, also cream, with red trimmings, against the wall. Nothing has been changed. Outside the garden is overgrown with shrubs – ginger-coloured fuchsia and olearia block out the light in the kitchen. The grass is not knee-high but it looks rough and unweeded. A solitary, crazy bramble taps against the windowpane.

'Your father is dead,' her mother says.

'I know.' Polly has to talk, although talk will mean nothing to her mother. Can she lip-read? Probably not, with those glasses. 'I heard.'

'And I'm deaf,' her mother said, without rancour. 'In case you didn't notice. I can't hear a thing you're saying. I can't hear anything at all. Are you speaking Irish? It's all the same to me what you speak.'

After the examinations, as June was drawing to a close, there was licence. Released from school, work, examinations, young people were given leeway to enjoy life. They were, for a while, expected to act their age, to explode with fun and vitality and youthfulness, by sharp contrast with what had been expected of them just weeks ago. The rules changed completely; studious quiet types were out of fashion now and the correct thing to be was wild and exuberant. Polly's mother loosened the reins.

'Enjoy yourself!' she said. Her mother was weeding vegetable beds, hunting slugs from the lettuce, freeing the cabbage and parsley and onions from choking bindweed. 'Have a good time!' It was, Polly knew, an order. Well, she would obey it, though not in the way her mother imagined.

An advantage of summer was that there was a bus twice a day, linking the valley to the town. In the new dispensation, Polly was able to take this bus every day, and could spend hours away from home. All her mother required to know was when she would return (on the last bus – there was not much choice about this). Occasionally Polly mentioned that she was going swimming with her friends, and occasionally she was.

Most of the time she spent with Paddy. He was going to work in the fish factory, but had postponed this for two weeks. He was fishing at this time, for salmon, but usually the fishing expeditions took place during the night, leaving him free to be with Polly during the day.

They avoided the town as much as possible. There was still about their relationship a furtive air, since Polly had not told her parents about it, and as it progressed it seemed increasingly impossible to imagine confiding in them. It was no longer just her belief that her parents regarded all boys as out of bounds, indeed seemed to believe that any sort of relationship between the sexes was essentially wrong, and, what was worse, in extremely bad taste. It was not just that Paddy was everything her mother would abhor: English-speaking, poor, a fisherman, a member of a family which had turned its back on every value that she held dear. It was more that the nature of her relationship with Paddy had become, literally, unspeakable. Polly could not describe it in any words she knew, in any language, and her connection with her mother was, it seemed to her, only by means of words, the formulae Polly selected from her rich store of clichés to dish out, sparingly, to keep her mother at bay.

She got off the bus in the main street, outside the pub which served as a bus-stop. Everyone got off there, and usually there were several neighbours to be nodded to, as well as some tourists – young people from Dublin or America, usually, backpackers with long floating hippy clothes, long curtains of hair, flowers in their hair. (Polly's dress was beginning to be modelled on what they wore, although she could not obtain the right things here. She had a T-shirt and a long cotton skirt which she had made herself, and in these hot days she wore a purple scarf tied over the top of her head and under her hair at the back). She walked down towards the central part of town, just like everyone else, and usually bought some bread and cheese, and cans of minerals, at a small grocery before continuing to the end of the town and turning up the road that led to the hills. This was a narrow road, winding between a few farmhouses and a few bungalows, then rising until it passed through the mountain range far above the town. The road was always busy with tourist cars passing, and that was why Paddy and Polly went there. When she met Paddy, they hitched a lift. All cars were going to the mountain pass. There was a car-park there, with a viewing point, where all visitors stopped and looked at the valley on the other side of the gap, and took photographs. Local people hardly ever visited this place.

At the viewing park, Paddy and Polly said goodbye to whoever had given them the lift – a German woman travelling with her son, joking and eating chocolates, a lonely man from Boston who had come to Ireland to play golf – and said they were going for a walk. The visitors usually smiled indulgently and waved goodbye, and Polly could see that they did what she could not imagine anyone in the valley doing, they approved of her and Paddy, they were looking at them and thinking, this is a handsome young couple, authentic Irish folk, in love, how delightful. She knew these people from America and England and Germany viewed her and Paddy as components in the landscape, partly, like the sheep, and also as ambassadors from the universal land of youth, the land of love.

At the top of the hill, they turned and walked back in the direction of their own town, the direction from which they had just come. They turned off the road and down a turf track. Within seconds, the trail of cars vanished, and they were in a wilderness. Nothing but the rough heather, the clumps of bracken, sheep bleating all around them.

They lay in the heather and kissed and pressed their bodies together. 'With my body I thee worship,' Polly said to him, tracing the line of his profile with her finger. Where had she heard those lines? 'They are in the wedding service,' she said, because she had read this in a novel.

'Are they? I never heard them,' he said. He had not been to many weddings and neither had she, and it was years later that she discovered he was right, nobody said that, not in Catholic weddings. It was the English service, the Church of England, and when Polly realised that if you married in Ireland, which she never did, you did not mention anyone's body, she felt acutely let down, and bitter, feeling it was typical. How could she have imagined her mother uttering such a line? In Irish? Or English or Latin? In the Catholic Church, as it happened, all you had to say at a wedding was 'I do'. The priest said everything else, speaking on your behalf.

She loved his body. The dark brown hair, thick and spiky – spiky with salt. The salty taste of his brown skin. His deep grey eyes, which reminded her of the sea as well, of the stillness, as she imagined it, the calm of fish, although when Paddy encountered fish they were anything but calm. She liked the dark hairs sprouting on his arms, thick like a bear's, and later she found those hairs on his legs and elsewhere. She loved his wide, generous mouth. It seemed she could not tire of exploring this body, even though it was one body, a tiny thing on the mountainside. It was a world, it was a continent, as John Donne said, in a sonnet she had found somewhere in the library. 'You are a continent,' she said, again tracing the line of his profile. Hill, rock, river. 'You are a map of the world.' He liked that better than the line from the wedding service.

They talked, endlessly, about themselves. She told him about her family, covering up the worst aspects but letting him understand that they would find him surprising, when they finally had to meet him. He understood that, he was used to being disapproved of, especially by schoolteachers and people of that kind. The priest. His father was a native, a speaker of the language, but his mother was from a suburb of Dublin, not a very posh one, and that was the trouble. Not only did she speak English, she spoke it with a working-class Dublin accent. Paddy had a touch of this himself. She went to bingo religiously, and she went to the pub on Sundays with her husband, something which shocked even Polly. Her mother would have preferred to die, she was quite sure of this, than enter a public house.

'What does she look like? Your mother?'

He had difficulty describing her. 'She has black hair.'

'Short or long?'

'Kind of shoulder length. And she's about five five. Medium build.'

'What sort of clothes does she wear?'

Paddy laughed: 'What is this? Is my mother wanted for some crime? Not speaking Irish?'

'No, sorry,' Polly kissed him and caressed his hair.

He said, in her arms, 'I don't know what sort of clothes she wears. Normal women's clothes. Jeans and jumpers mostly. She has shorts, actually, for this weather.'

Shorts. Polly imagined a short, fat woman with dyed jet-black hair, red lips, white legs bulging from red shorts. She imagined her with a cigarette dangling from her lips and with gold earrings, a sort of gypsy. She did not know where this picture came from.

This is what she does all day.

She tells stories.

The next time Polly comes, which is the next day, she does not bother ringing the doorbell, but just walks into the kitchen, not making much noise. She wants to have a good look today before she lets her mother know she's here. She explores the parlour, goes back and has a look at the bedrooms. It's all like the kitchen, plain, 1970s style, nothing cute or old or cute and new, like the house Polly is staying in. It seems her parents gave up on interior decorating, on their aim to be the best in the valley, a long, long time ago. A big photo of Polly is on the piano in the sitting room, Polly when she was twelve and making her confirmation, in a pink tweed suit and a white straw boater.

When she slips into the kitchen, her mother is in her chair in front of the television, talking. There's nobody else there, just herself, but she is engaged in a long monologue. Polly stands just inside the door and listens. It takes her a while to get accustomed to the flow of words, which seem to pour out of her mother's voice in a stream, not monotonous but unbroken, fluent as a river.

It's a story, about a girl and a boy. The boy is called William, but the girl does not seem to have had a name, oddly enough.

She was rich and beautiful, however, a landlord's daughter. Lots of rich young men came courting her but she wouldn't have any of them. And one day a poor farmer's son came and wasn't he the one she fancied? She'd have nobody but him. Well now, her father was none too pleased at this turn of events as you can well imagine, and what did he do but send his daughter away, away to her uncle's house, so that she would have no more to do with the poor young man.

She went, and was far from happy with her fate. And while she was there the poor young man, William, pined away and died. But she heard nothing, nobody bothered to let her know. And she stayed on at her uncle's for months. A year went by. And a marriage was arranged for her with another young man, more suitable than William. And she was going to bed one night a few days before the wedding was to take place when a knock came on her window. And it was him, it was William. He was outside the window on horseback and he asked her to come with him. 'Let's go away to somewhere where they won't bother us,' he said. She didn't need asking twice. Out she came through the window and onto the back of the horse and off they went, galloping across the fields. It was a bright night, the moon was shining, and she was as happy as could be.

Then her mother turns and catches sight of Polly.

'That's not the end, is it?' Polly asks.

'I forget how it ends,' says her mother. 'It's just old rubbish.' She's embarrassed at being caught out. 'I do it to pass the time. I used to hear those old things when I was a child and I thought I'd forgotten them.'

'I'd like to know how it ends,' says Polly.

'They were buried in my head somewhere and when I told one the others came back, one after the other. Funny, isn't it?' She stops talking and stares out the window. Then she adds, 'Usually I just watch the television. Most things are subtitled.'

Polly's picture of Paddy's mother was completely inaccurate, as she discovered a few weeks later when she saw her. This was at Paddy's funeral. He was drowned at the beginning of July, while out fishing. The weather had not broken, there was no storm or sudden calamitous change to explain what had happened. But his boat had got into difficulties, for no apparent reason. The rest of the crew were saved but Paddy was not. 'He was knocked overboard by a freak wave,' was the explanation circulating in the community. 'He was swept against the Red Cliff.' Drownings occurred every few years in this area, and the Red Cliff was notoriously dangerous. 'His number was up,' a fisherman said, shrugging casually, in Polly's hearing. More people said 'The good die young.' They had a proverb or a cliché for every occasion, and dozens of them for the occasion of death.

The entire school population of the peninsula turned out at the funeral, which was attended by hundreds and hundreds of people. Polly's friends hugged her and squeezed her, trying to sympathise, horrified at the idea of what had happened to Paddy and to Polly but unable to grasp the enormity of it. Polly's parents were not at the funeral.

They knew about Paddy now. When he had died and become a celebrity, someone had revealed the secret. But they did not take it seriously.

'I believe you were friendly with the young man who drowned, Lord have mercy on him,' said her mother.

'Yes,' said Polly. She was paralysed. She could not believe that

Paddy would not be there, at the spot where they met, if she took the bus and walked along the hill road. He was linked with the place, he could not move from it, in her imagination. She had seen his coffin, carried by six boys from the football team through a guard of honour, to the graveyard across the road. She had seen his coffin descend into the earth, and heard the clay fall on it. But she could not believe he was gone for good. How could he be, so quickly? This was four days after they had sat on the hillside discussing his mother's clothes. In that time he had changed from being a goalkeeper, a lover, a fisherman, to this: a corpse in the ground.

'It's a great tragedy for his family,' her mother then said, pursing her lips and tut-tutting. She turned her attention to the table cloth she was embroidering with pink roses. Polly said nothing, but left the room.

She purses her lips again, in just that way, when Polly tries to tell her about her living arrangements, showing her photos of her house, and of her partner, Karl. Her mother asks if she is married and Polly shakes her head. In Denmark, there is no major legal disadvantage to this, and she and Karl have been together for twenty years. They don't think of themselves as unconnected or likely to part, and getting married is not something Karl believes in. 'I am an old fox,' he says. That's what they say in Denmark, fox not dog. You can't teach an old fox new tricks. He looks like a fox, though, Polly is reminded when he says this. He has reddish hair, still, and a sharp face. He's a schoolteacher, like her father, but the principal of a large secondary school in one of Copenhagen's best suburbs. They live in a house in the grounds, a privilege for the headmaster. Polly is telling her mother this – she can lip-read, a bit. She is trying to tell her something about Copenhagen, mentioning Tivoli, which is as a rule the one thing people have heard of. She talks about the fishing boats at Dragor, how she goes there sometimes to buy flatfish from the fishermen on the quay, how you can get huge flounders for a few crowns. 'They are still alive when you buy them,' Polly says. 'Huge flounders, fat halibut, dancing around in the basket.'

'They don't have the Euro in Denmark,' her mother breaks in. She hasn't heard a thing. 'They have more sense, I suppose.'

When Polly found out that she was pregnant, about six weeks after the funeral, just before the Leaving results came out, she felt not as dismayed as she should have, although she knew it was in any practical sense a hopeless, insuperable tragedy. She had Paddy's baby. It was as if fate had awarded her some compensation for losing him. But it wasn't great compensation, in the circumstances.

'Tell you mother,' Siobhan said. 'You'll have to. I mean, what are you going to do?'

'How could I tell her? She'd die,' said Polly.

Siobhan shrugged. 'Sometimes things like that are easier than you think. When you do them.'

This advice sounded good. Siobhan saw the lift in Polly's expression and pressed her advantage. 'Things are usually easier than you think they'll be,' she reiterated. 'They're always easier, when they happen.' She convinced Polly. Anyway she had to tell her parents, as Siobhan said. The best thing that could happen would be that they would understand, and help, although at the moment Polly's mind could not wrap itself around the reality of what that help should consist of. A ménage of herself, her child and her parents was not imaginable, even as a dream.

She confronted her mother the next day, in the kitchen. They had been to the beach together. Polly had swum in the breakers, finding the cold shock of water comforting; it demanded so much immediate attention that it diminished her problems. Her mother did not swim but sat, in her full cotton sun-dress, on a folding chair on the beach, reading the newspaper, *Inniu*. Afterwards they had lunch together, salad and tea, and now Polly was smoking a cigarette, something her mother did not disapprove of although she did not smoke herself. It seemed like a good moment to break the news.

Her reaction could not have been more surprising, but it was not surprising in the way Siobhan had anticipated. Instead it surprised, shocked, terrified Polly that her mother was capable of

such anger. She screamed abuse and insults. She hit Polly with
her fists and seemed to want to flog her in some ritualistic
punishment of humiliation, degradation. But her father would
have to administer this treatment, and fortunately for himself and
Polly he was not available, having gone to the city for the day to
buy new textbooks for school. Polly was to be locked in her room
until he returned. She was to be starved. When all this was over,
it was not clear what her mother's plans for her were, but they
did not involve bringing up her grandchild in a normal family
environment. Homes, adoption, hiding, were words which occurred, in a medley of Irish and English, a macaronic stream of
abusive language which had never emanated from Polly's mother
before. It seemed that one language did not contain enough
invective to express the full depth and range of her anger. Clearly
this was the nadir of her existence. Nothing as tragic, as evil, as
shameful, as her only child's pregnancy, had ever befallen her.

Afterwards Polly had simply left the house; as it happened
there were no locks on any of the room doors. She ran away
without even a toothbrush, catching the afternoon bus to town
and going on to Dublin on the train. She had some money, it was
not so difficult. Her Leaving results she got from Siobhan a month
or so later. Siobhan came to Dublin to visit her, to Polly's gratification and surprise, and tried to persuade Polly to go to college,
as she had planned: she would have some money from her
scholarships; if she padded it out with a job she would get by.
Polly tried it, and her parents were unable, or did not bother, to
prevent her. But she had Conor, the baby, in April, just before the
first-year examinations. She missed them and no quarter was
given, no special provision could be made. She lost her scholarship and left college. She got a job in a bank, lived in a bedsitter,
and kept the baby, Conor, although Siobhan tried to persuade her
to be sensible and give him over for adoption. She couldn't part
with him, although she soon found out that keeping him was
quite astonishingly difficult, in every possible way. There was no
money, there was no time, nobody even wanted to rent her a
place to live; mothers with babies were blacklisted by most
landlords in Dublin. Everyone colluded in making her life as

hard as it could be – her parents, the state, the system. Siobhan, who was in Dublin herself, studying to be a nurse, continued to help, finding flats in her own name and installing Polly and Conor when the lease was signed.

When Conor was three Polly got a chance to move to Copenhagen with the bank, and she took it. As she had hoped, nobody cared whether you were a single mother or not in Denmark. In fact it seemed that most mothers were single, at least the ones she came across; it was almost something to brag about. They had grimly bobbed hair, dressed in corduroy pants and big green parkas, and smoked cigars. Some of them had jobs in the bank, but usually they were doing degrees in impractical subjects, Women's Studies or Ethnology or Greek and Roman Civilisation. The state paid for their education, and paid them social welfare and child welfare while they were in college. All the talk was of feminism and women's rights and the country was packed with crèches and kindergartens where children were looked after free, by students and nurses and women from Turkey, in what looked like luxurious surroundings. After a while Polly left the bank and went to college at last, like all the other single mothers. She chose film studies, and eventually became a script writer, writing soaps for the Danish television channel, then documentaries which brought her all over the world: Faroes, Shetland, Greenland, Iceland. In Greenland she met Karl, who was hiking around the old Norse settlements, taking photos, and did not mind that she had Conor although he had no intention of having any children himself, as Polly found out soon enough. By then Conor was twelve. He grew up, became a scientist, a marine biologist. After working for a few years in Denmark he went on a round-the-world trip, and ended up in Australia, and got a visa and a temporary post at a university doing research on the breeding habits of pilot whales. He is still there.

Polly sits at her window, in her own cottage, and listens to the fire whispering in the grate, to the wind whispering outside, whistling around the eaves. She has been here for a week, longer than she had planned to stay, and has decided to stay for one more week. She is going to begin work here, sketching the basis for a programme of some kind about the region: the Gaeltachts of Ireland, maybe, a topic she is well suited to covering but has always avoided. The house is warm and cosy, and now the valley seems to hold her too. People she runs into in the shop nod to her and say hello, do not avoid her, as she thought they were doing initially. A few have recognised her and chatted to her about old times. Nobody mentions Paddy Mullins, or asks about the baby, but when Polly mentions that she has a grown-up son they don't seem surprised. Siobhan probably spilled the beans, or Katherine. It doesn't matter, they are interested in him too, they want to hear about Australia and the whales. Lots of the local young people do round-the-world trips as a matter of course, in their gap year; half the population of twenty-somethings seems to be in Thailand or New South Wales. Nobody cares about what used to be called unmarried mothers now either. There are heaps of them, even in the Gaeltacht. Still, nobody mentions Paddy Mullins. Maybe they forget he existed.

Polly tries to tell her mother about Conor, since she has told almost everyone else. 'I have a child,' she says. Her mother cocks her head, and smiles uncomprehendingly. Her ability to lip-read is most erratic. 'He's Paddy's child,' Polly continues. 'Paddy Mullins, the boy who drowned. Do you remember?'

'Would you like a cup of tea?' asks her mother. It is the first time she has offered Polly any refreshment. She gets up and walks across the kitchen to the electric fire.

'I was in love with Paddy Mullins,' Polly says. Her mother smiles and says, 'I was thinking of baking an apple tart. I still have apples in the garden. It's the only apple tree in this parish.'

She finds the end of her mother's story.

When they had gone a few miles William said, 'I've a terrible headache, love.'

'Stop,' she said. 'Stop and have a rest. What hurry is on you?'

'I can't stop,' he said. 'There is a long journey ahead of us. I'm taking you home.' So all she could do was take out her handkerchief

and she tied it around his forehead and she gave him a kiss. His head was as cold as ice and she felt frightened when she touched it. But she said nothing. And he galloped on and on until they were passing her own father's house. And she shouted and asked him to stop.

'Why would you want to stop?' he asked.

> *'The moon shines clear,*
> *The horseman's here.*
> *Are you afraid, my darling?'*

And he spurred on the horse.

But the horse would not move an inch. The horse stopped at her father's gate and refused to move. He spurred and he whipped but it didn't matter. The horse had a mind of its own.

So – 'Go on inside,' he said, 'and sleep in your own bed tonight. And I'll be here waiting for you first thing in the morning. I'll sleep in the stable, myself and the horse.'

She kissed him goodnight and did as he told her.

And when she went inside her father was there and he was surprised to see her. But she took courage and told him what had happened. She said William had come for her, and she could not live with anyone else.

Her father turned pale. 'William?' he said.

'Yes,' said she. 'He's outside, asleep in the stable.'

'That's impossible,' said her father. 'William died a year ago.'

She didn't believe him. How could she, the poor girl? So her father took her out. He had to do it. He took her to the graveyard and he took a shovel and he dug and dug. And there was William, in his coffin, dead and decayed. And around his poor head her handkerchief was tied, the handkerchief she'd tied around his forehead only the night before. Yes. And it was stained with blood. So she had to believe him then.

The story is in a collection of German ballads, which she finds in one of the bedrooms. So how did her mother learn that? Had she read the book, or were the stories flying around in the air like migratory birds, landing wherever they found suitable weather conditions, a good supply of food? What a gloomy story! Polly shivers and shuts the book firmly, feeling the dead hand of William like ice on her forehead.

That night Polly rings Conor, the baby, and tells him she is here. She hopes he will say he will come over, but since he lives in Brisbane, he is not likely to come today or tomorrow. It's nice to talk to him, though, and to tell him what she is doing. She does not tell the truth, that her mother will not listen to her story. He listens, with appreciation, although it is early morning in Australia and he has just woken up to a summer's day. He appreciates the drama of her news, Polly can tell that, and suggests that she go and visit Muriel, if she is still alive, Muriel his paternal grandmother. Maybe Muriel is not deaf? Polly finds herself saying yes, she will do that, and then she rings Karl to tell him she will stay on in Ireland for another week or perhaps two.

Something happens in the valley now, that takes Polly by surprise.

The Christmas lights go on.

All the little houses come alive.

Coloured lights fill every window, are strung along the edge of the roof, are draped in the hedges. Santa Clauses climb up fairy ladders to the chimneys, reindeers glow in the bare gardens. Red and green and blue lights flash and twinkle in the deep dark of the winter valley; some of the bungalows seem to be jumping, they flash so much.

In the old days, there was one candle, lit on Christmas Eve in every house. When you walked through the valley to Midnight Mass you saw these candles flickering in every window, the stars flickering overhead. Now the houses are flashing and jumping in a myriad colours glowing against the black sea and sky and mountain, brash and it seems to Polly, beautiful. 'We're here!' the lights seem to proclaim, 'We've survived, we're not going away!'

She finds Muriel easily. She lives in the house she lived in thirty years ago, Paddy's house. It is, as Polly expected, decorated, though not as extravagantly as some of the other houses. There are coloured lights on a hedge by the gate, and another string around the door.

Muriel is watching TV when Polly calls. She's alone. Polly

guesses, correctly, that Paddy's father is dead. It strikes her that the valley is full of widows. Muriel is wearing jeans and a jumper, and she is still small and thin. To Polly's surprise she speaks Irish, but with a north Dublin accent. 'Of course I speak Irish,' she says. 'I've been here for fifty years. I'd have been out of the loop altogether if I hadn't learnt it, wouldn't I?' Her manner is chirpy, friendly but with an underlying toughness, an urban edge which is different from anything you get around here. She offers tea and biscuits straight away; she turns down the TV but she does not turn it off. Polly opens her mouth and starts to explain why she is here. It is not as hard as she thought it would be, now that she is here. Muriel listens, half smiling, her eyes thoughtful rather than sad. Then she takes Polly in her arms and holds her for a minute, against her woolly jumper, her thin body. Polly, of course, cries. She cries and Muriel pats her head and says, 'Yes, love, yes.'

Then they drink the tea.

Muriel talks herself, about Paddy. He was a very quiet boy, but always good-humoured, she could talk to him more easily than she could ever talk to anyone, much more easily than she could talk to his father. His father is dead now too. He – Paddy – had a depth of understanding. He was more like a daughter than a son. On the night he drowned, he had kissed her goodbye, which was unusual, but she only remarked on it afterwards. It was a calm night, he had been out in much rougher weather and returned home unscathed. The truth about his death would not be known, but she had heard there had been a row on board, another young man had attacked Paddy, Paddy got thrown overboard and hit his head on a rock. The real story would never be told, the other man was the son of the owner of the boat, Paddy was dead anyway and the fishermen would never inform on one of their own. The whole story about going aground was made up, a sham. Fiction.

There are no tears from her. She tells the story calmly, pausing occasionally for dramatic effect or to let a shocking point sink in. It is a story she has told before, many times, in spite of her protestations that it is confidential, a secret. Probably she told it to Paddy's father, and to who else? Her best friends, her close relations? The story is polished. What is true is its terrible core, that Paddy, the son she could talk to, is dead. And even this no longer disturbs her. But of course it all happened so long ago. Paddy drowned thirty years ago. How could she cry? Tears do not last that long. Paddy has been transmogrified into a hero: a brave, strongly-drawn character in a story that she has half-remembered, half-invented.

So Polly tells her story of Paddy, and for her it is a fresh story, it is the very first time she has told it to anyone, and so her tale is not as polished, not as well-paced, not as neatly composed, as Muriel's. Still it takes on a certain formality: Polly has to decide, as she sits on the fireside chair, keeping her eyes off the silent TV screen, where to start. The bus, the pier, the park? School? She decides, or memory decides, or Muriel, or the pressures of the moment, the pressure to relate, the pressure to sympathise, the pressure to attract compassion, the pressure to confess, the pressure to create, what to leave in, what to exclude.

The fact is no matter what she decided, Muriel would be fascinated by this story of her son, which she had not heard before, not at all, although of course kind tongues had let her know of Polly's existence, had hinted at the reason for her sudden departure from the valley. But those were rumours, snippets of malice and gossip, that had the power to disturb but not to enthral, console, nourish. So now she listens intently, her whole body still, concentrated on listening. For this story she is the perfect audience, and the story is shaped by her listening as much as by Polly's telling; Paddy's story belongs to the two of them. And why did Polly not understand that until Conor pointed it out?

When the story is finished Muriel and Polly sit in silence. The coloured lights on the fuchsia bush twinkle against the black sea and the black mountain and the black sky. They sit in silence. They let the story settle. And for minutes it is as if he is here again, on this earth. Alive, seventeen. He is not on the pier or in the park or on the mountainside, but on the bus. He is sitting on the bus, silently staring out the window, motionless as a seagull on a rock, lost in a boy's dream.

NIALL McARDLE

Heavy Weather

I do not know if it is possible for temperature to have weight, but I am slowly developing a theory that it might, for the heat here possesses a heaviness I have never experienced. It presses down upon you like the simple giant who smothers a small child unawares. The days are passed sluggishly. Drink, the guidebook reliably informs us, will do nothing to relieve one from the oppressive heat, and it may well do more harm, but we are doing our level best to disprove this well-known scientific truth.

The only things worse than the heat are the bugs. I lie to myself, sometimes convincingly, that I could stand the temperatures were it not for the mosquitoes. I feel as if I am the main course in an insect banquet: they feast upon me nightly, having stealthily got past the fine mesh of the net that hangs above our bed. I wake up a mass of sores and bumps, some bleeding. My skin is – what's the word? – mottled. Sometimes as I lie there futilely trying to get back to sleep, I wonder is there only one bug in our room, or has the word gone out over the bloodsuckers' telegraph and I am supporting the island's entire insect population: a one-man ecosystem?

Laura says it is because I am so sweet that the bugs love me so much. She has a theory that bugs are attracted to sweet and warm skin, and so she refuses to wear any insect repellent since this merely increases body temperature. This mixture of practicality and nonchalance – she also disdains sun cream, yet her body is positively golden – is typical of her. Typically too, though I am loth to admit it, she is probably right. She strolls around the island like a goddess taking a constitutional on Mount Olympus, the sun shining upon her as if by command: lightly and with devotion. I trudge behind, my lungs wheezing with each fiery breath, and with the bugs as company. We must look, I know, a strange pair; were we figures in a painting it would be called 'The Lady And Her Retainer', European nobility and its grotesque manservant.

When we first arrived here the heat and the bugs and the drinks were all I could think about. Laura and I had planned to see the sights and visit the historic temples. Behave, as she put it, like proper tourists. After a week of finding excuses not to do any of those things, a week of 'It's too hot', a week of 'We're on holiday, let's relax', a week of 'The sights aren't going anywhere, another drink?' we both tacitly agreed to give up the pretence. We let a quietness seep between us as we lounged on the beach. An acceptance of things unsaid. Conversation became limited to offers of cocktails, and with each drink the sights seemed like a distant memory and even the bites eased up on their itching, as if they understood the need for the relief that alcohol offered.

The cocktails are exotic enough, given the setting. They have colours to match the ocean. Turquoise, aquamarine, ultra-violet. They even come with little umbrellas and swizzle sticks, as if it would be an offence to the tourists to try them unadorned. One night we tried a tasty number called a phaser, named in honour, apparently, of one of the *Star Trek* actors who once stayed there. 'I have no idea what's in it,' said Laura after three of them, 'but beam me up, Scotty.' She has adopted it. I, on the other hand, have more mundane tastes, and take immense pleasure in the fact that a gin and tonic is a gin and tonic pretty much anywhere you go.

At the start of the second week we both danced a little too much having drunk a little too much. We tipped the waiter over the odds and the band played a few more songs. The music, I recall, had a soft, sensuous touch as it wrapped itself around us on the dance floor. I cannot tell you now what kind of rhythm it was that night that lightened the air and buzzed around us as we kissed. Samba? Reggae? Salsa? Or some other, perhaps more appropriate Eastern melody? No matter; I will remember it always only as Island Music. It gently prodded us closer together like an eager matchmaker. We hugged clumsily at first, then used each other to hold ourselves up. When I think back on that night I see Laura and me as one of those couples in old sepia photos of dance marathons during the Depression: lumbering, eyes tired, legs like jelly. Laura laughed. She has the kind of laugh that men dream about their wives having; it starts high in the throat and breaks like crystal into a languid, tear-filled sigh. I held her close and she was the ocean lapping on the shore behind us, salty and promising depth.

That was the night she got the bite.

It was small and round and pink and quite precisely centred on the sole of her left foot. It woke her up gasping. Her insistent poking roused me. I had been dreaming of water. It was warm and blue and the feel of it on my skin was like a balm. Laura had been there too, naked and shimmering, like a dolphin leaping playfully. It was a dream I was reluctant to be pulled away from, for with the dream came memories of our lovemaking.

We had come at each other like wounded animals; slow careful movements made after long deliberation for fear of hurting the other. A series of kisses. A slight tonguing of one another. We pressed against each other with cool passion, postponing the moment of coupling until I felt as if I would simply fall apart, and she was breathing hard and fast and needing me. The final togetherness was brief and smelled of orchids and there were white spots in front of my eyes. She dug her nails into my hand and breathed 'I love you.'

Need I add it was our first time in many months?

Now we were perched on the end of the bed examining the mark that had disproved her ideas about bugs and shown her to be vulnerable. Flawed.

'Your foot must've fallen outside the net. Perhaps you're sweeter than you believe.'

'I doubt it. What is more likely is that they've had enough of yours. They seek variety. A balanced diet is healthy, nutritious and very important.'

'Even for a mosquito?'

'Yes, especially the ones here. Think about it: they suck the blood of dusky Thais most of the year and pasty Brits and Paddies like yourself the rest of the time.' Had I mentioned Laura is Portuguese? At least, a part of her is, way back. She betrayed her ancestry by rationalising the bite, while at the same time fulfilled every stereotype about Latinos by sulking at the injustice of it.

'How the hell am I supposed to walk around now? It'll itch like crazy. Why couldn't I have got bit somewhere practical, like my arm?'

Something is happening to us. Neither of us wishes to admit it, and we pad around the edges of it like insects skirting a carcass, unsure if it is really dead. It started the day after the bite. Laura wanted to swim. She swims like a fish; she was born for the promise of water. I sat half-reading a book and watched her slink in and out of the ocean. It was not a sea. There is a difference and it is, believe me, important. Seas are defined by the land they touch. They tend to be on the small side, and their memories, therefore, are short and muddled. The ocean, however, creates the coastline it pummels. It has – I am sorry for this – depth. It doesn't forget easily. I watched my wife gliding in and out of the Indian Ocean and it was as if she had been reclaimed. Christ, she's beautiful, I thought. My island queen.

You must understand that she and I are not given to excess sentimentality. When we first got together we were both running away from bad relationships that had left us with wounded hearts. Part of our mutual attraction, I am sure, was this romantic refugee status. Early on we had agreed to curtail the usual over-sweetness that characterises so many relationships at the beginning. Statements of everlasting love were outlawed, as were saccharine romantic gestures. Flowers were banned. Birthdays were marked by the giving of presents that were truly needed. One year I gave her a food processor, a gift that my friends assured me would result in a long cold winter spent sleeping on the couch. She was delighted, for she had, after all, asked for one.

Valentine's Day, of course, was our chance to smirk at the rest of the world's folly. We would sit in the park and watch as people rushed around clutching bouquets, boxes of chocolates, airline tickets for those romantic getaways. We did nothing to hide our contempt and revelled in our superiority. For us, Valentine's Day had transmuted itself into anti-Valentine's Day. We bought each other wreaths. Or cactuses. One year I did not have time to find one (it had become a tradition). Luckily, dinner that night was roast chicken. I removed the cooked onion from inside its guts, stuck cloves into it and presented the blackened hideous thing to her in an eggcup. She cried laughing.

So we had learned over time to stay within the limits of our love. Yet as I watched her emerging from the water, the sunlight dutifully glistening upon her back and water droplets like pearls falling off her, I heard myself say the word 'nymph'. How tired was that? Even though it was true, and there was no other word more appropriate, I told myself there was no excuse. But then she smiled at me and I felt my chest tighten. The heat was getting to me.

Later, after dinner, she fell into a gloomy silence. I made an effort at conversation for a time, then gave up. We sat there scattered like two discarded chess-pieces. Or bookends. Or something. I was looking at the moon in the ocean. She was half-turned the other way, twisting her napkin with controlled distraction. The band was warming up on stage. They launched into a cover of 'Fly Me To The Moon'. It was the rumba version. I glanced at Laura and smiled. 'Wanna dance? It'll be fun.' I heard the way I'd stressed 'fun' and instantly regretted it.

'I'll pass, honey.' There was ice in her voice.

'Frank'll be spinning in his grave. I thought that would appeal to you.' I reached for her hand in a way that I thought was nonchalant and cool, but was probably eager and clumsy. She gazed at it like it was a strange dish served to her by mistake, then looked away.

Now it was my turn to sulk. The band was working through the entire Sinatra catalogue. They were murdering 'It Was A Very Good Year' in a way that possibly helped to define kitsch. I was awash with the irony and cynicism of it all, yet I felt nothing other than childish petulance. I could not understand why she was being so distant. I did not want to bother comprehending. I felt insulted. I was still remembering the night before. I was on the verge of speaking, of saying something I would probably later regret. In the end it was Laura who broke the silence.

'Can we go to our cabin?'

It was the tone of her voice. It was not that it was remote or displayed anger. It seemed to come from somewhere deep inside her, and was unsure of itself in the outside world. It sounded lost.

We walked back to the cabin and nothing was said. 'How Lucky Can One Guy Be?' was samba-ing its way across the garden. We continued walking in silence. Just as we reached the door, she turned and kissed me with a violence I could never have anticipated.

'You know I love you, don't you?' Her voice was slightly thawed.

'Yeah, sure, yeah.'

What was I thinking? 'Yeah, sure, yeah' was what you said when the barman asked if you wanted another. What the hell was happening to us?

In bed I ached. She drew me into something even now I have difficulty in describing. It was not that it was animalistic, although it was that too. There was something in her kisses and the movement of her hips against mine that was aloof. Removed. As if she were studying me. I half-expected to turn around and see a group of scientists peering at us through a microscope, noting every thrust with an approving tick of pencil on paper.

Afterwards, spent, I lit a cigarette. This too is a cliché, but I beg your indulgence. We both lay back and stared at a gecko stealthily making its way across the ceiling. We could see its gills throbbing with each breath. It effortlessly tongued a fly and chomped at it noisily, jaws grinding as it efficiently tore it to pieces.

'Do me a favour, would you?'

'I'm not sure I can, love, the little fellow needs time to recuperate.'

She laughed. The sound of glass breaking. 'No, no that.' Her voice dropped to a conspiratorial whisper. 'Scratch the bite.'

I am convinced now that she knew. Somehow she knew.

Maybe she had already experimented herself, or just happened upon the knowledge in an absent moment. Perhaps something occurred earlier in the water that triggered it. I moved to the end of the bed and gently stroked the bite. The bump was tender. She gave a low throaty moan, barely audible, but there was a distinct sexuality to it. Gradually, the more I stroked her sole, the harder the groans became.

'Are you okay?' I asked rather stupidly.

'Shut up and don't stop.'

And I didn't, for a long slow hour. Tenderly, softly, hard, fast, slowly until she lay back on the bed in a mess of sweat and tears and screams. She had ripped the sheets with her nails.

How many times had she come? Is it important? Yes, I think it is. Twelve, thirteen maybe, not counting the multiples. My memory of the experience is dominated mostly by the sense of strangeness that I felt. My face no doubt hinted at further horrors. She saw it and smiled. It was a smile I did not care for. More surprising was the realisation that I too had erupted several times, and I was faintly astonished at how quickly I had recovered. Yet my pleasure was naught in comparison with hers, and the prior coupling had been to placate me. I felt . . . I know this sounds ridiculous . . . I felt left out. A tool. Used.

The morning after was still. The clouds were gathering off the coast and hung, heavily and dark, above the other island to the south. There was evidently a storm coming. I should, you would imagine, have spotted the rather dreadful metaphor a mile off. What can I say in defence? My critical faculties were dulled by the heat and the booze.

It took several days for the weather to break. Five to be precise. Five days of heavy, muggy, sultry . . . sultry what? Be exact, man. Okay then, the weather was muggy. And damp. I sluggishly moved through the heat like a bumbling moth searching for the flame. Even our resident lizard seemed a little unsure of things. He would simply hang upside-down all day surveying the scene beneath him. Occasionally he moved to catch a fly, but it was not an effort he was overly willing to make.

Laura and I would lie gazing out the window at the ever-darkening sky. Days groaned by in this manner. We did not dare make love, the memory of the other night still fresh. We opted instead for tender caressing, slow kisses and long, almost passionate embraces that transformed into stiff tableaux. Once or twice, testing the water, I would touch the bite, and she winced in ecstasy and grabbed at me and made a sound that was a lot like love.

Then the typhoon arrived. Or was it a hurricane? It may have been a cyclone. Or perhaps the slightly disappointing, lesser-sounding tropical storm. I think it was a typhoon. Does it matter? When the roof is being whipped off and the scene outside bears remarkable similarity to something apocalyptic, you don't argue the technicalities. Despite how long it had been looming, the suddenness of it did surprise us. Even our new friend, the gecko, huddled in one corner from where he made tiny pathetic noises of despair.

I let myself be tossed about by the wind for a while as I tried in vain to keep the rain out. I hammered windows shut and placed a chair against the door as it struggled to blow open. I don't think I accomplished much. The room was sodden by the end of it all. So was I.

'You look windswept,' said Laura from the centre of the bed, which she had been valiantly defending all evening. I glanced at myself in the mirror that had been hurled across the room. My hair was matted to my head. Rain was dripping off me in a way that made me look rather heroic. She had a point; I *was* windswept.

'I feel tropical.'

'That's funny, you still look quite temperate to me.'

I gave her a look. She returned one back that was better. She is good at doing that.

Afterwards we returned to the promises that the bite afforded. There was much in the way of 'I love you' and lots of stifled, clenched-teeth breathing. My chest tightened. My thighs throbbed with pain. Her foot had now become the major, indeed only, zone of pleasure in her body. Even to me; I had learned to love the thrilling sounds touching it brought out in her. Her breasts, which I had previously had cause to gaze upon in rapt attention and devotion, were now ignored in favour of that tiny bump. Not even the delta between her thighs was considered. I made an attempt to go there and was rudely pushed away and back to her foot, which she demanded I touch, kiss, lick, stroke, press, do anything I could think of to. The bite was the only point in her body which was capable of – please forgive me in advance – capable of transporting her into paroxysms of delight.

I am deeply sorry for that. I never intended to write sordid Victorian pornography. This is, after all, not a happy story. It is rather a document of maddening despair. What shall we call it, an affidavit of loss?

The storm continued for three more days. The island was turned into a wind-lashed raft, and we were the stragglers clutching to it, desperately searching for land. Both the tourists and the natives were levelled by the winds. Equal before the forces of nature, we pulled together to batten down the hatches and hold onto the provisions. There was an eager glee to all of this, and you can imagine the sheer mateyness of it all: the ever-smiling staff scurrying to and fro, rescuing precious marijuana plants, the Westerners trying to remain cool and failing utterly, opting instead for general bewilderment and awe at the power of the natural world. 'Oh my God' and 'Wow' are the two expressions I remember hearing most that weekend as the rain drummed on the tin roof of the bar and the sky was lit fluorescent by a hundred simultaneous flashes of lightning, so bright we had sporadic seconds of daylight in the midst of the consuming darkness.

The Americans among us predictably assumed control, and did a very efficient job of persuading the staff to liberate the fridge as the storm had knocked out the power. I dare not think how much beer was drunk that weekend, for I know that after half an hour the manager gave up trying to keep tabs on us. Instead in that quiet way of his he ordered the band to play, and Island Music once again sashayed across the room and we danced and drank and smoked until, finally, the clouds rolled back and three magnificent rainbows were spread across the blue of the ocean like a family of whales coming up to breathe.

The day after, everyone pitched in once more to clear up the debris. Laura wandered off on her own to go treasure hunting. She scrambled among the rocks or shuffled through the shale at the foot of the beach. This had been a hobby of ours from years back: heading to the shore off Malahide looking for shells and pebbles. Crick-cracking our way around. She would explore, skipping along, I would trundle in her wake. She ran down to the water. I used to hang back, perch on a rock, smoke, glare at the clouds. That was our Sunday routine. Back in our old life.

Now here I was letting the water cool the anguish of my skin. She returned after an hour with something in her hand. A dead crab. A victim of the tempest. It had been smashed against the rocks; its back was broken and one of its claws dangled uselessly.

'What on earth do you have that for?'

'It's a sacrifice.'

'A what?'

'An offering to the gods.'

Spirit houses are a predominant feature of this part of the world. These elaborate mini-temples, like overgrown dollhouses decked out in garish fairy lights, offer protection and watch over us. They are placed high, usually on stilts or fastened to the tops of walls. Food is placed in front of their little doors. Joss sticks seem to be permanently lit, yet in all our time there I have yet to see anyone actually make an offering. But they must work: the hotel survived the deluge, and the main spirit-house itself remained unharmed, as if it existed in a vortex that the typhoon could not penetrate.

We stood in front of our cabin. I fought to hide laughter as I watched Laura carefully place the crab's corpse on an old dish. Beside that she put a lighted candle, an incense stick and a glass of whiskey. Then things got strange. She took her Swiss army knife from her pocket (I told you she was practical) and sliced open her finger to let the blood drop over the mess on the deck and liberally around the doorway. As a finishing touch she placed a little card with a scrawled picture above the doorframe. I peered at it. This was, I now realised, a shrine to a mosquito.

'You have got to be joking.'

'I think the lizard ate him. I'm praying for his return.'

'Reincarnation?'

'Yeah, okay, if that's an easier way for you to understand it.'

It wasn't, as a matter of interest, but Laura is always thoughtful that way.

'What do you think mosquitoes come back as anyway? Lice? Or if they're good, do they get to ascend and return as bluebottles?'

'You're being sarcastic.'

'My wife is bowing, no, kneeling to a dead crab and some sort of voodoo altar, and I am being sarcastic. I can't imagine why.'

'Part of the joy of travel is meeting and learning about other cultures, is it not?'

I thought about the temples we had not visited, the statues we had not seen, the traditional crafts we had not bought. I said nothing; Laura was starting to look a little upset.

'I miss the mozzie. The bite is . . . healing, you know? So shut up, show some respect, get on your knees and bow or I won't take you in my mouth tonight.'

That night, smoking some quite decent dope, courtesy of the barman, we lay and watched the gecko through the gauze of the net. He was looking particularly nervous, and we wondered why until we realised he had a visitor. The two lizards faced off against each other along the roof beam. Laura and I settled in for a rumble in the jungle.

'My money's on our guy,' said Laura between inhaling.

'Okay, fifty baht says the challenger kicks his arse.'

They went for each other, and there was a lot of noise – a sort of high-pitched chirruping. But we had both been wrong. It wasn't a fight; they were making love.

I have witnessed a fair amount of animal sex. It is impossible not to in an age which reveres wildlife so much. Television documentaries featuring it are unavoidable, and there is a deep-seated assumption on the part of film-makers that viewers desire nothing more than to watch the rutting of lions in the Serengeti, or Amazonian rhesus monkeys humping noisily in the treetops. Most of this activity is rushed, furious and seems often brutal.

Yet as we continued to watch in silence, it was obvious that the two geckos were involved in something quite beautiful and tender. They took their time. The male mounted his partner carefully, and only after a good twenty minutes of foreplay, he very gently probed her. I could have sworn I heard a moan from one of them. They carried on this way, delicately swinging on the beam, upside down, a ballet of fucking. At the end, the male dismounted (again, carefully) and before departing, turned and touched her mouth with his.

'Kiss me,' said Laura. There was a sob in her voice. I did kiss her, and soon we were back to where we had been every night for the past week, in an agony of happiness and pain and joy. I am embarrassed to admit this, to being turned on by seeing two reptiles fuck, yet something, a small voice at the back of my mind, insists this is relevant and cannot be excluded.

But there is something else, and probably you have already guessed. The power of the bite had diminished. Its effects were wearing away; Laura had been right about that. I wonder had its potency been passed on to our gecko, which we now realise is a lady. Is there some hidden link between mosquitoes and female pleasure? In any event, what does it matter? The bite no longer seduced us into states of ecstasy. It was still wonderful, of course, yet we both sensed that it could only be a matter of days before we would have to return to our old-fashioned, fumbling, graceless ways. As if to mark the occasion, to signal that we had approached the end of a journey, a distant roll of thunder sounded across the bay, a deep, faintly sad rumble. Laura and I stared at one another. She kissed the tears in my eyes. We hugged and allowed sleep to wash over our twisted limbs like the great Indian surf.

October

The bar is quiet. A wet Saturday afternoon in October, and the minor patronly hum is tolerable, pleasant even. I've been coming here, the Bear and Staff off Charring Cross, for three weeks now. You get a lot of tourists wandering in and out, in their bluff and fatigued shower of shopping bags and unsuitable clothes, some with kids, some without, worn out by the treadmill terrain of strange place names and hard sidewalks. The pub's decor is dim and suited to London at this time and in this place. Shabby, beautiful, unholy and skint. I am so tired these days that the soft lack of effort is of great comfort to me.

I'm a tourist myself, of course. I was only supposed to be here for a week, on business, but I am not a businessman any more. Now I am a tourist and I don't think I shall ever be going home.

They are both in their late fifties, perhaps early sixties. He is not a good-looking man but he is well dressed. He shakes the droplets from his umbrella. She is very beautiful, with a glaze of unfussy wrinkles on her neck and around her eyes, and fractured wisps of untouched grey in her hair. He takes her hand as she sits, a polite glide of grace, and leans in close to her.

'What would you like?'

'A double Scotch on the rocks, please.'

Her voice is a soothing beige of sound, and the accent rolls over me like a sorrowful blessing. It is my own accent, exactly. I'm only two tables away but they seem oblivious to my presence. He goes to the bar and I am struck by how well he moves. Perhaps he was a football player in a previous life. No, that roll carries with it, definitely, the don't-care intensity of a baseball man. Suddenly I feel homesick. No matter.

He returns with two tumblers of Scotch and ice and sits down here in the smallish alcove. They stare at each other and I can discern no discomfort between them. They seem to breathe in rhythm. The near-silence, rain-splattered only, is one of the best. I have stopped reading my paper and am staring out of the window at the passers-by, while the devout couple nearby begin to talk. In Bear Street, outside, a young man is asleep in the doorway of the pizza restaurant. His trouser leg is hiked up and everybody passing can see the abscesses on his shins. It is disgusting but from here, here in the damp warmth of the bar, it is a silent, serene scene. It is the kind and very point of disarray, to console the rest of us tinkers. And I am consoled.

I don't normally eavesdrop, but here and now there seems no point in not. The man and the woman are in a world of their own. I am only yards away but I am invisible to them. The dimness of the alcove, with its naff pictures and assorted tacked-on knick-knacks, reeks of a local common sense that tourists like myself find kindly and hateful at the same time. The couple look at each other and they light each other's cigarettes. They begin to talk and I lean back and close my eyes, and listen to the aural stencil of their conversation for a little while.

My chest hurts these days, but it's nothing to do with my health. It's just in a crumpled and bone-tired way these days. There is no parochial piffle any more. No domestic and lovely liabilities. Sometimes I feel as if I can't breathe properly. But listening to the inelegant gurn of some strangers and the spring-heeled possibility of others, has made me think that listening is not, in itself, a sterile occupation. That there are some stories that need sniffing from the ether, pleasant or no, and those stories might provide me with the wherewithal to avoid disappearing altogether.

Stories with prized blunders, unintended.

With hearts splintered and celebrated.

I am tired and my chest aches.

But there is still the couple, and now they are leaning in and talking, with creaks of handbag and trousers and the clunk of uneven tabletops, and they are talking to each other.

'Are you okay?'

'Yes. Of course. And you?'

'Yes.'

A long pause. A motorbike rumbles by outside.

'Ah, well then,' he says. She nods, and I see that she is tracing the outline of the wood grain of the tabletop with her ring finger, round and round and along.

'So. Well then,' she said.

I pick up my paper again, trying to minimise the noise of crinkle. They don't notice. They stare at each other, but not in that pinpoint, awkward way. Their eyes just softly rove over shoulders and neck and eyebrows and eyes and back again. They must have been together for decades, to do that. I read my newspaper and I read that a doctor has been convicted of negligence for removing the wrong kidney. The guy is still alive but his days are numbered. I don't know why, but I feel more sorry for the doctor than I do for the guy. What is wrong with me? I feel so tired these days and I know there is a reason for that, but that's no excuse for misplaced sympathy.

'I just don't know what happened,' she says, and she laughs.

It is an astonishing sound, a lofty and reasonably dirty noise. The kind of sound children make when they giggle because they don't know what noise a polite diaphragm is supposed to produce. He laughs too, but in his throat.

'Me neither,' he says, and he takes her hand.

They don't say anything for a bit, but just look at each other, with a serious, silent applause, and with fingers roaming over fingers. My God, how can two people be that much in love? And at that age? I have the newspaper raised sturdily up to cover my face, but the typeface is a wash of unwatched nonsense. They aren't even aware of me, but even if they were, it wouldn't make any difference. I try to concentrate on reading the paper. There's a story about a dentist. Some kind of malpractice suit. My mother was a dentist. She attended a conference in New York in 1984, about the early detection of AIDS. I think it was 1984. Dentists were the first to spot the signs. Gum lesions, to be exact. I was only a kid but I could tell that the whole weekend had upset her. I remember my father taking her out for a nice dinner downtown. She was more cheerful after that, for a while.

I turn the page of my newspaper as carefully as I can.

The man takes a hefty swig on his drink. She takes a sip.

He trails a finger along her cheek.

She smiles and with both hands takes a gentle grip on the damp collar of his coat, and waggles it, this time not so gently. He sways his upper body, in on the joke, and she lowers her head onto his chest. He rests both his hands on either side of him, on the leather seat, palms upwards. Like a flip prisoner or, equally, like a grave and helpless thing.

The rain is really coming on now. Outside, the people without umbrellas are just strolling along, soaked in a kind of mesmeric apathy. You can only get so wet. Past that, it really doesn't matter.

'So what do we do now?' she says.

'Sweetheart,' he says, and his voice is bristling with love, done and dusted, 'I don't know.'

'Thirty years is a long time.'

'Yes. Well, anniversaries . . .'

'That was a very good year.'

'This isn't Sinatra. Or Harry James either.'

'Sorry.'

'Well okay, then.'

'Okay, so.'

I find that I am leaning in closer to hear what they are saying. But there is no need for that. There is no jukebox music, there are only a few other customers and no bar staff scurrying around. Every svelte syllable wafts across as easily as all get out. I can hear every word, and either they know it and they don't care, or they don't know it. I fold up my paper and drop it on the table, fold my arms and stare at them both.

They don't give me so much as a second, grubby glance. I go back to my paper. I don't mind being ignored. Invisibility, these past two weeks, has bestowed upon me, unbidden, a kind of boom-boom, idiotic charity, where there is nothing to give me away but my accent, and where my accent has made usually sensibly people cry. It is ridiculous.

The rain is coming down even harder now, a beatific tattoo, so loud that for alternate moments their voices aren't so clear. There is a roll of thunder so loud the window rattles. A woman passes by outside. She is using a copy of the *New York Times* to cover her head. The weight of it, and the rain, has her bent forward at the waist, but she runs like a proper runner, bouncing on the balls of her feet. The sight of that distinctive masthead has me almost out of my seat, but then I settle back and crane around and watch her disappear into Leicester Square.

I pick up my paper again and read. A man in Southwark is being taken to court by the Council's planning department. He has covered the outside of his house (Grade II* Listed) with eighty-one flags from all around the world. There's a photograph. It's stunning. He won't take them down and he won't give a reason. It was just something he felt like doing, apparently. They're going to haul his ass through the courts, it's going to cost him a fortune, but he doesn't care. It's the absence of an excuse that's driving everybody crazy. He just won't say why he did it. Not a word by way of explanation. Well, good for him.

'You are the only man I have ever loved. Did you know that?'

'I knew it. That's good. And you are the only woman I have ever loved. You know that too, don't you?'

'Yes. Good.'

'What the hell do we sound like?'

'A couple of teenagers. It's ridiculous.'

'Ah, well . . .'

'I need another Scotch.'

'Me too. Coming right up.'

I watch him go to the bar. He leans over it, the bills mashed in his fist, while he looks at his knuckles. She stares at what I think is me, but it isn't really. She is staring through me, to the street outside. She raises a hand, wrist curved Hepburn-like, to draw back a strand of grey hair. She is astonishingly lovely. Through me, she is watching the wash of passers-by and the pretty funk of rain on glass. My paper tells of cat breeders in Wisconsin, genetically mutating cats to have short legs. Just like dachshunds. She takes off her wedding ring, looks at it, polishes it on her sleeve. And puts it back on.

I don't have a wedding ring. I used to have one. I was married up until three years ago, but my weight went up and down so much over the years that the ring first fitted, then didn't, then did, then didn't again, until I just decided to keep the damn thing in a drawer. I'm as skinny as a rake these days, so it probably would just slide off, uselessly, even if I could find it.

Tourists are odd creatures. I know I'm one, but I don't feel alien here any more. I feel as if I don't belong anywhere and that, in a strange and synaptic way, makes me feel as if I belong everywhere. Bars are bars the world over. Tables and chairs, sidewalks, billboards, skylines high or low, they're all the same. The only difference lies in the texture of the grain beneath your feet, the volume of the traffic, the bossy ruffle of other tourists, flickering by, on their way to other places, the feral utility of the locals, sometimes kindly, sometimes not. But it's all basically the same hymnsheet. The world over.

I have been to forty-seven countries in seven years. I have spent more time packing and unpacking suitcases than I have sleeping, and I never got it down. It should have been a fine art after a couple of years and it wasn't. Every goddamn trip was a vicious shindig of unironed shirts and lost tickets and lost luggage and missed flights and arguments with my wife. A nightmare of sad and deranged airport bars, Powerpoint presentations put together at the very last minute, of bad food and headaches and indigestion and fears of deep-vein thrombosis and the occasional numb whore. And I did it because I preferred it to staying at home. No wonder she decided that she'd had enough.

But at least we stayed civil about the kid. Weekends were sorted out without rancour. At least, there, we didn't disgrace ourselves too badly. That gut-precious girl, she was made frighteningly aware of how much we both loved her. Sometimes I think we may have overdone it. At the age of twelve, she began to drift away from both of us, with a kind of soft, imbecilic resistance that we were powerless to tackle. She turned into the worst kind of teenager. In the last three months she spoke exactly thirty words to me. Fifty to her mother. I counted. It's obviously not an accurate count, but it's close enough. I actually liked the tattoo, but if I had said so she probably would have cut off her own arm. Truth be told, she frightened me. Even when she was tiny, there was a stillness about that girl which unnerved me and I never had the grace to get over it. She was the bravest, vilest, jauntiest, most horrible person I ever had the good fortune to beget, and she packed more into her eighteen years than either I or her mother could ever have imagined. She was gone, long gone, before she actually went, really. Well, good for her.

Her mother has been calling the hotel a dozen times a day for the last two weeks. It must have been a task, finding out where I was.

But what can she tell me that I don't already know? That I haven't seen on television over and over again?

She must be frantic.

I can't help.

She is a religious woman. She knows that God does, in fact, answer all our prayers. And that sometimes the answer is no.

'Thanks. I don't normally go beyond one whisky. But today is a different day, isn't it?'

'Yes. Today is different. Are you warm enough, honey? Do you need your shawl?'

'No, Richard, I'm fine. You?'

'Mary, I'm okay but, truth to tell, I'm a little tired.'

The silence between those words and her reply lasts fifty-nine seconds. I didn't count. I watched the clock on the wall.

The rain, well, now it's just getting stupid. It's coming down so heavily that hordes of folk are crowded into the lobby of Wyndham's Theatre, looking like a bunch of drowned rats. It is hard to see out; the window is a near opaque, caustic sauna of streaks and dribbles. I lean in closer to the glass. My breath steams. I can't get a fix on them. The people are a solicitous squall of unreasonable colours and melting shapes, a mashed community in limbo. And they are all just waiting for the rain to stop. Strangers waiting and getting all pally, there in the doorway, with nothing but the svelte dynamic of the city to keep them company. Limbo. There's a thing. Patience has a lot to be said for it.

And then, it stops. The rain. Suddenly. Just like that. And everybody looks up, gormless. The bar staff stop moving around, the customers stop talking, and we all look out the window, silent and embarrassed by our own silence, astonished by the alchemical silence of the deadpan skies. I can see the people opposite. They shake themselves, their colours now proper and clanking, and shiver away from each other, this way and that, folding umbrellas and saying goodbye. Cheerio and goodbye then.

They disperse, unlistenable, to the four corners, to parts unknown, immaculate and shambling.

I turn the corner of the newspaper and the rattle rattles people out of their brief stupor. The waitresses begin to glide and shift, the tills ring, but quietly. Everybody starts to talk again.

'Richard, my heart is breaking.'

'I know it. I feel as if I've been punctured, or something.'

'As if your head is wrapped in cotton wool?'

He laughs, and it is a soft, broken bark. I can't move. I'm hiding behind the paper.

'Yes. Is this real, Mary? Is this really going to happen to us? To you and me?'

'We've been there. It's been coming for a long time. I'm tired. We're both tired. It's time.'

'But, thirty years. Jesus, God.'

'Drink your drink, Richard.'

'I know. I'm just scared.'

'No. You're nervous. There's a difference.'

'And you're not?'

'No, I'm not nervous. I'm terrified.'

She laughs, and it is a soft bruise upon my ear. I still can't move. Please let this be something other than what I think it is. She is folding a piece of paper, over and over.

'But we'll stay in touch.'

'No, Richard. This is it. We'll never see each other again.'

'Mary?'

'Of course we'll stay in touch, you moron. That was a joke. Remember jokes?'

'Oh, Jesus . . .'

'Besides, it's Dana's thirtieth birthday in a week, and we both have to be there for that, right?'

'And in November, it's their anniversary.'

'January, it's the child's eighth birthday. You see? You see the way it works?'

'I see.'

'Richard, sweetheart. It doesn't have to be a battle. It never did.'

'I get it. I know.'

'Well, there you go then.'

'Yes.'

'Will you be okay, Rick?'

'Yes. No. Oh, Christ, probably.'

'Me too. Good enough to be going on with, yes?'

'Yes. Christ, Mary, I have never been so exhausted in my life.'

'Yes, well. Splitting up with your wife after thirty years will do that to a body . . .'

'Are you tired?'

'Yes. I'm tired.'

'Shall we go? Now. Shall we go?'

'Let's go see a show.'

A very long pause.

'Mary, you want to go see a show? Right now?'

'Yes. And I want it to be a comedy.'

'A comedy. Okey-dokey, how about *Noises Off*?'

'Fine. Whatever. We could do with a laugh, no?'

'But I am never going to stop loving you. What am I going to do about that?'

'And I will never stop loving you. And we're not going to do a damn thing. Let's go.'

'Let's go.'

And then she says 'Ah, well.'

And then he says 'Ah, well.'

And they get up and they leave.

Just like that.

They leave.

He takes her by the elbow and she glides, again, upwards and they leave. They go out the door, arms around each other, with a nod and a smile to the bar staff, and a quiet word about something or other, and a big tip left on the table, and their body language is a thing, entire, of sheer joy. There is no other word for it.

So here I am.

Damn, I was almost enjoying that. I thought they were going to be together for ever. I thought that's where this thing was going.

I place my newspaper down because I've read every story and now my fingers are blackened with ink. Christ, I've been rubbing my hands over my face for the last two hours. I must look like some kind of street urchin.

Well, at least the rain has stopped.

A young waiter is hovering over me. He looks embarrassed.

'Sir?'

'Yes?'

'This is for you.'

'A bottle of wine? I didn't actually order that, thanks.'

'It's for you anyway. And the rose, too. And the note.'

Now he's turning puce.

And there it is.

A rose, wrapped in a blue bar napkin. A red rose. And a bottle of white wine. I don't know much about wine, but it looks like a fine one, quite expensive.

'The couple opposite asked me to give them to you. After they left, like.'

'Thank you.'

'Okay, then.'

He turns on his heel and I can almost smell the relief off his skin.

I settle back and I look at the wine. And at the note. I pick up the rose and I press it to my nose. All the thorns, I notice, have been removed. The stem is smooth as a willow stem and the aroma is such that I almost pass out, it's that beautiful.

An hour later, I am still drinking the wine and sniffing the flower. The rain starts again, but now it is a soft mist. It is another hour before I unfold and read the note.

It's written on the Bear & Staff's headed paper. Small, tear-off notepad paper. Cheap.

It is a short note.

The handwriting is a woman's, with several very interesting flourishes: it manages to be terse and lanky at the same time.

They were watching me the whole time.

Talking their lives and watching me at the same time. Keeping some kind of flip ley-line going from their table to my table and back again, and breaking each other's hearts and healing each other's lives, all at the same time. They were a goddamn tag team, a mute and slinky team, able to do their own thing and still take an interest.

And I thought I was the one doing the watching.

They were watching every move I made, every twitch, every expression, and they never missed a damn beat. They were watching me more than I was watching them.

It is a very nice note. She speaks of home and of love, a little, and of a reassurance occasionally winnable. She speaks of time in a way that makes me believe it actually can heal. If I were a different man these days, I would have been insulted.

I fold the note and put it in my wallet. I finish the wine.

I get up to leave. Now my back hurts, a little, but my chest feels better.

I leave the waiter a £10 note as a tip. I fold it up the way you do when you're slipping it into the garter belt of a pole dancer. 140 millimetres by 17 millimetres.

I'm feeling generous.

I stand in the doorway for a bit, face up, eyes closed, the vagrant and addled sunshine busting a gut to come out properly. I take the note from my wallet and read the last few lines again.

'Once again, I apologise for what may seem like unforgivable rudeness.

But you seemed to be so dreadfully sad, and I can't bear to see that these days.

Just because it's personal doesn't mean it's important.
Kind regards.
M. & R.'

I walk back to my hotel room and, this time, I pick up the phone.

JULIA O'FAOLAIN

The Corbies' Communion

Liam sat, glassed-in, on a half landing crammed with photographs. It was easy to heat, which was why he came here
when he couldn't sleep. Lately he had been feeling the cold.

Images of himself gleamed mockingly but could, if he twitched
his head, be dissolved in light-smears or made to explode, milkily,
like stars.

'Sap!' he told a young Liam. 'What was there to smirk about?'

Kate had mounted bouquets of snaps in which she – why had
he not noticed? – was often less than present: half-hidden under
hats or bleached out as if too easily reconciled to mortality. The
solid one was himself, who had seized his days with a will visible
even in creased press cuttings. Cocky and convivial, the past
selves could be guises donned by some mild devil to abash him.
Flicking whiskey at them, he managed to exorcise the Liam who
was accepting a decoration from the country's ex-president
and an award from someone he could no longer place.
OLD POLEMICIST HONOURED bragged a headline. GREAT
MAVERICK RECONCILED AT LAST. Black-tied, white-tied,
tweedy in a sequence of Herbie Johnson hats, alone, on podia
and at play, the personae zoomed in and out of focus. Liam at the
races. Liam on a yacht. Some wore whites as though for cricket,
a game no Irishman of his stripe would have played. That ban
was now obsolete. By humiliating the old masters, West Indian
bowlers had freed the sport and its metaphors.

'You had a grand innings!' a recent visitor had exclaimed.
'Close to a century!' Liam, loath to be sent off to some pavilion in
the sky, pressed an imaginary stop-button. Rewind. Replay. But
replays were nightmares and Kate featured in them all.

'Was I such a bastard to you?' he cajoled one of her half-averted faces. It was bent over a picnic basket, counting hard-boiled eggs. 'Neglectful? Selfish?' The face would not look up.

'I could kill you for dying,' he told her. His watch hands pointed to four.

He had been twice to bed, started to sleep, funked it and returned here. Catastrophe was tearing up his sky and panic circled, black as crows. Keeping it at bay, he topped up his whiskey and, from habit, hid the bottle behind a fern. Outside, the dawn chorus made a seething churr. He was alone by choice, wanting neither minders nor commiseration.

'You were plucky,' he told a likeness of Kate, smiling in an old-time summer dress. 'But you cheated on me! Became an invalid! Querulous! If you were alive now we'd be fighting!'

Two nights ago she, contrary to what statistics had led him to expect, had died. He had counted on going first. She had always been here till now, hadn't she? Even when it had spoiled his plans! The thought startled him and his crossed leg pulsed. 'Kate!' he mourned, amazed. For years he, not she, had been the adventurer.

'I know you resented that,' he told a snapshot in which a child's head bobbed past her face. 'But you were happy at first. And later wasn't so bad, surely?' He scrutinised snaps taken in restaurants and on boating holidays on the River Barrow. '*Was* it?' Helpless, he brushed a hand across dapplings from awnings and other people's menus. Cobweb grudges, forgotten tiffs. 'Damn it, Kate, did you put bad photos of yourself here to torment me? That could make me hate you!'

Spying the whiskey bottle behind its plant, he reflected that hating her would be a relief – then that she might have planned the relief.

His checked hand reached the bottle and poured more anyway. Nobody to stop him now! If she'd died twenty years ago he'd have remarried. Maybe even fifteen? Now – he was ninety. Had she planned *that*? Wryly, he raised the glass.

'To you then, old sparring partner and last witness to our golden youth!'

Losing her was radical surgery. Like losing half his brain. Like

their retreat, years ago, to this manageable cottage. In the background to several snaps, their old house made a first, phantom
appearance as a patch in a field, its roomy shape pegged out with
string. Pacing the patch strode Kate. Expansive, laughing, planning a future now behind them, she waved optimistic arms

'Shit!'

He banged his head against the wall. More exploding stars.
Watch it, Liam! You're not the man you were.

A civil-rights lawyer who had become a media figure in his
prime, an activist who had brought cases to Strasbourg and the
Hague, he had let her take over the private sector of their lives.
This included religion. A mistake? Religion here was never quite
private, and their arrangements on that score jarred.

The Requiem Mass which was to have comforted her would set
his teeth on edge. It was a swindle that the Faith, having brought
him woe – sexual and political – when he was young, should now
pay no dividends. None. He had said so to the parish priest, a
near-friend. Running into each other on the seafront, or watching blown tulips reveal black hearts in the breezy park, the two
sometimes enjoyed a bicker about the off chance of an afterlife: a
mild one, since neither would change his bias. Liam was past
ninety and the PP was no chicken either.

Brace up, Liam! The things to hold onto were those you'd lived
by. Solidarity. The Social Contract. Pluck. Confronting a mottled
mirror, he acknowledged the charge reflected back. Funerals here
were manifestos. His conduct at Kate's must, rallied the mirror,
bolster those who had helped him fight the Church when it was
riding roughshod over people here. You couldn't let *them* down by
slinking back for its last vain comforts. How often had he heard
bigots gloat that some Liberal had 'died screaming for a priest'?

They'd relish saying it of him, all right! Addicts of discipline and
bondage, the Holy Joes would get a buzz from seeing Liam
dragged off by psychogenic demons. Toasted on funk's pitchforks!
Turned on its spit! Tasty dreams. In the real world, they'd settle
for seeing him back in the fold – and why gratify them? Could
Kate have wanted to? She who, in the vigour of her teens, had
marched at Republican funerals, singing: 'Tho' cowards mock

and traitors sneer/ We'll keep the red flag flying here'? Hair blowing, cheeks bright as the flag. Sweet, hopeful Kate!

On the other hand, how refuse her her Mass? Anyway, how many of the old guard were left to see whether Liam stood firm? Frail now, and rigid in the set of their ways. He ticked them off on his fingers: a professor emeritus, some early proponents of family planning, secular schools and divorce, a few journalists whose rights he had defended, his successor's successor at Civil Liberties: a barrister long retired. Who else? Half a score of widows confirmed the actuarial statistics which had played him false. Would they make it to Kate's funeral? Not long ago, he had drawn a cluster of circles which she mistook at first for a rose. It was a map showing the radius within which each of their contemporaries and near-contemporaries was now confined. Those who still drove kept to their neighbourhoods. Those who did not might venture to the end of a bus route. Not all the circles touched.

The Mass, though, would be accessible to most, being in the heart of town, in Trinity College chapel: a case of an ill wind bringing good, since the choice of venue – made when he, Kate and the twentieth century were a mutinous sixty – had lost pizzazz. Ecumenicism was now commonplace, and the old Protestant stronghold had Catholic chaplains. The Holy Joes had him surrounded. For two pins he'd call off the ceremony – but how do that to Kate?

'For Christ's sake, Liam!' he raged at himself. 'There is no Kate! Hold onto your marbles! She's gone!' He poured his savourless whiskey into a fern.

Anger, a buffer against worse, had made him insult the PP when he came yesterday to condole. Priests, Liam had hissed, were like crows. They battened on death. Then he recited a poem which he remembered too late having recited to him before. Never mind! Rhymes kept unstable thoughts coralled.

> *There were twa corbies sat in a tree,*
> *Willoughby, oh Willoughby.*
> *The tane unto the t'ither say*

'Where shall we gang and dine this day?
In beyond yon aul fell dyke
I wot there lies a new-slain knight . . .'

Liam wasn't dead yet, but here was the first corby come to
scavenge his soul in what the priest must think was a weak
moment. If he did, he thought wrong. When asked about the
Mass, Liam said he might call it off. He'd see when his daughter
got here. Ha, he thought, the cavalry was coming. Her generation
believed in nothing. Kitty was tough – Kate's influence! The two
had ganged up on him from the first, saying he was all for
freedom outside the house and patriarchy within. How they'd
laugh – he could just hear them! – at his seeing himself as slain
when the dead one was Kate.

Ah but – the thought stunned him – the living are also dying.

'Naebody kens that he lies there,
But his hawk and his hound and his lady fair.
His hound is to the hunting gane,
His hawk to bring the wild fowl hame,
His lady's ta'en anither mate
Sae we may mak' our dinner swate.'

Kate's remains had gone – as would his – to medical research. It
felt odd not to have a corpse.

'You'll need some ritual,' said the PP. 'To say goodbye. Kate
liked rituals. I used to bring her communion,' he reminded, 'after
she became bedridden. Your housekeeper prepared things. You
must have known.'

Liam remembered a table covered with lace. Water. Other
props. Of course he'd known. He had kept away while she made
her last communions just as, to please *his* wife, Jaurès, the great
French Socialist, let their daughter make her first one – to the
shock of the comrades for whom fraternising with clerics was a
major betrayal.

A weakness?

Liam sighed and the PP echoed the sigh. Many Irish people,

mused the priest, went to Mass so as not to upset their relatives. 'It was the opposite with Kate. Her religion meant a lot to her.'

'How do you know?'

'I know.' The PP made his claim calmly.

His lady's ta'en anither mate, thought Liam, and called the priest a carrion crow. 'The way the corbies took communion,' he ranted, 'was to eat the knight's flesh. Tear him apart!'

Suddenly tired, he must have dropped off then, for when he awoke the PP had let himself out. Liam felt ashamed. 'Tear him apart,' he murmured, but couldn't remember what that referred to. The word 'ritual' stayed with him, though. It floated about in his head.

'I'm not doing it for Him!' he told his daughter, Kitty, who now arrived off a plane delayed by fog. As though her brain too were fogged, she stared at him in puzzlement.

'HIM.' Liam tilted his eyes aloft. 'I mean HIM.' He shook an instructive fist heavenward, only to see her gaze ambushed by a light fixture. She – Kate could have told him who to blame – was indifferent to religion and always nagging him about the wiring in the house.

'Who's "him"?'

'God!' More fist-shaking. 'Bugger HIM. I don't believe in HIM! I'll be doing it for HER.'

'Doing what?' Living in England had made her very foreign.

'Taking,' he marvelled at himself, 'communion at your mother's Requiem Mass. I'll do it for her. For Kate. She'd have done it for me.'

His bombshell failed to distract Kitty from the fixture in the ceiling. Wires wavered from it like the legs of a frantic spider. He couldn't remember how it had got that way. Had someone yanked off the bulb? His temper, lately, had grown hard to control.

'I'm calling an electrician.'

Liam, on getting no argument from Kitty, started one with himself. Holy Joes aside, the prime witnesses to his planned treachery would be the betrayed: those who had dared confront a Church which controlled jobs, votes and patronage. With surprising courage, vulnerable men – rural librarians and the like – had, starting back in the bleak and hungry '40s, joined his shoe-string campaigns to challenge the collusion between dodgy oligarchs and a despotic clergy. Old now, many campaigners were probably poor and surely lonely. Not pliable enough to be popular, they were unlikely to be liked. Honesty thwarted could turn to quibbling, and brave men grow sour. He wondered if they tore out light bulbs?

Startling Kitty, he whispered: 'They can put their communion up their arses.' Luxuriating in blasphemy: 'Bloody corbies! God-and-man-eating cannibals!'

He had grown strange. Her mother had warned her, phoning long distance with reports of his refusal to take his salt substitute or turn off his electric blanket. 'He'll burn us down,' she'd worried. 'Or spill tea into it and electrocute himself. Stubborn,' she'd lamented. 'Touchy as a tinderbox. He's going at the top!'

Kitty reproached herself. She had not seen that these fears – transcendent, fussy, entertained for years – were justified at last. Poor mother! Poor prophetic Kate!

Sedated now, he was dreaming of her as a bride. 'Slim as a silver birch!' he praised her in his sleep. True, wondered Kitty, or borrowed from those Gaelic vision-poems where a girl's naked-ness on some rough mountainside dazzles freaked-out men?

'Kate,' whimpered the sleeper. 'Kate!' His tone rang changes on that double-dealing syllable.

Saliva, bubbling on his lip, drew from a jumble in Kitty's memory the Gaelic word for snail: *seilmide*. When she was maybe four, he and she used to feed cherry blossom to snails. White and bubbly, the petals were consumed with *brio* as the surprisingly deft creatures folded them into themselves like origami artists.

Kitty wiped away Liam's spittle. Had she chosen to forget the tame snails, so as to feel free to poison the ones in her London garden, a thing she now did regularly and without qualms? She grew arugula there, and basil and that heart-stopping flower, the blue morning glory, which looks like fragments of sky but shrivels in the sun. The snails got the young plants if you didn't get them first.

She drove him out the country to take tea in a favourite inn. Sir Walter Scott had stayed here and a letter, testifying to this, was framed in a glass case. Across from it, iridescent in a larger one, was a stuffed trout.

Liam buttered a scone and smiled at the waitress, who returned his smile as women always had. 'Women,' he remarked, watching as she moved off in a delicate drift of body odour, 'are the Trojan mare! *Mère.*' In his mouth the French word seethed breezily. He cocked a comical eye at Kitty and bit into the scone. 'They don't like to be outsiders, you see. That's dangerous.'

The drive had perked him up. He loved these mountains, had rambled all over them and could attach stories to places which, to Kitty, were hardly places at all. It was late September. Bracken had turned bronze. Rowan leaves were an airborne yellow and a low, pallid sun, bleaching out the car mirror, made it hard to drive. Dark, little lakes gleamed like wet iron and Liam, who in his youth, had studied Celtic poetry, listed the foods on which, according to the old poets, hermits, mad exiled kings and other wild men of the woods had managed to survive.

He paused as though a thought had stung him. Could it be fear that some wild man, slipping inside his own skull, had scrambled his clever lawyer's mind?

'He's not himself,' Kate had mourned on Kitty's visits. The self Liam was losing had been such a model of clarity and grace that his undoing appalled them. He had been their light of lights, and even now Kitty could not quite face the thought that he was failing. Now and again though, the process seemed so advanced as to make her wonder whether it might be less painful if speeded up? A release for him, who struggled so laboriously to slow it down.

'Yew and rowan berries,' she heard him drone like a child unsure of his lesson – not the clever child Liam must have been but a slow-witted changeling – 'Haws, was it,' he floundered, 'and hazel nuts, mast, acorns, pignuts . . . sloes . . .'

It was an exercise of the will.

'Whortleberries. . .dilisk, salmon, badger fat, wood sorrel, honey. . .'he faltered, '. . . eels . . .Did I say venison? Porpoise steak . . .' His face was all focus: a knot, a noose. Its lines tautened as he grasped after two receding worlds: the Celtic one and that of the Twenties when he and other Republicans had gone on the run like any wild man of the woods. They'd hardly have lived on berries, though. Local sympathisers must, she guessed, have provided potatoes and bastable bread spread with salty butter. 'Trout?' he remembered, and his mouth gasped with strain as if he had been hooked.

Now, though, tea and the stop in the inn had once again revived him. The old Liam, back and brave as bunting, was going through one of his routines. He had always been a bit of a showman.

'In what way,' Kitty asked encouragingly, 'are women Trojan horses?'

'Not horses,' he corrected her. 'Mares! Fillies! They conform. That's why. Anywhere and everywhere. Here, for instance, they go to the Church and, behold, it catches them. *It* gets inside *them*. It's as if Greeks inside the wooden horse inside the walls of Troy were to breathe in drugged fumes. They'd become Trojans, collaborate . . .'

Twinkling at her over his tea cup. The old teasing Liam. Back for how long? As with an unreliable lover, she feared letting down her defences. But wouldn't it be cruel not to? Yes and no? Kitty was a professional interpreter. She worked with three languages, and liked to joke that her mind was inured to plurality and that the tight trio she, Kate and Liam had made when she was growing up had led to this. Her mother, going further, had blamed it for the rockiness of Kitty's marriage, an on-off arrangement which was currently on hold.

'We were too close,' Kate used to say. 'We made you old before your time.'

And it was true that Liam had modelled rebellious charm for

her before she was eight. How could the boys she met later compete? Add to this that the house had been full of young men about whom she knew too much too soon: his clients. One was a gaol bird and a bomber. Surprisingly domestic, he helped Kate in the kitchen and taught Kitty to ride a bike, running behind her with one hand on the saddle. This, unfairly, made her suspicious later of helpful men.

'A penny for them?'

Liam's blue, amused eyes held hers. 'We,' he repeated, 'send our women into the Church and *it* slips inside their heads!' She recognised an old idea, dredged from some spilled filing system in his brain.

'You sent me to school to nuns.' She had once resented this. 'Was I a Trojan filly? A hostage? Would you have lost credibility if we'd found a secular school? Or were there none in those days?'

Liam smiled helplessly. He had lost the thread. That happened now. Poor Liam! She gripped his knee. 'Darling!' she comforted.

But he reared back with a small whinnying laugh. 'I know what you're thinking!' he accused. 'Liam, you're thinking, it's been nice knowing you. But now you're gone! Your mind's gone.'

'It's not gone. You were very sharp just now about how the Church captured me and my mother.'

'Oh, they didn't capture you the way they did her.'

'They didn't capture her either.' Kitty wanted to be fair. 'She was open to doubt. They don't like that.'

'True enough.' He seemed cheered.

'She was never a bigot.'

'So you think we should go ahead with the Mass?'

'Why not?'

A mash of red-raspberry faces lined the pews, which were at right angles to the altar. Stick-limbed old survivors tottered up the nave to condole with Liam and remind him of themselves. Some had fought beside him, seventy years ago, in the Troubles or, later, in Civil Liberties. They had seen the notices Kitty had put in national and provincial papers and travelled, in some cases, across Ireland, to this shrunken reunion. A straight-backed Liam stood dandified and dazed. Ready, Kitty guessed, to fly to bits if the shell of his suit had not held in his Humpty Dumpty self. The suit had been a sore point with her mother.

'Riddled with tobacco burns!' had been her refrain. 'For God's sake throw it out!'

He wouldn't though. And his tailor was dead. So Kitty's help was enlisted. She had scoured London for the sort of multi-buttoned, rigidly interlined suits which he recognised as 'good' and which might well have repelled small bullets. His sartorial tastes were based on some Edwardian image of the British Empire which he had chosen to emulate, as athletes will an opponent's form. Nowadays, Japanese businessman seemed in pursuit of a modern approximation of it, for she kept running across them up and down Jermyn Street and in Burberry's and Loeb.

Liam refused to wear the new clothes. Perhaps he missed the dirt in the old ones? Its anointing heft? Embracing him this morning, Kitty had sensed a flinching inside the resilient old cloth. Tired by their outing, he had regressed since into a combative confusion.

'Kate!' he'd greeted her at breakfast, and had to be reminded that Kate was dead. He'd cried then, though his mouth now was shut against grief. Anger, summoned to see him through the ceremony, boiled over before it began. When the Taoiseach's stand-in, his chest a compressed rainbow of decorations, came to pay his respects, the mouth risked unclenching to ask, 'Is that one of the shits we fought in twenty-two?'

'No,' soothed Kitty, 'no, love, he's from your side.'

She wasn't sure of this. Liam, a purist, had lambasted both sides after the Civil War and pilloricd all trimming when old friends came to terms with power. Today, mindful perhaps of the Trojan horse, he was in but not of this church and, ignoring its drill, provoked disarray in the congregation as he, the chief mourner, stood attentive to some inner command which forbade him to bow his head, genuflect or in any way acknowledge the ceremony.

He softened, however, on seeing his own parish priest serve the Mass. This had not been provided for, and the PP had come off his

own bat. 'For Kate,' Liam whispered to Kitty who, in her foreign
ignorance, might fail to appreciate the tribute.

Suddenly, regretting his rudeness to Kate's old friend, he
plopped to his knees at the wrong moment, hid his face in his
hands and threw those taking their cue from him into chaos.

Afterwards, two Trinity chaplains came to talk to him. No doubt –
the thought wavered on the edge of his mind – they expected to
be slipped an envelope containing a cheque. But Kitty hadn't
thought to get one ready and he no longer handled money. Its
instability worried him. Just recently, he had gone to his old
barber for a haircut and, as he was having his shoulders brushed,
proffered a shilling. The barber laughed, said his charge was five
pounds then, perhaps disarmed by Liam's amazement, accepted
the offer. Liam, foxily, guessed he was getting a bargain – though,
to be sure, the man might send round later for his proper
payment to Kate? Perhaps the chaplains would too? No! For Kate
was . . . she was . . . Liam could not confront the poisonous
fact and the two young men backed off before the turmoil in his
face.

As Kitty was leaving – she had work waiting in Strasbourg –
Liam, enlivened by several goodbye whiskeys, told of a rearguard
skirmish with the Holy Joes. It had occurred in a nursing home
where, though he had registered as an agnostic, a priest tried to
browbeat him into taking the sacraments.

Liam's riposte had been to drawl: 'Well, my dear fellow, I can
accommodate you if it gives you pleasure!' This, he claimed, had
sent the bully scuttling like a scalded cat.

He rang her in Strasbourg to say he wished he was with her and
Kate. Unsure what this meant, she promised a visit as soon as she
was free.

'I'm hitting the bottle.'

'I'll be over soon.'

Her husband, when she rang to say she couldn't come home
yet because of Liam, warned, 'You can't pay him back, you

know. You'd better start resigning yourself. You can't give him life.'

Returning to Dublin now was like stepping into childhood. Liam, barricaded like a zoo creature in winter, had holed up in an over-heated space which evoked for Kitty the hide-outs she had enjoyed making when she was five. Its fug recalled the smell of stored ground sheets, and its dust-tufts mimicked woolly toys. The housekeeper, counting on Liam's short-sightedness, had grown slack.

Interfering was tricky, though. Last year, neighbours had told Kitty of seeing Liam fed porridge for dinner while good food went upstairs on a tray to the more alert Kate. The housekeeper was playing them up. Liam, when asked about this, had wept. 'Poor Kate! Running the house was her pride and now she can't.' Rather than complain and shame her, he preferred to eat the penitential porridge.

'Was I a bad husband?' he asked Kitty, who supposed he must be trying to make up for this.

He had a woman. The fact leaked from him as all facts or fictions – the barrier between them was down – now did. 'She's nobody,' he told Kitty. 'Just someone to talk to. I have to have that. I don't even find her attractive, but, well . . .' Smiling. Faithless. Grasping at bright straws. Weaving them, hopefully, into corn dollies.

'She' – once or twice he said 'you' – 'takes me on drives which end up in churches.'

'Ah? The Trojan mare?'

'Last week we lit a candle for Kate. They were saying Mass.'

'It's your soul she's after then, not your body?'

'Cruel!' His *memento-mori* face tried for jauntiness. 'Well, *you* can't have me to live, can you, with your fly-by-night profession! Triple-tongued fly-by-night!' he teased. 'There's no relying on you! Where are you off to next?'

'Strasbourg, for the meeting of the European Parliament.'

'See!'

*

He was terrified of death. 'I want,' he confided, 'to live and live.'
Terrified too of relinquishing his self-esteem by 'crawling' to a
God in whom he didn't believe. 'Why do people believe?' he
wondered. Then: 'Ah, I know you'll say from fear: phobophobia.
They want immortality.' And his face twisted, because he wanted
it too.

On her next visits, he was a man dancing with an imaginary
partner. A sly mime indicated the high-backed, winged armchair
in which, he claimed, her mother sat in judgement on him. 'Don't
you start,' he warned. 'I hear it all from her!'

This, if a joke, was out of control.

'Psst!' he whispered. 'She's showing disapproval.'

Courting it, he drank but wouldn't eat, threw out his pills, felt
up a woman visitor, fired his housekeeper who was cramping his
style, and behaved as though he hoped to rouse his wife to show
herself. Like believers defying their God. Or old lags wooing a
gaol-sentence to get them through a cold snap. Spilled wine drew
maps on Kate's Wilton carpet and, more than once, the gas had
to be turned off by neighbours whose advice he ignored. After
midnight, their letters warned Kitty, he stuffed great wads of cash
into his pockets and set forth on stumbling walks through slick
streets infested with muggers.

'Things have changed here,' cautioned the letters, 'from when
you were a girl. Even the churchyards are full of junkies shooting
it up.'

Liam too seemed to be seeking some siren thrill as he breasted
the darkness, his pockets enticingly bulging with four- and five-
hundred-pound bait.

Splotched and spidery letters from him described a shrunken –
then, unexpectedly, an expanding world.

Two angels – or were they demons? – were struggling over
him. An old friend and neighbour, Emir, engaged in what he
snootily dismissed as 'good works', hoped to enlist his support.
'Therapeutic?' wondered one letter touchily. 'For my own good?'
But Emir's causes were the very ones he himself had promoted

for years. And who was the other demon/angel? The one who
had taken him into churches was, it seemed, a nurse. Used to
older men, she maybe liked him for himself, 'though I suppose
she's too young for me'. Clearly he hoped not, and that it was
not his soul which concerned her. She was persuading him to
return to the bosom of Mother Church. Any bosom, clearly, had
its appeal, but Emir, though more congenial, was not offering
hers.

The nurse – Kitty imagined her as starched, busty and hung
with the sort of fetishes to which gentlemen of Liam's vintage
were susceptible, came regularly to tea. The letter stopped there.
Liam had forgotten to finish it, or perhaps been overcome by the
impropriety of his hopes.

More urgent letters came from neighbours. Even in Kate's day,
they revealed, Liam's mind had been wobbly. Kate had covered
up, but something should now be done. There had been
'incidents'. Near-scandals. No new housekeeper could be expected to cope.

Kitty dreamed she was watching a washing machine in which
a foetally-folded Liam, compact as a snail, was hurtled around.
She could see him through the glass window but, in her dream,
could not open this. White sprays of suds or saliva foamed over
his head.

Did 'do something' mean have him locked up? Put in a nursing
or rest home? He would not go willingly. While she wondered
about this, there came a call to say he had caught pneumonia,
been admitted to hospital and might not live.

She was in California, where it was 2:00 a.m. and the telephone bell, pulsing through alien warmth, jerked her from sleep.
Outside, spotlights focused on orchids whose opulence might or
might not be real, and night-scented blooms evoked funerals.

However, when next she saw him, Liam, though still in hospital, was out of immediate danger.

'The corbies are conspiring,' he greeted her. 'Caw caw!' His
eyes were half-closed and a brown mole, which had been repeat-
edly removed, had overgrown one lid. After a while, he tried to

sing an old schoolyard rhyme: 'Cowardy, cowardy custard, Stick
your head in the mustard!'

Mustard-keen priests had, it seemed, persuaded him to be
reconciled and take the sacraments. Or was it the nurse? Emir,
dropping in for a visit, said that the fact had been reported in an
evening paper.

'A feather in their caps!' She shrugged. 'Sure, what does it
matter now?'

It did to Liam, who whimpered that he had perhaps betrayed . . . he couldn't say who. 'Am I – was I a shit?' His mind
meandered in a frightened past. 'Cowardy Custard,' he croaked
guiltily.

'Don't worry,' Emir rallied him. 'It's all right, love.' She spoke
as if to a child.

Kitty couldn't. Unable to discount or count on him, she went,
fleetingly, half-blind. Colours and contours melted as if she were
adapting to a reversible reality in which, later this evening on
reaching his house, she might find his old spry self smiling at the
door.

It smelled of him. It was a cage within which his memory paced
and strove. Trajectories of flung objects – a wall smeared with
coffee, a trail of dried food – were his spoor.

'He wants to die,' Emir whispered next day. 'He told me so.'

The two were sitting with a somnolent Liam who had been
placed in an invalid chair. Lifting his overgrown eyelid, he
scratched it weakly and asked Kitty, 'Why are you blaming me?
Your face is all blame. A Gorgon's!'

'No, love,' soothed Emir. 'She's worried for you. It's Kitty. Don't
you know her?'

'Why can't you give me something?' he asked. 'Wouldn't it be
better for me to die now – and for you too?'

You never knew what he meant.

'Kiss him,' Emir whispered. 'Say something.'

But to Kitty this wasn't Liam, and she felt her face freeze. She
was unresponsive and stone-stiff: a Gorgon which has seen itself.

'I'll leave you together,' Emir tiptoed out.

Liam opened an eye. 'You'll die too,' he told Kitty with malice. 'You'll succumb.'

'We all will, darling,' she tried to soothe.

'You're punishing me.' His face contracted venomously. 'The survival instinct is a torment. Why did you inflict it on us?'

She marvelled. For whom did he take her now?

He mumbled and his bald skull fell forward as though his neck could not support it. Confronting her, it was flecked with age-spots like the rot on yellow apples.

Earlier, two nurses, lifting him to the chair, had held him by the armpits and, for moments, his whole self had hung like a bag on a wire. Vulnerable. Pitiable. Limp. She couldn't bear it. Slipping an arm around his neck, she felt for the pillow. Her fingers closed on it. Would he let her help him, now they were alone? Let her snuff out that remnant of breath which tormented but hardly animated him? No. He was a struggler. Even against his interests, resistance would be fierce. Yet the old Liam would have wanted to be freed from this cruel cartoon of himself. He surely would have. Was what was left of him content to be the cartoon?

But now, touched off perhaps by her closeness, energy began seeping perceptibly through him. The bowed head jerked up, showing a face suffused with relish. His chapped mouth, lizard grey on the outside, was strangely red within. As if slit with a knife, it was the colour of leeches and looked ready to bleed. 'Ah,' murmured the mouth, 'it's you. You, you, you! I feel your magic. Give me your hand.' And greedily, it began to rush along her arm, covering it with a ripple of nipping kisses. Like its colours, its touch was alternately lizardy and leechlike. 'I betray everyone,' said the mouth, interrupting its rush. 'I *want us* both to betray them. I want to run away with you, you – who . . .' Abruptly, perhaps because of Kitty's lack of response, doubt began to seize him. Again, he managed to jerk his head upwards, his eyes narrowed and his face hardened. 'Who are you?' he challenged. 'You've sneaked in here. You're not who I – who's betraying whom?'

'Liam, nobody's betraying. Everything's all right, I promise.'

'No, no! We're sunk in treachery. Treachechechechery! Who
are you? Who? Who? Are you Kate?'

'Yes,' she told him, 'yes. But it's all *right*, Liam.' Her arm was
still around his neck. Her breath mingled with his.

'So what about the other one, then? You can't be in agreement.
Where's she gone?' Twitching. Eyes boiling. Mouth twisting.
'Life,' he told her, 'is a mess. It's a messmessmess! Where's she
gone?'

'I'm her too.' Kitty held the pillow experimentally with two
hands. She needed three, one to hold his head. 'I'm here,' she told
him. 'And I'm Kitty as well. We all love you, Liam. Nobody
disapproves. Nobody.'

'A treachechecherous mess! Telling on me, all of you! Going
behind my back! Trinities of women . . .'

She soothed him and he asked: 'Are you God?'

'Yes,' she said helplessly. 'I'm God.'

'You made a fine mess,' he told her. 'Life's a . . .'

'Don't worry about it now.'

'How can I not worry? *You* should know! What can we do but
worry? Are we getting an afterlife, yes or no? Not that I believe in
you. Are you a woman, then?'

'I'm whatever you want.'

'Another bloody metaphor! Is that it? Like cricket! Like fair
play!' The leech-lips protruded, red with derision, in the grey,
lizardy expanse. 'Not that fair play and you have much in
common!'

Kitty took her hands from the pillow. 'You always knew that,'
she told Liam. 'Which was why you went your own way!'

'I did, didn't I?' He was awash with pride. 'Bugger you, I said.
Man made you, not the other way round. That's why *you* never
promised fair play. Not you! "The last shall be first" was your
motto. Treacherous. Like me. Buried in treachechech . . . Egh!'

His hands plucked at his dressing gown and his throat seemed
to close. Was he dying?

'Liam!' She rang for the nurse. 'Liam, love, try some water.
Here. Open your mouth, can you? Swallow. Please. Listen. You're
not treacherous. You were never treacherous. You just loved too

many people. And we all love you back. We love you, Liam. There, you're better now. That's better, isn't it? Let me give you a kiss.'

And she put her lips to the protuberant, raw, frightened mouth which was pursed and reaching for them with the naive, greedy optimism of a child.

Tomorrow she'd try with the pillow. Or a plastic bag? Would Emir help, she wondered. Might it be dangerous to ask her?

BIOGRAPHICAL NOTES

JACKIE BLACKMAN was born in Dublin in 1956. She left school at sixteen to get married, then studied Dress Design and Tailoring at the Grafton Academy, and later the History of European Painting as a mature student at Trinity College. She won an Arts Council Scholarship and is now working towards an M.Phil in Creative Writing at TCD.

LORCAN BYRNE was born in Dublin in 1956 and is a graduate of UCD. A prizewinner in the Martin Healy Short Story Award in 1998, he won the *Irish News* International Short Story Award in 1999, and in the following year was short-listed for the *Sunday Tribune/* Hennessy *New Irish Writing* Award for Emerging Fiction. He lives in Bray, Co. Wicklow and works as a secondary schoolteacher.

MARY J. BYRNE was born in Ardee, Co. Louth, and won a Hennessy Literary Award in 1987 for her first story which was published in the *Irish Press New Irish Writing*. She graduated from UCD and worked in Ireland, England, the USA and many other countries. She was invited by Lawrence Durrell to collaborate on his final book of essays (Faber, 1990) and was awarded the *Bourse Lawrence Durrell de la ville d'Antibes* in 1995. She has just completed a novel set in Ireland.

SEAN COFFEY was born in England in 1959. His family relocated to Mullingar, Co. Westmeath, in the early Sixties, and he was educated there. He did a Degree in electronic engineering at the University of Limerick, eventually finding refuge as a lecturer in that subject in the Galway-Mayo Institute of Technology, where he now works. His stories have been published in *Books Ireland, Force Ten* and *West 47*.

GERARD DONOVAN was born in Wexford in 1959. His family moved to Galway when he was six, and he attended the local Jesuit College and Galway University, graduating in 1984. His first publication was a poem, which appeared in the *Irish Press New Irish Writing* in the same year, and in the year 2000 his third collection of poems was nominated for the *Irish Times* Literature Award. In the same year, his story 'Glass', now published in this Phoenix edition, was a finalist in the *Chicago Tribune*'s Nelson Algren Short Story Award, and he recently completed his first novel.

PAUL GRIMES was born in London in 1952. He left school at sixteen and had numerous careers, ranging from factory work to a senior manager in the London Ambulance Service. He did a degree in Sociology as a mature student, and followed this with a Masters in Philosophy. His wife, born in Ireland, persuaded him to come and live in Ireland six years ago, and they live in the Burren, in Co. Clare, and together teach and practise in the field of alternative medicine. Some two years ago he wrote his first short story, which was published in the *Sunday Tribune New Irish Writing*. Since then he has completed a collection of stories and is now revising a novel.

CLAIRE KEEGAN was born in 1968 and raised on a small farm in Wexford. She studied English Literature and Political Science in New Orleans, and graduated from the University of Wales with a Master's Degree in the Teaching and Practice of Creative Writing. One of Ireland's most widely acclaimed new writers, she has won many short story awards, including the 2000 Rooney Award for her debut story collection *Antarctica*, published in both Britain and the USA. She is now working on a new collection and a novel.

NIALL MCARDLE was born in Dublin in 1971, and was educated at University College, Dublin and in the USA. His story *Heavy Weather* is his first to be published.

BLÁNAID MCKINNEY was born in Enniskillen, Co. Fermanagh in 1961. A Political Science graduate of Queen's University, Belfast, she has been a leading executive officer in a number of British Government

Departments. Her first short story appeared in *Phoenix Irish Short Stories 1998*, and her widely-praised debut collection, *Big Mouth* was followed by her first novel, *The Ledge* (Weidenfield and Nicolson), which confirmed her reputation as another of Ireland's most important new writers.

MARY MORRISSY was born in Dublin in 1957. Her first story appeared in the *Irish Press New Irish Writing* in 1984, and in that year she won a Hennessy Literary Award. Further stories were published in newspapers, magazines and anthologies, and her debut collection *A Lazy Eye* (Jonathan Cape) appeared in 1993, followed by two widely-praised novels. Last year she gave up her post on the *Irish Times* and went to live in Cobh, Co. Cork to devote all her time to writing.

ÉILÍS NÍ DHUIBHNE was born in Dublin in 1954. Her first story appeared in the *Irish Press New Irish Writing* in 1974, and in 1976 she graduated from UCD with an M. Phil degree in Medieval English/Folklore. She is one of Ireland's leading writers with novels, story collections, children's books, plays and TV scripts for RTE and Telefís na Gaeilge, and she has for many years worked as a curator in the National Library of Ireland.

FRANK O'CONNOR was born in Cork in 1903 and died in Dublin in 1966. He has long been regarded as one of the world's greatest short story writers.

JULIA O'FAOLAIN was born in London, brought up in Dublin, educated in Rome and Paris. Married to the prominent historian Lauro Martines, she commutes between London and Los Angeles. She has a worldwide reputation as a short-story writer, a novelist, and an incisive commentator on many widely different social and historical subjects.

CÓILÍN Ó hAODHA was born in Galway in 1975. He attended St Mary's College there before studying at UCD, graduating with a degree in English and Philosophy. He won the 1998 Francis

MacManus Award and his first story was published in *Phoenix Irish Short Stories 2000*. He lives in Galway.

DERMOT SOMERS was born in Co. Roscommon in 1947, and moved to Dublin when he was thirteen. His career has included building, broadcasting and writing. His two published collections of short stories have won awards in Britain and Canada. A climber for twenty-five years with worldwide experience, he has written extensively on mountaineering, and has written and presented, in Irish, three TV series for RTE and TG4 on mountain landscape, adventure and tradition. Recent projects include documentaries in Siberia and the Sahara.

Previously unpublished short stories are invited for consideration for future volumes of *Phoenix Irish Short Stories*. Unsuitable MSS will not be returned unless a stamped, addressed envelope is enclosed. Writers outside the Republic of Ireland are reminded that, in the absence of Irish stamps, return postage must be covered by International Reply Coupons: two coupons for packages up to 100g, three for packages 101g to 250g. All communications regarding MSS which require a reply must be accompanied by a self-addressed envelope and return postage. MSS and letters should be addressed to David Marcus, PO Box 4937, Rathmines, Dublin 6.